The Gypsy Cried

Writers Apex

Gateway Towards Success

+13176596889   476 Hamilton Park Circle
www.writersapex.com   Saint Cloud, 34769
8063 MADISON AVE #1252   407-593-8138
Indianapolis, IN 46227   *Email: rsteck5@yahoo.com*

THE GYPSY CRIED

A Writer's Fantasy

WRITTEN BY:

RACHEL F. STECK

*Dedicated to my amazing sons
who are a blessing from above*

CHAPTER ONE

Christmas Eve, 1988 - Tarpon Springs, Florida

Although Suzie wouldn't allow any emotion to show on her beautiful face, she felt a sadness as she watched her youngest son, Jason, soon to be eighteen, leave to enjoy the holiday festivities with his best girlfriend, Sarah. Her oldest son, Douglas, had already left to spend the holiday with his fiancé, Tracy, and her parents.

Suzie glanced around the suddenly lonely room, admiring the Christmas decorations she had meticulously placed throughout the apartment. Although David wasn't able to spend the holidays with her, she had outdone herself with the decorating. The tree was exceptionally beautiful with its twinkling miniature white lights, meticulously placed white and gold ornaments, gold beads, clusters of baby's breath, and large gold bows.

The beauty of the room was wasted by the emptiness Suzie felt. Now that she was alone, her mind overflowed with memories of David. After all, it was Christmas Eve.

"Christmas is a romantic time...." she whispered, taking a deep breath to fight the tears that welled in her deep blue eyes. "David, if you really love me as much as you say, why aren't we together tonight?"

Suzie turned on the stereo and lay down beneath the Christmas tree. When Elvis' "Blue Christmas" started to play, she closed her eyes to allow her tears to spill onto her cheeks.

Finally, exhausted and depressed, she fell asleep and started to dream. In her dream, David was holding her lovingly in his arms. The dream seemed real. His kisses awoke the long-neglected passion within the deep crevices of her soul.

Suzie was awakened as a climax racked her body, with relieving satisfaction. At first, she couldn't believe what had happened. "I didn't think it was possible for a woman to be sexually relieved without manual stimulation or lovemaking! I thought only men had 'wet' dreams!" she said to herself, mystified by what had happened.

The magnitude of her dream was overwhelming. It seemed as if David was actually holding her, making love to her. His body seemed to be pressed against hers in a never-ending embrace. Miraculously, the loneliness and depression was now gone. Suzie felt happy, refreshed, loved.

"David, I love you too much!" she whispered to herself. "I want you more today than when we were twenty years old. Since the day we met, I've never stopped loving you, wanting you, and needing to hold you in my arms, to be held. But, maybe I'm not as special to you. You made the decision, not once, but twice, for us not to be together. You said we could have had a successful relationship; that we could have made it work. You said my children should have been yours. Oh, David, it's not too late, is it?"

Suzie pondered, savoring the dream, hugging herself as she remembered the sweetness of David's love. "If I can't have you, David, I'll remain alone forever!"

Feeling inspired by her dream, Suzie picked up a pen and note pad. The words to a free-verse poem were flowing through her mind so rapidly that she couldn't get the pen to write fast enough. She quickly jotted down the poem:

DREAMS

Tonight was so wonderful!
Hearing you peacefully sleeping,
Oh, the sensuous warmth of your skin,
The faint aroma of your musky cologne,
Your kiss as your lips crushed mine,
Inflamed by your massive embrace,
As we adventure passion beyond belief!

BUT

Then I awoke from my ravishing dream
To the desolate darkness of this lonely room!
Since we no longer sing a lover's serenade,
Please visit me often—in my dreams!

Suzie read and re-read the lines of the poem, making minor changes. Yes, the words were a reality of her life. In her dreams, David was still her lover. He still held her in his arms in her dreams. Their passion had been so realistic; she actually had experienced sexual satisfaction.

Confused by it all, she began to pray: "Dear Father, please help me. You created me in Your image. You've given me this sexual desire, which, at times, has gotten me into trouble, leading me astray. Thank you, Father, for forgiving my multitude of sins. Help me control this burning passion. I don't want to be a carnal Christian! Lord Jesus, I don't know what to think about my sensuous dreams. I feel as if I should thank You for the sexual release. I must have had a need. Your Word tells me YOU fulfill ALL my needs."

Suzie laughed at herself, and then prayed the Lord's Prayer. She sat motionless for several minutes, deep in thought, staring at the Christmas tree, thinking about Jesus' birth. He IS the reason for the season...."

She wanted to feel joyous, to put David completely out of her mind. She rebuked the devil..."This is satan's devious trick to steal my Christmas joy!"

Praying again, "Lord Jesus, why have You allowed so much love to be in my heart for David? Can we, will we, ever be together? Does he realize how much I love him? Oh, Lord, I pray for David's salvation. Prepare his heart, convict him of his sins, and work Your Will in his life. Give him another chance to accept you as his Savior."

She sighed and continued, "Your Word tells me You will give me the desires of my heart. It's my desire for David to be with me in Heaven. Search my heart, Lord; see that my motives are true. If I have to, I can survive without him on this earth if I know we'll spend eternity with You in Heaven. Thank You, Lord, for saving me, for giving me the assurance that I WILL spend eternity in Heaven. In Jesus' Holy Name, I pray. Amen."

The Carpenters' song, "Christmas Bride" was now playing on the stereo. Suzie's arms were prickled with goosebumps as she listened. Oh, yes, she wanted so much to be David's Christmas bride. She didn't want anyone else but him.

Still inspired, Suzie felt compelled to write a love story, using bits and pieces of her love affair with David as the basis for the novel. The story would be fabricated, of course, but the emotions would be real. She would write their story. The characters would be believable, but stronger than life.

"David's character will be an Adonis," she whispered, "and the character I create for myself will be much stronger emotionally than I am. Let's see, what kind of problems can I create for them?"

"There's a problem, though, this will be a difficult novel because I don't know how things will end up between us... the real lovers!" She whispered, as she began to write:

"UNTITLED"
A Writer's Fantasy

Written by Michelle Wynne

Spring, 1963 - A Small Town in Midwestern Ohio
(onset to the sexual revolution)

April Morgan was celebrating her twentieth birthday by going to Frisch's Drive-in Restaurant with her best friend, Sandy.

"Well, April," Sandy said, "how does it feel to be a woman?"

"What do you mean?"

"Well, hey, you're twenty years old today. You're no longer a giggling teenager. You're a woman, now!"

"I don't feel any different. I wonder what the next ten years will bring us, Sandy. Who do you think we'll marry? What do you think our wedding night will be like? You know, the big event! The night we can finally give in ... lose our virginity?!" April said wistfully.

"Well, speak for yourself, Girl. I'm not planning to save myself until the wedding night. When I meet that special guy, he won't have to wait until we're married."

"Well, you know why I feel so strongly about staying pure until I'm married. My Dad! Do you know what I heard from my cousin? She said my Dad requested prayer for me at church in Tennessee the other day because he thinks I'm sleeping around with a different guy every night. I can't believe he did it 'cause he seldom goes to church. He thinks I'm promiscuous simply because I have my own apartment. Why does he say those terrible things, Sandy? I've always been good..."

"Gee, if he knew about your reputation, 'Miss Cool Cucumber,' he'd thank his lucky stars. He's a bum, April. If he knew the truth, that you won't let a guy kiss you until the third date, the shock'd probably kill him! Really, April, that's pretty tough on a guy."

"I'm afraid to let my hair down, Sandy.... afraid I'll lose control of my emotions. It's like I have a volcano smoldering inside me. I think about making love all the time."

"What I wouldn't give to be in your shoes, you lucky dog! You're so cute. You've got a perfect figure ... everything's proportioned, a curvy figure eight. You're not too tall, just the right size, in my opinion. Look at you, you get asked out all the time. You could have a date every night, if you wanted. Believe me, if I looked like you, and had my own apartment, I'd have a ball!"

"Well, Sandy, you know I had to get my own apartment when my parents split up. After all, I had a good job at the bank and didn't want to move to Tennessee. It's not easy making ends meet on my meager salary, though. You know I don't make much money."

"Well, April, from where I'm sitting, you have it all!"

"Sandy, I'd gladly give it up for the right guy. I don't want a career. I can't wait to get married, to have children. I've got so much to give a good man. I wantta be a good wife, a good mother, a good homemaker—in that order. But, for tonight, my birthday, let's forget all those negative things my Dad has said and have some fun."

"Yeah, put him out of your mind. It's your birthday. The guys go ga-ga over you. Marty's got a major crush on you. The guys keep asking you out, even though you keep telling them 'no.' Why don't you date a guy more than once or twice?"

"Well, to be honest, by the second date, I know if he's husband material or not. If he's not, I stop seeing him. I've got to keep my emotions under control, so I'll still be a virgin when I get married."

"Why?"

"I've just got to ... because of my Dad."

"Well, good luck; you're going to need it; but for tonight, you need to laugh. Maybe there'll be some cute guys at Frisch's."

"Well, hopefully, we'll see 'cause we're almost there. I want to laugh, have some fun. Tonight, I have an overwhelming feeling that I'm being followed by a lucky star!"

As April pulled into Frisch's parking lot, she saw an old friend, Tom Wilson.

"Sandy, I'm going to park next to Tom. You remember him, don't you? He was on the wrestling team in school. He used to pull my pigtails in the third grade."

As soon as she had parked, Tom walked over to her car. "Hi, Good Lookin'," he said, as he leaned into her car window to kiss her gently on the cheek. "Happy Birthday! I was hoping I'd see you tonight, so I could give you a birthday kiss."

"Thanks, Tom, for remembering. Good friends, like you, make it a special day. You remember Sandy, don't you ... from school?"

"Sure. Hi, Sandy. How'ya doing?" he asked, still looking at April.

Sandy smiled and nodded and then continued to chat with a couple of friends who were parked on her side of April's car.

"Where have you been keeping yourself, Tom?" April asked.

"Oh, I've been around. I've been dating a new girl. She's kind of special."

Tom's attention was suddenly drawn away from their conversation. Everyone in the drive-in restaurant is laughing.

"Well, I guess Jared Walker got his new car. Would you look at that nut?" Tom remarked, pointing towards the car which had entered the parking lot.

They all watched as a shiny maroon Corvair convertible backed up in front of the security guard. The driver of the car sprayed the guard with water from his windshield washer, and sped away.

It was an amazing sight, and everyone laughed hysterically as the security guard wiped his face, shaking his night stick as he shouted, "Don't try that again, Walker!"

April glanced at Tom, as the car drove around to where they were parked. "Who is that, Tom?"

"Jared Walker. He's our age, but graduated from Jefferson. His dad bought him that car for his 20th birthday last month. It was a special order. I guess he just got it today."

Jared parked his car at an angle behind Tom and said, "H-e-l-l-o!" April knew he was talking to Tom, but he was looking directly at her, with a broad smile.

"Jared, do you know April Morgan? She's a friend of mine." Tom said, introducing them.

"No, but it's a pleasure to meet ya'. Hey, April, how ya' doin'?" he said as he got out of his car and walked over to them.

April smiled, and then looked away as Jared and Tom discussed the new car. When she could resist no longer, she observed Jared as he talked with Tom. She liked what she saw. He was almost six feet tall, slender, built like a man is supposed to be built ... broad muscular shoulders, and slim waist. He had curly, almost-black hair, with a light olive complexion, definitely had an Italian look. Jared and Tom were almost the same height and frame; but, Tom had straight blond hair, similar in looks and stance to Troy Donahue.

"Come on, Tom," April heard Jared say. "Let's go for a ride in my new car."

April watched as they got into Jared's car. She tried to refrain from turning her head to watch them leave; but she found she was captivated by Jared Walker's natural looks. She escaped, momentarily, into a fantasy. Emotionally, she could never remember feeling so much so quickly after meeting a new man. Although she'd been sexually attracted to other men in the past, she was awestruck by this dynamic man, Jared Walker.

"Hey, April, come on, let's go to the restroom inside." Sandy suggested, breaking April's trance.

"Okay, I need to freshen-up."

"Oh, pooh! You look great."

As they walked inside, April remarked, "Jared Walker is really cute. Do you know him?"

"Well, I know about him. He has a way with women—makes them feel like they're the most important girl in the world when he's with them; but I've heard he won't get serious unless a girl's willing to go all the way with him..."

"Are you sure? Have you ever dated him?"

"No-o-o! but, he used to date Carol Simpkins. She told me all about him."

"Oh, tell..." April pleaded.

"Well, we both know about Carol; she's dated everyone who looks her way. According to her, she and Jared really got it on for a while."

After they had finished in the restroom, April and Sandy walked outside to return to her car. Halfway there, Jared drove his car alongside them.

April blushed, as he looked her over approvingly. He whistled softly, and sensuous chills swept over her. She tried to ignore him as she hurriedly got into her car.

When Jared dropped Tom off next to April's car he smiled at April, and then said, "Hey, Tom, I'll see you soon."

April wondered if he was talking to her. After all, he was looking at her when he said it. She gave Jared a smile, and waved as he drove away.

"April," Tom said, "Jared asked me for your phone number. I told him that he couldn't have it 'cause I have MY eye on you."

"Oh, Tom, you know we're too good a' friends to date." she said, waving her hand, slapping his forearm playfully. "You're special ... just like a brother."

"Sometimes that's the best way to start a love affair... by being best friends first, then lovers." Tom quirked hopefully.

"And, what about this special girl you were just telling me about a few minutes ago?" she smirked.

"Sweetheart, I'd drop her in a minute if I thought I had a chance with you." Tom said seriously. "You won't even let me get close to you."

April knew Tom was serious, and that he had had a "crush" on her since grade school. But, she couldn't let herself think about that right now. She was in a daze. Her mind was racing at the prospect that Jared Walker wanted HER telephone number. She didn't say anything in rebuttal to Tom at first. She didn't want to hurt his feelings. It wasn't in her nature to be cruel to anyone.

"Oh, Tom, come on. You're leading me on! You'd just break my heart!" she teased.

"No way, April, I care too much about you to hurt you." He replied, looking deeply into her eyes.

"You're sweet, Tom ... just like a brother."

"Okay, I give up for now. Well, then, do you want me to give Walker your phone number? He's going to call me later."

"Sure, I guess it's okay," she said, not wanting to sound too anxious.

"If he calls, be careful. I'm not at all sure you two travel in the same circles."

"Oh, pooh, it'll be okay, Tom." she assured him.

"Well, listen, I've gotta go. Have a happy birthday!" he said, as he kissed her on the cheek. Then, in a loving gesture, he kissed her hand, which was resting on the car door. "Are you sure? It could be really great between us."

"You're the greatest, Tom! I wish things were different."

"Darlin', if you ever change your mind, if you ever need me, I'm all yours. It'll be terrific, I promise."

She blew him a kiss and watched as he walked away. She had to admit Tom Wilson was a remarkably attractive man.

"Hey, April, why don't you go out with him? He's a doll! Tall, blonde, and, oh, God, those gorgeous blue eyes. You two would make a great-lookin' couple." Sandy said, urging April to reconsider.

"Unfortunately, he's too much like a brother. Besides, I prefer guys with dark hair, like Jared Walker. Do you think he'll call, Sandy?"

"Oh, I'd hate to see you with him. Give Tom a chance, please. He's more your type."

"Why don't I fix YOU up with Tom? He's going to the University of Cincinnati. He's going to be an engineer ... says he wants to build bridges."

"Maybe, I'd go out with him, if things don't work out with Rick. We've been dating for a couple months now. But, really, April, why don't you reconsider? Its obvious Tom's crazy about you."

"Well, who knows, maybe someday I'll go out with him. I can't think about that right now. Jared Walker's crowding him out of my mind."

"Tom would be much better for you than the likes of that Jared Walker." Sandy smirked.

"Well, time'll tell...." April said, confident that she'd have a chance to find out, first-hand, about Jared Walker.

* * *

Every time the telephone rang the next week, April jumped. Sandy called twice, just to gossip. Joe Sweeney, a friend from the bank called to ask April to see a movie with him on Friday night after work. She refused because she wanted to keep her weekend open in case Jared wanted to take her out.

Somehow she knew Jared would call. After all, she WANTED him to call! Positive thinking is nine-tenths of the battle, she reasoned.

Finally, on Thursday evening, as April was giving herself a manicure, the phone rang. Feminine intuition told her it was Jared. April answered on the first ring. Ut oh, a mistake, she thought to herself. I should have let the phone ring a few more times before I answered it.

As soon as April heard Jared's deep voice, she said his name. Oh, no, another stupid mistake, she thought.

I should have been coy, pretended not to know who was calling.

After several minutes of small talk, Jared asked, "Would you like to see a movie with me on Saturday night?"

"Yes, of course, I'd love to...." she said quickly. Then, she closed her eyes in regret, thinking to herself that she'd goofed again by agreeing so quickly. She knew she should have been less available at this late date—just two days notice!

"Great! What's your address?" Jared asked. "I heard you live in an apartment complex downtown."

"That's right," she said, wondering who had told him. She surmised it must have been Tom, and she gave him the address and directions to her apartment complex.

"Is seven o'clock okay?" he asked.

"Sure, that'll be fine, Jared."

"I'm lookin' forward to our date, April. I'll see you Saturday night at seven."

The phone line went dead. April cradled the receiver in her hand for several minutes. "Imagine that! I have a date with Jared Walker. I can't believe it!" she said. She hung up the phone, got up and danced around the room joyfully. "Me, April Morgan," she said, pointing to herself, "I have a date with the handsomest man in the whole wide world...."

April quickly called Sandy to tell her the great news. Sandy, to say the least, was not overjoyed by the news, but tried to be happy for her best friend.

* * *

Friday seemed like the longest day in history. April was amazed when her window balanced on the first count. All she could think about was her upcoming date with Jared Walker.

After work, she and Sandy drove to Frisch's for Big Boys and cherry Cokes. Other than that, it was an uneventful evening. She had hoped to see Jared; but, he was nowhere to be found. Sandy agreed to go shopping with her the next morning to find a new outfit to wear on her dream date.

When April got home, she was too excited to sleep. Although she was extremely tired, and she knew she needed her "beauty" sleep so she'd look great for Jared, she couldn't drift off.

When she finally fell asleep, she dreamt about a prince on a white stallion, who came charging in to slay the wicked dragon. The prince swept her away to forever happiness. Strange, she thought, that handsome prince resembled Jared Walker.

April woke up late on Saturday morning; but she immediately rejoiced—it was Saturday. That night, she had a date with Jared Walker. Glancing at the clock, she stumbled to the telephone and dialed Sandy's number. Mrs. Reid, Sandy's mother, answered the phone. "She's on her way to your apartment, April."

Just as April hung up the phone, the doorbell rang. She quickly let Sandy in and said: "I overslept. Please fix us some coffee while I get ready."

* * *

Shopping was tedious and frustrating .... Everything seemed inappropriate or too expensive. April finally decided to buy a pale blue cashmere sweater with white piping. She'd wear it with her black wool skirt and black heels.

"My budget doesn't allow much for clothes, Sandy; but, this sweater is too beautiful to resist."

"Yes, the sweater is very pretty; but, from what you told me, this is three months' clothing allowance. Are you sure?"

"It's soft and dreamy, and the same color as my eyes. And, Sandy, it's on sale. If it wasn't, I could never afford cashmere."

"Is Jared Walker really THIS special?"

"Yes, he is. Luckily, I got some birthday money from my Mom, or I wouldn't be able to buy it." April remarked, as she handed the store clerk three twenty dollar bills.

Exhausted from shopping without breakfast or lunch, April suggested they stop for a bowl of chili at Frisch's on the way home.

Then Sandy dropped April off at her apartment, saying, "Well, Kid, I hope he's worth all this trouble. I'm not sure you're the same April I've known for the past ten years. I've never known you to be this excited about anything, 'Miss Cool Cucumber'. Be careful."

"He's different, I just know it." April said.

"Yes, I know; but, can YOU handle him?"

"Oh, Sandy," she smirked, ignoring Sandy's remark. "I've got so much to do ... my hair, my nails; my makeup has to be perfect. And, I've got to clean up my apartment.

"Well, if you ask me, which you're not, he's nothing special ... just an ordinary guy."

"I've always heard love is blind..." April said, nonchalantly.

The Gypsy Cried

"Well, then, put on your glasses, April. Take a good look; but, since you've got *so much to do*, I'll head on home; Rick's coming over tonight." Sandy said sarcastically. "Be careful, and have a good time, if that's possible. I'll call you tomorrow."

"Okay, thanks, Sandy." April said, as she waved good-bye to her longtime friend. She knew what Sandy meant when she said to be careful; but she couldn't think about that right then.

April spent the next two hours straightening her already-immaculate apartment, and getting dressed for her date.

She styled her light brown hair into a pageboy fluff, swept back on one side. The soft blue cashmere sweater complemented her blue eyes. The freshly-pressed black wool skirt enhanced her cute figure. The seams up the back of her hose were perfectly straight, as she stared into the full-length mirror.

She meticulously applied her make-up, and then smiled at her image in the bathroom mirror. "I'll knock him dead! He'll fall for me at first sight.... I hope!"

April glanced at her watch; it was seven thirty-five. No Jared. Where could he be? she wondered, as she looked out the window that overlooked the parking lot. No Corvair convertible to be found.

Oh, relax, Girl, she thought to herself. He's just running a few minutes late. It's no big deal. He'll be here soon.

By eight o'clock, April was panic stricken, and fighting the tears that pooled in her eyes. "Oh, no, I'm going to be stood-up. How embarrassing! I've never been stood-up in my life."

The sound of the ringing telephone jarred her back to reality. She grabbed the receiver and said angrily, "Hello."

"April, this is Jared. I'm sorry to be late. I've been driving around for over a half hour trying to find your apartment complex."

Relief was evident in April's voice as she again gave Jared directions to her apartment. She quickly ran to the bathroom to repair the damage her tears had caused to her make-up.

* * *

Five minutes later, the doorbell rang. She smiled to her image in the mirror and said, "Well, there's your Prince Charming. Your magical night is finally beginning...."

CHAPTER TWO

······························

April opened the door and Jared quickly stepped inside. He smiled at April, and then glanced around her living room, which was comfortable-looking, and softly feminine in style.

"Wow, April, you look great!" he said, taking her hands and admiring her from head to toe. "I'm sorry I'm late. Will you forgive me? Hey, you have a nice apartment."

April blushed, diverted her eyes, and glanced to the floor coyly, trying to hide her excitement. "Thanks, Jared. I'll forgive your being late this time, I guess."

"Well," he said, glancing at his watch, "if you are ready, we'd better hit the road. The movie starts in a few minutes."

As they walked to Jared's car, they chatted nonchalantly. He opened the car door for April, and helped her get into his car. April quickly wrapped her hair in a blue chiffon scarf since Jared had the top down in his convertible. While they drove to the theater, April turned sideways in the bucket seat, leaning against the car door, staring at Jared, who was very handsome, wearing black dress slacks and a black watch plaid shirt with a button-down collar.

His dark curly hair was well-styled, very becoming, and cut somewhat shorter than most men were wearing their hair.

As they drove along, April told Jared things she had never told anyone, things about her Dad and his mistreatment of her. She even mentioned her goal to remain virginal until her wedding night. She was thrilled when he seemed to agree with her goal, seemed to understand.

As she talked, Jared would turn his head to look at her as often as he could and still keep the car on the road. Her innocent beauty overwhelmed him. He hoped he was communicating that fact with his amorous glances.

His adoration and chills of excitement which swept through her body thrilled April. Yes, she had been attracted to men before, but never like this!

April assumed they were going to an inside movie theater; so, when Jared pulled into a drive-in movie, she gulped. After all, drive-ins had a reputation for being "make-out pits." This was their first date. She was somewhat appalled and wondered how she should handle the situation, the dilemma.

Relief, however, became obvious when Jared pulled his small car to the front row of the theatre. He laughed when he saw her surprised expression.

"Hey, the simple fact is, I can't see very well. Besides, the cops never check out the front row!" he explained.

"Well, Jared, I have to tell you. I, uh, usually don't go to a drive-in with a guy ... and, certainly not on the first date."

"Don't worry, April, you can trust me. You'll see. I'm a gentleman. After all, I didn't head for the lovers' lane rows in the back, did I? Really, you can trust me."

* * *

April didn't have time to respond as the screen burst with light, and they laughed at the "Tweety Bird" cartoon.

"Do you mind me having the top down on the car?" he asked. "Would you rather have it up?"

"No, of course not. This is fine."

"Well, let me know if you get cold...." he said

The first movie began to play. Frankie Avalon and Annette Funicello were staring in a beach movie. As they watched, April couldn't help but note a resemblance between Frankie and Jared.

"Has anyone ever said you look like Frankie Avalon? You could be his brother." she asked.

Jared turned his head and smiled, looking intently at April, not saying anything. He touched the fluffiness of her hair. It was soft. Her hair was not stiff and lacquered with hair spray, as most girls' were.

"Yes, don't you know? He's my brother! I'm afraid I've heard this before. So I just decided to adopt him for a brother. And, you know, with your hair styled like this, you kind of look like Annette ... you have beautiful eyes ... and those cheeks..." he whispered, as he touched her plump cheek affectionately.

April smiled, and realized he was "heading" in the direction of making a pass. She swallowed hard, turned her head abruptly, and pretended to watch the movie, which gave her a chance to regain her composure.

"We could pretend their love story is OUR love story...." he whispered, as he continues to stroke her cheek, trailing her jawline to her neck. He ran his hand down her arm and softly whispered, "You smell so great, and your sweater is so soft.... I really like it."

April was thrilled by his touch, and tingles of excitement swept through her. She wanted to throw herself into his arms. Quickly regaining her composure, she looked at Jared and smiled, "Watch the movie, Frankie...."

Jared laughed, and for several minutes they stared at the screen. April felt the warmth of Jared's hand, which was now resting on the car seat, just centimeters away from hers. She was aware of every breath he took, and was influenced by their lookalikes on the screen—two young lovers who were falling in love. Whenever Frankie kissed Annette on the screen, April longed to feel Jared's arms around her, to have his lips pressed against hers in a never-ending kiss.

April mentally chastised herself, asking herself what was wrong with her. She mentally commanded herself to regain her composure. She pretended to watch the movie, trying to clear her mind of amorous thoughts. Maintaining her composure was difficult, but she forced herself.

Finally, the movie ended. Jared broke their silence. "Would you like a Coke?"

"Oh, yes, that'd be great!" she replied, with a smile.

"I'll be right back, then," he said, touching her hand. "Would you like anything else? Do you need the restroom or anything?"

"No, a Coke's fine ... and I'm fine. I'll wait here."

After he walked away, April used the few minutes of solitude to clear her mind. She tried to figure out why she was so shaken by Jared's good looks. Although she had probably dated better-looking men than Jared, none of

The Gypsy Cried

them had affected her like he had. He excited her like no other man.

Jared returned, carrying two soft drink glasses, handing her one of them before he got back into the convertible. The Cokes were cold and refreshing and the conversation was interesting as Jared told April about himself.

"I was a change-of-life baby. I have seven brothers and sisters who are all well established in life, with careers and families of their own. I am the only one who's still single, still living at home."

"Oh, I see. You're the 'baby' of the family, and used to getting your own way. Spoiled rotten, no doubt." she teased.

Although she was kidding with her remark, the thought did scare her somewhat. She sensed his desire, his sensuality. He maintained eye contact with her, and stroked her shoulder or arm as they talked.

"April, the moonlight shining on your hair makes you look like a beautiful princess. I just love this sweater. It's so soft." he mumbled.

"Well, that might not be moonlight, Jared, it could be the theatre lights..." she said, with a laugh.

He laughed at her remark and shook his head.

"Hey, thanks for the compliment. I like this sweater, too. It's new. I bought it at Rike's today with some birthday money I received."

"Your birthday? Today's your birthday?"

"No, not today. I was celebrating my birthday the night we met. Remember? Frisch's restaurant? I was celebrating my twentieth birthday that night."

"Well, Kid, happy birthday! This is a beautiful sweater for a beautiful lady. I love your hair; it's so soft. Oh, April..." he whispered, moving closer to her.

Luckily April's attention was drawn to the screen. The second movie was beginning. Jared leaned over and kissed April gently, sweetly, which caught her totally off-guard.

"Happy Birthday...." he whispered, as the kiss ended.

She was noticeably shaken by the tenderness of the kiss. Mentally, she again chastised herself because she had broken her most important rule and allowed him to kiss her much too soon in their relationship. What's wrong with me? she asked herself. I've got to stay cool until my wedding night. Then, I can relax and make love to my man for the rest of my life. I cannot let passion lead me astray. My Dad would kill me.

Neither Jared nor April could concentrate on the second movie, which was a strange spy movie with foreign subtitles.

Finally, Jared took her hand in his, kissed it lightly, and said, "Do you like this movie?"

April was afraid to answer his question. If she admitted she didn't like the movie, would she end up fighting him off before the evening ended, she wondered. She chose not to respond to his question.

"I take that as a negative! Tell you what. Why don't we get outta here? Wantta get a sandwich at Frisch's?" he suggested. He had sensed her anxiety, and wanted to reassure her that she could trust him. He knew it was too soon to make advances.

Jared's mind raced with confusing thoughts as he raised the convertible top. He had never met anyone like April Morgan. She oozed with sexuality; but she turned cold at the first touch. If he can be patient with her, he felt confident that he would be able to break down her resistance, and teach her the thrills of lovemaking. Tonight, however, was not the night, he reasoned.

The Frisch's Buddy Boy sandwiches and cherry Cokes were delicious, and they continued to lighten the mood and chat about their lives. April was hoping some of her friends would drive into the restaurant, because she wanted them to see her with Jared as they sat in his car, again with the top down, noticeable by all.

When Tom Wilson pulled into the parking space next to Jared's car, April waved to him. He waved back, giving her a surprised, and then disappointed look. He got out of his car and walked around to Jared's window.

"Well, what do we have here?" he asked, looking at April. "I'm tellin' you, Walker, April's pretty special. You'd better behave yourself, or you'll answer to me."

Tom and Jared looked at each other for several minutes, not saying anything, knowing the "line had been drawn in the sand," signaling their battle to win April's heart.

"Hey, Man," Jared smirked, as he took April's hand. "A gentleman always behaves himself when he's with a lady..." He kissed her hand gently, still looking at Tom. Then, he looked over at April and whispered, "I know a good thing when I see it. I'm going to treat her like the princess she is...."

April blushed and smiled, then glanced away to relieve the intenseness of the conversation.

"Well, then, I'll leave you two alone...." Tom said. "You take care of yourself, April." As he walked away, he shook his head, bewildered at seeing April with Jared.

"Are you ready to go?" he asked.

"Yeah, I'd better get home. It's getting late." He again raised the convertible top because the night air had become somewhat cool.

Neither Jared nor April said much as he drove the short trip to her apartment. They were both preoccupied by their thoughts, pretending to listen to the soothing sounds from the stereo. Neither wanted the evening to end. April secretly longed to have Jared to take her in his arms and hold her forever. She wondered what would happen when they got back to her apartment.

Jared was toying with the idea of making another pass. Then, he decided he had better not take a chance on messing up their great date. He decided he would play it "cool" so he would not scare her away. He knew by her reputation that he had already gotten more than most guys on a first date with her. He wanted another date, another chance. He knew that if he "played her game" and got her to fall in love with him, eventually he would get what he wanted. April was "hot" property among his peers. Most of them would kill to be where he was that night ... on a date with "Miss Cool Cucumber!"

"April, this has been a lot of fun. I'd like to see you again. You're really sweet," he said as he turned into her parking lot.

"Thanks, Jared. I enjoyed it too," she replied nonchalantly. She was preoccupied with her thoughts, and somewhat apprehensive as they walked to her apartment.

Jared took April's hand protectively as they crossed the courtyard to her building.

"You know, April, you're the only girl our age that I know of who has her own apartment. How do you swing the rent alone? You can't make that much money at the bank."

"Well, I have a tight budget. I have to watch my nickels and pennies very carefully..." she said, with a chuckle.

Jared laughed, and squeezed her hand affectionately.

By the time they arrived at her front door, April was trembling both from the chill of the night, and somewhat fearful she would mess up with Jared. She fumbled with the key in the lock. Her hand trembled and she dropped the keys.

Jared quickly picked them up and said, "Here, let me do that...." He calmly unlocked the door and opened it, swinging the door wide open. "Hum-m-m, where's the light switch?" he asked.

April felt inside the door and flipped the switch to flood the room with light. Jared handed April her door keys and looked around the living room.

"I just want to make sure there's no intruder ... to be sure you're alone here."

Not knowing what he meant by his remark, April frowned.

Jared quickly explained, "To be sure no one has broken in, or anything..."

April laughed, shaking her head as affirmation.

Jared became quiet and looked directly at April, maintaining eye contact. He wanted to kiss her again. Tom had warned him that April NEVER kissed on the first date.

Since he had already gotten a small kiss, should he press his luck?" he wondered.

"Your eyes are so blue... like pools of water on a warm sunny day. I'd like to dive in and swim around in there forever," he whispered, and then became embarrassed by the corniness of his remark. He looked away as his face turned bright pink in color.

"Hey, I'd look pretty funny with a man swimming around in my eyes, wouldn't I?" she teased, laughing sensuously. She touched his hand reassuringly, letting him know his remark was quite a compliment.

Using this as a "go ahead" signal, Jared touched April's cheek with the tips of his fingers.

"I'd like to stay for a little while..." he whispered but sensing sudden alarm in her eyes, he explained..."You know, to make sure you are in no danger ... to make sure there are no intruders."

"Oh, I think the only danger is YOU! Some other time, maybe." she said, steering him towards the door.

Jared put his arms around April, and their lips touched in a sweet, passion-filled kiss. She couldn't help herself ... she moaned, put her arms around his slim waist, and returned the passion. As they embraced, Jared's hands slipped underneath her sweater and the touch of his hand on her bare back sent thrills through them both. Suddenly frightened, April pulled away.

"You're special, April. I'll call you soon.... Maybe we can go out Friday night."

"I'll see; I have to work until about seven o'clock on Friday nights. Sometimes I don't get off until after eight, and then, I'm usually pretty tired," she replied, proud of herself for regaining her composure so quickly after the breathtaking kiss.

"Well, I'll give you a call later in the week. Maybe we can just take a ride, get a sandwich, or a pizza."

"Maybe, I'll see. Call me, okay?"

"You bet!" Jared said. He had decided not to take a chance on messing things up by becoming too aggressive. He'd gotten a passionate kiss, and the underlying promise of more to come. But, feeling suddenly confident, he cradled April's face in his hands and kissed her again. She abruptly pulled away.

"That's enough for tonight, Jared Walker!"

"As long as it's just for tonight..." he said, looking intently into her eyes. April looked away and opened the door to her apartment.

"Goodnight, Princess. Catch ya' later. Sweet dreams." He said as he walked away. He stopped suddenly, and turned to look at April, saying nothing. He sighed deeply, shook his head, and gave her a questioning look, hoping for an invitation to stay.

Remembering her dream, she asked. "Jared, why did you call me 'Princess'?"

"That's a good question. I don't know. You just seem like a beautiful princess."

April smiled and closed the door halfway. "Thanks, again, Jared. I had a great time."

Jared smiled, not saying anything. He gave her a longing glance. "I'll call you next week..." he whispered.

Jared listened as she closed and locked the door. He smiled to himself as he walked down the hallway to leave the apartment building. Once outside, he turned to look at

April's window. She was standing in the window, watching him leave. He waved, feeling very cocky and confident. After all, he had gotten a very passionate kiss on his first date with "Miss Cool Cucumber!"

"Well, what do you know about that! Miss Cool Cucumber will kiss on the first date. Walker, you got that charm..." he said to himself as he ran across the parking lot and leaped into the air with delight. "I wonder what else she will do? Do I dare kiss and tell? Nah, no one will believe me; and, if she found out that I had bragged about it, she would never speak to me again. I plan to turn that little kitten into my tiger!"

Jared started the car, giving himself a challenge as he glanced at his image in the rear view mirror. "Jared Walker, I challenge you to melt that little iceberg. Pick that cherry while it's sweet, and ripe for the plucking...."

As was the usual practice for the guys after their dates on Saturday night, Jared drove back to Frisch's. Tom was still there, and was glad when he saw Jared drive into the parking space next to his. He motioned for Jared to get into his car.

"Well, Walker, how was your date with April? I see she sent you packing early.... GOOD! Good for her. Did you get a kiss?" Tom asked smugly, expecting Jared to say that he had not.

"That's none of your business, Wilson; but, for the record, as a matter of fact, I did!"

"You're shittin' me, Walker! April Morgan never kisses on the first date."

"Don't worry about it, Man. She's a nice girl. That's obvious. Don't worry yourself. Her precious virginity is still intact. Why don't you stop asking silly questions and order us a Coke, Man?"

Tom ordered the soft drinks as instructed, and they continued to talk for a few minutes about local sporting events. Then the conversation turned serious again.

"Jared, April Morgan is REALLY very special. We've been friends for years... ever since we were kids. To be frank, I've got my eye on her to be my wife someday, after I've sewn a few wild oats."

"Sorry, Man, not if I get there first. Right now, the ball seems to be in my court." Jared bragged confidently.

"Well, April's not like most girls. She really IS pure, and yet, she's a little wildcat. She's MY idea for a perfect wife ... calm, cool and collected on the outside, probably red hot in the bedroom. She can cook, and her apartment is always clean. I know because I've been there several times."

"So far, I agree with everything you say." Jared remarked.

"Man, she looks like a dream. Every hair's in place. I'd love to mess up her hair. She's the greatest, Man, the greatest!"

"Yes, I agree. She's something else...." Jared replied.

"I'm tellin' you that I've staked my claim on her. I don't want her spoiled by the likes of you, Love-em-and-Leave-em Walker!"

"Well, may the best man win, Tom, but I'm the one who has a date with her Friday night. I have the home court advantage. Besides, you have Carol."

"You know exactly why I'm dating Carol. You've been there ... she's just a momentary amusement. I'd never marry her. She used to be hung up on you, right?"

Jared smiled sarcastically. "Yeah, she's okay."

"She's okay... but, she's not April, though."

"Well, Tom, you and I have been friends for a long time. You've never introduced me to April before. Either you've been hiding her, or you don't know her as well as you say. But, as far as I'm concerned, as of today, it's open season on April Morgan."

"Yes, we have been friends a long time. Let's not let a woman end our friendship." Tom said, trying to change the subject because the conversation was becoming too intense.

"Let me say this, my friend. April's yours, if I don't get her first!" Jared challenged.

"She'd better be untouched when I win her over to my side." Tom counter-challenged, jokingly. They laughed, knowing they were both serious, and making harmless banter between long-time friends. They changed the subject, and began to discuss the Cincinnati Reds game.

Back at April's apartment, she could not sleep. When she was finally able to drift off, she dreamt about her prince. Her knight had a face now... Jared Walker's face. He had even called her "Princess."

CHAPTER THREE

. . . .

THE NEXT DAY:

The next morning, April was awakened by ringing church bells. She picked up the clock on her bedside table, and blinked hard until her eyes focused. It was almost eleven o'clock. She didn't have enough time to get dressed for church, and Reverend Barkley frowned on late arrivals.

She was still consumed by a passionate longing to give herself to Jared Walker, in a satisfying surrender, to have complete knowledge of his secrets, his body; so, her thoughts on that sunny Sunday morning could hardly be conducive to her pastor's sermon. All she could think about was Jared's kisses.

As she fixed herself some breakfast, her old familiar self-doubts returned. What if Jared doesn't feel the same about me? After all, we live in two different worlds. I'm the product of a broken home, and have been forced to get my own apartment.

Jared comes from a wealthy, secure environment. He's spoiled...used to getting his way. He probably thinks I'm an "*easy touch*" and, judging from my behavior last night, that's an easy assumption, she reasoned. I let my guard down, because he turned me on. He awoke a passion so deep inside me ... a passion I've never experienced with any other man.

She stared at her image in the full-length mirror. "Girl," she warned her reflection, "You'd better get a hold of yourself. Daddy said he'd kill you if you disgraced him by getting pregnant out of wedlock. Just like your Dad said, maybe you *ARE* hot-to-trot! Do you think it would occur to him that you're still a virgin? Why does my Dad assume I go all the way with my dates?"

Remembering her father's harsh destructive words, April began to cry. Finally gaining courage, she wiped away her tears, and dialed Sandy's phone number. She answered.

"Hey, Sandy, I missed church this morning. Do you wantta drive around for awhile...?"

"Okay, sure. Give me time to clean up. By the way, April, how was your date with Jared Walker last night?"

"It was great. Really great! You know, I could easily fall for him. I've got to watch myself, though, 'cause, I don't want to be just *another notch on his belt,* if you know what I mean."

"From what I've heard, he's the *love 'em and leave 'em crying type.*

"Don't worry, I'll be careful. Let's talk about this later. Tell you what, Sandy, I'll jump in the shower, and pick you up in about thirty minutes. Okay?"

"Okay. See ya."

April quickly showered and put on her favorite jeans with a royal blue pullover sweater. After she fixed her hair and makeup, she drove to Sandy's house. They drove around, uneventfully, for almost three hours talking endlessly about nothing.

April's mind was cluttered with self-doubts. She wondered if she had enough self-confidence to get Jared. She didn't mention her negative self-doubts to Sandy. They were both somewhat somber.

Nothing much was happening that afternoon, and Sandy was sick of April's moodiness said, "Today's a bummer. I've gotta get home. I told Mom I'd be home for dinner tonight 'cause my sister and her family will be there. Why don't you come over and eat with us? Mom wouldn't care. You know my mom really likes you. She thinks you're a good influence on me!"

"Nah, ever since my parents split up, I have a problem with family dinners. Thanks for asking, though. Tell everyone I said 'hello'."

"Okay, well, then, I'll see you tomorrow at work. Call me later if you need to talk." Sandy said as she got out of the car, slamming the door behind her.

"Okay, see ya." April drove away.

April couldn't stand the thought of going back to her dreary apartment. She stopped at a phone booth to look up Jared's address so she could see where he lived.

After finding the address in the phone book, she knew exactly where his street was located, in the swanky part of their town. April quickly drove to his street.

Although she was panic-stricken by the thought that Jared might see her, it was something she had to do. She slowly drove down Jared's street, noticing the beautiful mansions. Several people were outside in their yards.

Suddenly, she spotted Jared's Monza convertible parked in one of the driveways, behind two Cadillacs. Jared's house reminded her of the mansions she had seen in the movie, "Gone with the Wind," with its tall pillars, and winding driveway. She drove by quickly.

Her courage waned. She mentally asked herself, how could I ever expect to marry him? I'm fat, ugly, and poverty-stricken. *Jared's an unattainable dream!*

Unbeknownst to April, inside the house, Jared was dialing her phone number for the fifth time. He sighed, hung up the phone, and rejoined his parents in the dinette where they were having coffee and reading the Sunday newspapers.

"Still no answer?" he said, matter-of-factly.

Mr. Walker teased his youngest son, "Ut, oh, Son, she's out with someone else..."

"Dad, the girl I went out with last night's pretty special. She just turned twenty, and has her own apartment. She's got a good head on her shoulders; and, she's pretty to boot. Wow, she looks like Annette, you know, the movie star!"

"She MUST be special. Why don't you bring her over to meet us, Son?" his Mother suggested.

"Hum...maybe I will." Jared replied, thinking about the possible ramifications. He didn't recall his parents ever asking to meet one of his girlfriends.

As April drove back to her apartment, tears streamed down her cheeks. She felt hopeless. What she wanted seemed to be so unattainable for her.

Relieved to be home, she walked into the bedroom and pulled off her clothes. She stared at her naked image in the mirror. "I'm ugly...so fat. I'll never get Jared." she smirked, pulling a measuring tape out of the drawer. "I bet I've gained weight!"

She measured her waist...21 inches. Then, she measured her hips...36 inches! In the fullest part of her bust, she measured 35-1/2 inches. The numbers seemed gigantic to her.

"I'd better give up before I become the *hot-to-trot slut* my dad said I'd be! If my own Dad didn't love me, how can I ever expect another man to love me? I can't remember Daddy ever kissing me good-night. All he ever did was make wild accusations and put-downs. Hers is a hopeless cause, she surmised. "I'm totally unlovable. Give it up, Girl!" she told her mirror-image as she pulled on a lacy nightgown.

April began to cry hysterically. She ran to the bathroom and vomited into the basin. Stepping onto the scale, she weighed 119 pounds. She'd never eat again! In her mental image of herself, she WAS fat! And, to boot, she didn't have enough confidence in herself to fight for what she wanted.

Finally, exhausted and depressed, she stumbled back into the bedroom and crawled into bed. Within minutes, she fell into a deep sleep.

SAME NIGHT - JARED'S HOUSE

"Jared, are you ready to go?" Carl Walker asked his son. "If we're going to make our plane, we've got to leave soon."

"Yes, I'm packed; but, I've *got* to run an errand. It'll take about a half hour. It's really important. Do I have enough time?"

"Are you sure it can't wait until you get back on Thursday?"

"No, it's really very important."

"Okay, but, get a move on. Don't take a minute longer."

"I'll be right back, I promise, Dad. I'll go ahead and put our luggage in the trunk of your car, so we can leave as soon as I get back. Okay?"

Without waiting for a response, Jared grabbed their luggage. As an afterthought, he grabbed a fresh long-stemmed red rose from a vase on the credenza. Thinking a minute, he grabbed a pen, a piece of paper, and a roll of scotch tape from the drawer of the credenza. He quickly wrote a note, folded it and ran to his car.

When he got to April's apartment building, there were no lights on in her unit. Since she had not answered the telephone, and there were no visible lights, Jared assumed she wasn't home. After all, he reasoned, he had called several times already with no answer. He taped the quickly-scribbled note, and the beautiful red rose, to her apartment door, without ringing the doorbell.

When Jared got home, his Dad was already sitting in the car. He quickly started the engine, and motioned for Jared to get into the passenger side.

He quickly responded to his Dad's command, knowing he was being groomed to take over the family's sporting goods business. His brothers didn't want it; and Dad had voiced his desire to retire many times.

The flight to Chicago was uneventful. When they checked into their hotel, Jared was surprised to discover his Dad had rented *two* rooms. He looked at his Dad questioningly.

"I'll explain when we get to our rooms, Son."

After they were ushered into Jared's room, Carl Walker handed the bellhop a five-dollar bill and said, "Take this bag to Room 502, please. I'll be right there."

Jared waited until the bellhop had closed the door, and then asked his Dad why they weren't sharing a room.

"Son, you're twenty years old—you're a man, now. You're not a teenager anymore. I suspect you have the same '*problem*' I do with women. I married your Mother without sleeping with her. Don't get me wrong, Son, I love her deeply, but we're not sexually compatible. Oh, I'd never leave her - not in a million years. She tries, bless her heart, or you wouldn't be here. Son, you're young, handsome, and ripe for amorous adventures. Go, have some fun with some willing woman. I may do the same!"

"You're kidding...." Jared said, jaw-dropping, not believing what he heard.

"Son, sometimes it takes money for willing women to do what you want them to do, *if you know what I mean.* Here, have some fun!" he explained, handing Jared five one hundred dollar bills.

Jared's mouth fell open again in astonishment. Never, in his wildest imagination did he expect to hear those words from his Dad. "But, what about Mom?"

"All I can say is ...don't buy a pair of shoes *without trying them on* 'cause they might not fit. What if you love the shoes? Marriage is a lifetime commitment in the Walker family. It doesn't work well *if your shoes are too tight!*"

Jared had often wondered if his Dad was true to his Mother all those years, on all those buying trips.

"So, the old man's still got what it takes, huh? Good for you, Dad." Looking at the money, the hotel key, the large king-size bed, he said, "This sure beats the back seat of my car!"

Carl Walker slapped his son on the back and laughed, leaving the room with a twinkle in his eye.

After his Dad left, Jared unpacked, and freshened up by splashing some cold water on his face. After brushing his teeth, he went back downstairs.

As he strolled the lobby, he couldn't believe the smorgasbord of women, who lingered everywhere, obviously available *at a price.*

Jared walked around for about half an hour. None of the women appealed to him; so, finally, he went into the cocktail lounge and sat down, pretending to watch the floor show.

"What'll it be, Bub?" the bartender asked.

"Jack Daniels on the rocks." Jared answered, nonchalantly, as he pulled one of the hundred dollar bills from his wallet and laid it in front of him.

The bartender stared at him for a minute. Jared remained calm. The bartender finally shrugged his shoulders and remarked, "You're twenty-one, right?"

"Right, Man." He was relieved that he didn't have to prove his age.

A brassy blonde sat down on the bar stool next to Jared and snuggled against him. "Say, Good Lookin', how 'bout buyin' me one of those?" she asked, pointing to the drink in front of him.

"Sure, but that's ALL I'm buying..." Jared smirked, trying to sound worldly. Motioning to the bartender, he ordered her a drink.

She picked up the glass, pressed herself against him, and purred, "Sure you're not lookin' for a good time?"

Jared looked at her, smiled and shook his head. She walked away saying, "Too bad, we could've had a ball!"

Within the next fifteen minutes, three more women approached Jared. Their heavy make-up, and overly-sexually exposure dresses turned him off. They were much too flashy for his taste. He looked around the lounge. There wasn't a "*lady*" in the place.

By the time he had finished his third drink, and being repulsed by everything he'd seen, Jared stood up to leave. He picked up his change, leaving a five dollar tip. Suddenly, he noticed a woman who had just entered the lounge, and watched as she looked around the smoky room. Her gaze stopped to look intently at him. She quickly looked away, saying nothing, as she nonchalantly sat down at the end of the bar. She ordered a *"pink lady"* from the bartender. She glanced at Jared, and then looked away shyly.

When the bartender brought the drink, Jared pushed a five dollar bill into his hand. "Here, let me get that for you." he said, smiling at the woman.

"Why, thank you!" she said, looking away quickly, rather shyly.

Everything seemed to go well for Jared as he slowly drew the woman into a conversation.

After a few moments, he suggested, "Why don't we get a bottle of Jack Daniels and go upstairs to my room where it's quieter. We'll be much more comfortable there, and can get to know each other better." he pleaded, giving her the look that he knew worked well to persuade a woman to do as he asked.

The woman looked at Jared, intently and responded, "Sure, but, *it'll cost you*. I'll do anything your heart desires, for a price."

Her voice had suddenly become seductive, passionate, and businesslike. She resembled April; but, yet, she wasn't anything like her. Jared hesitated because her sudden aggressiveness was a turn-off.

"What the hell, let's go."

After they reached Jared's room, he asked if she wanted a drink.

"No, I want you, Stud; but, I need the money before we can do anything, Honey." she answered in a professional manner.

"How much?"

"Fifty dollars ...depending on what you want."

"The usual, I guess; but, I want you to continue to act like a shy virgin," he instructed, handing her a fifty dollar bill.

"Thanks, is this your first time?"

"With a woman, NO; but, with a hooker, yes."

"You'll love it, I promise," she as she took Jared's hand and led him to the sofa.

"Pretend we're on our first date, and you know I'm a virgin." The woman suggested as she sat down stiffly, waiting for him to make the first move.

"Boy, it's hard to believe you're only twenty years old and have your own apartment...." Jared pretended, getting into the mood. He put his arm around the shy-acting prostitute and said, "Can I kiss you goodnight?"

She didn't respond. She looked at him passionately and then looked away shyly, pretending to be virginal.

Jared pulled her into his arms, and kissed her sweetly, at first, then with more ardor. She responded passionately, and began to fumble with his clothes.

"I can't do anything," she pretended, "I'm still a virgin— pure and innocent....never been touched by a man. You're so sexy!" she said, as she pushed him away roughly, to continue the fantasy.

Jared grabbed her, and kissed her again, while unbuttoning her blouse, freeing her now-naked breasts to his caress. She moaned seductively as he continued to caress her willing body.

He stood up and swept her into his arms, carrying her to the bed. After he'd gently laid her across the foot of the bed, he pulled at her clothing with one hand, undressing himself with the other.

"Here," she purred…"Let me do that!"

When she pulled off his under shorts, she gasped, "Wow, that's quite a *baseball bat* you've got there, Honey. I can't handle that!"

Jared looked at her questioningly, surprised by her remark.

"Here, let me satisfy you another way." she instructed as she started to orally satisfy him. Jared was thrilled as she masterfully brought him to satisfaction, not realizing that this was her preferred mode of business, since it required very little *"cleaning up"* on her part. She was handing him a line, big-time.

"Oh, God, what a trip!" he exclaimed when she had finished, trying to regain his composure. "I loved it!"

"Curl up with me for a minute and then I have to go?" she instructed.

"My time's up?"

"Almost; but, I'd like to lay here with you for a few minutes…no charge. That way, it doesn't feel so businesslike. In this profession, it's not often I meet someone as nice as you are—and close to my own age!"

Jared did as she asked and cuddled her in his arms tenderly. "Why are you a prostitute?" he asked.

"For the money.... I don't have anyone in this world that gives a shit about me. Most of my tricks are ugly; so, I don't care if I ever see them again—old men, trying to prove they've still got what it takes to satisfy a woman...most of the time I fake it!"

"Can I have a date with you for the next few nights at, let's say, ten o'clock? I would like you to pretend to be a shy virgin."

"Sure."

Jared pulled on his shorts and grabbed a robe from the closet. He lit a cigarette, took a drag and sat down on the bed, offering her a drag.

"I'll try to be here every night at the same time. Sometimes, I run a little late so don't worry if I'm not here right at ten."

"What's your name?" Jared asked.

"Tempest; but, you can call me whatever you like. You kept saying a girl's name tonight, while we were making out on the sofa. Let's see, what name did you say? Anne?" she said, thinking.

"I don't remember saying anyone's name." he said, surprised by the remark.

"You definitely called me some sweet name. It wasn't Anne, what was it?" she asked, rolling her eyes, trying to remember.

"I don't know an Anne; but, was it ... April?"

"Yes, that's it!" she exclaimed, snapping her fingers. "Well, April," she said, pointing to herself, "will be here tomorrow night, Honey, and she'll be pure as the driven snow."

Jared watched as Tempest left the room. He didn't remember saying April's name. He put the thought out of his mind as he remembered the incredible experience he'd just had with the hooker. He turned out the light, laid across the bed, and allowed himself to drift into a dreamless sleep.

Daytimes were spent endlessly buying fall merchandise with his Dad, followed by dinner together. Then, his Dad would smile knowingly; and, they'd go their separate ways, for their secret rendezvous of illicit sex.

The next three nights were repetitious of the first; but, each night, Tempest showed up in a different "virginal" costume. The last night, she wore a pink prom dress.

Nothing was mentioned between Jared and his father regarding their night-time activities, until Thursday night on the return flight home.

"Well, Son, did you get lucky?"

"Yes, Dad, I did. How about you?"

"For your Mother's sake, I'd better not answer that question." he said, although his smile gave him away.

Jared remembered Tempest's remark about old men trying to prove they still had what it takes to satisfy a woman. She'd said most of her tricks were OLD men.

Good God, Jared thought to himself, she might've left my Dad's bed, and simply walked down the hallway to my room.

"I'll tell you what, Dad. I'll NEVER pay for it again..."

The Gypsy Cried

"As I've told your brothers, just be sure to get a *good-fitting pair of 'shoes'* when you're ready to settle down. That way, you'll never have to go *shopping* again. In the Walker family, marriage is a forever commitment, remember that!"

CHAPTER FOUR

....

TIME FRAME PARALLEL TO JARED'S TRIP / APRIL'S APARTMENT

When April awoke Monday morning, her temperature was 102 degrees; she had a classic case of the flu. She called to let her boss know she wouldn't be at work because of the illness.

After taking some medication, she stumbled back to bed. After two-and-a-half agonizing days of aches and projectile vomiting, her fever broke. She had been so ill; she couldn't manage more than dragging herself from the bed to the bathroom. She hadn't even been upstairs to get her mail since Saturday. All she normally received was junk mail, and bills anyway.

She showered and got, dressed. When she opened the apartment door to go get the mail, she noticed the dried rose and Jared's note taped to her door and quickly removed it. Her breath caught in her throat as she read the note: "April, thanks for a great date. Don't forget to save Friday night for me. We'll do something simple; and, don't make any plans for Saturday night either. Going to Chicago with

The Gypsy Cried

my Dad on a buying trip. I'll call you when I get back on Thursday night. Jared."

April's heart skipped a beat. All this time the note and the dead rose had been taped to her door. What must her neighbors thing? she wondered.

She fixed herself some bacon and scrambled eggs, and poured herself a large glass of orange juice. She trembled with weakness caused both from reading Jared's note, and from not eating for three days. She felt stronger after she ate, more confidant. She tidied her apartment and re-read Jared's note every time she passed the bulletin board where she'd tacked it. She placed the dried rose in her Bible to preserve it. She couldn't remember ever feeling as happy as she did right then.....Jared was the man for her—for life! she just knew it!

"Take it easy, Girl," April said to her reflection in the hall mirror, "Things are happening too fast...."

She smiled at herself in the mirror, and noticed how pale she looked. She had dark circles under her eyes. "Your eyes are your best feature," she said to herself. "You'd better get back in bed and get some more sleep so you'll be irresistibly gorgeous on Friday night."

Thursday passed quickly since most of April's assigned duties had not been done during her absence. Before she knew it, she was back in her apartment, waiting for Jared's call. She was so anxious to talk to him; she didn't even take enough time to stop at the store to buy food. She didn't want to miss his call!

Supper that evening consisted of a dry fried egg—no margarine, no cheese, and no bread!

April scolded herself, "You've never waited for a phone call in your life! You wouldn't allow yourself enough time to stop at the stupid store. Girl, you're crazy! No man's worth this! In my heart, though, I think HE'S worth this meager sacrifice because, someday, someway, Jared'll be my love, my husband, my Knight in Shining Armor."

April paced the floor. By ten o'clock she was panic-stricken. No phone call! What if the airplane crashed? She turned on the radio to hear the news...no airline catastrophes. Finally, at ten forty-five, the phone rang.

April grabbed the phone on the first ring....oh, no, she thought to herself, remembering Jared's first call. I should've let it ring longer.

"Hey, April!" Jared said confidently, "How are you?"

"Oh, I'm fine," she lied, "How was your trip?"

"It was okay. It was just a buying trip for Christmas merchandise for our stores; but, I'm really tired from the trip."

"Oh, by the way, thanks for the rose; but, I've got to tell you I didn't see it until last night. I had the flu and didn't even leave the apartment for three days; but, I'm fine now. Today is the first day I've worked this week."

"I'm sorry you've been sick. Are you okay now? Do you feel good enough to get a pizza after you get off work tomorrow night?"

"Sure, why not. It sounds great! We'll have to make it an early evening though 'cause I have to work on Saturday to get my work caught up..."

"Okay. I'll pick you up at your apartment at, what do you say, eight o'clock?"

"Fine; but, if, by chance, I'm not home when you get here, wait for me. I can't leave until *all* the windows are in balance."

"Okay, well, catch ya' later, Princess. Sweet dreams."

"Bye."

As luck would have it, two windows were out of balance on Friday night. Everyone pitched in, of course, to find the errors; but, it was nearly seven forty-five before April could leave. She had hoped to have enough time to freshen her makeup before Jared arrived. Although she wasn't really dirty, she didn't feel fresh. It had been an unusually stressful day. It seemed as if all the customers were irritable. April remembered that she needed to stop by the store; but, there wasn't enough time.

Jared was sitting on the steps of her apartment building when April got home. She spoke and rushed past him, feeling frazzled and disheveled. He smiled. She couldn't help but notice how adorable he looked.

She unlocked her front door and said, "Wouldn't you know it...*TWO* windows were out-of-balance. What a day!"

As Jared walked into the apartment, April noticed he had one hand behind his back. She smiled to herself and turned on the lights.

"Since you didn't get the other rose until it was all dried up, I thought I'd bring you a fresh one." he said, moving his arm so she could see the beautiful red rose he was hiding behind his back.

"Oh, how sweet, Jared. Thank you! What a pleasant surprise."

"You deserve a roomful of roses, Princess."

Noticing her tearing eyes, Jared put his arms around her small waist and kissed her sweetly on the lips.

April pulled away..."Jared, I need a minute to freshen up. Make yourself comfortable. I'll be right back. If you like, turn on the television or stereo. All I have to offer you to drink is orange juice or ice water. Since I've been sick, I've not had time to go to the store."

"That's okay, April; but, you know, you *DO* have a lot more to offer me..." he teased, coyly, confidently.

April reacted nervously to his remark; but, she tried to chuckle as she said, "Here entertain yourself by watching television... and try to behave yourself!"

"Yes, Dear." he said, jokingly. The way he looked at her, his smile, the obvious longing in his eyes, sent chills of excitement through her psyche.

April went into the bathroom to refresh her make-up and spritz on some cologne. Then, she went into the bedroom and changed from her dress into much-more-comfortable jeans, and a dark green knit shirt, which accented her svelte figure. When she returned to the living room, Jared whistled under his breath.

"Wow! You look great, and much more comfortable. Green's one of my favorite colors... Are you hungry?"

"Starved!"

"Wantta just go to Ron's for a pizza? We can bring it back here and watch this movie, if you want...."

"No, Jared, not tonight, okay?"

"Sure, I thought because you've had a rough day, it would be okay..." he said. Then, remembering her cool reputation, he knew he'd better not move too fast.

Ron's was crowded, as usual, and the service was slow; but, when they finally received their pizza, it was so delicious, it was well worth the wait.

Jared held April's hand under the table, and told her about his buying trip. "I was always busy during the day at the Merchandise Mart. You know, it's not easy to think about Christmas this time of the year."

"Yes, I guess it would be. What else did you do?"

"Not much, but I kept thinking about you. I'm really glad to see you tonight. You've already become special to me, April." he remarked, somewhat nervously.

"Talk like that could turn a girl's head!" she said. Then, changing the subject, "Did you meet anyone interesting in Chicago?"

"As a matter of fact, I met a girl who reminded me of you. She wasn't nearly as pretty, or as nice; but, she was okay."

"Did you leave her crying at the airport?" April smirked, showing a little jealousy. Catching herself, she quietly turned the remark into a joke, and pretended to wipe a tear from her eyes. In the back of her mind, she wondered how much time he'd actually spent with the girl he had met.

"No, I didn't leave her crying at the airport." he smirked, mocking her. "I'm not sure I even know her real name...."

"Oh, is that right?" April teased. "Well, anyway, I guess we'd better get home. I have to work tomorrow, remember?" (Silence).

"I'm not ready to say goodnight, April. Can we take a drive or something?"

Feeling suddenly brave and somewhat confident, April suggested, "Why don't we get some soft drinks and go back to my apartment, and see what's on TV?"

"Back to your apartment? But, I thought...." Jared replied, surprised by her boldness. "Sure, let's do it!"

April nodded her head, and smiled at his obvious surprise.

Once they had gotten back to April's apartment, she turned on the television. All the channels were broadcasting the evening news. "Do you want to listen to the news?" she asked.

"No, not really," he replied, walking to the stereo. "Why don't we listen to some music? Do you have any Elvis albums?"

"Sure he's one of my favorite singers" she said, putting a stack of her favorite records on the player.

The smooth love songs put them in a mellow, relaxed mood. At first, Jared sat on the sofa, while April sat across from him in an armchair. They talked about their jobs, their favorite movies, their best friends, old school memories, everything April could think of to continue their conversation. Remarkably, they discovered they had a lot in common.

"What's your favorite song?" she asked.

"Besides ANY Elvis song, my next favorite song is a new release called 'The Gypsy Cried' by Lou Christie." he said. "Have you heard it?"

"No, I haven't."

"I just like the way it sounds. I'm not crazy about the lyrics; I just like the music." he explained.

April sat quietly, thinking of something else to talk about.

"Why don't you get over here and sit beside me on the sofa, so I can hold you for a few minutes before I leave?'" he suggested, patting the sofa beside him. "It's getting late. You said you have to work tomorrow."

"Yes, I have to get up at six-thirty in the morning."

"Well, it's after midnight. Come on, get on over here...." he urged.

Somewhat reluctantly, April moved to the sofa beside Jared. He immediately put his arm around her, and she gently positioned her head so it rested on his shoulder.

They sat quietly, at first, and then he cupped her chin and tilted her head up. Their lips meshed into a sweet kiss at first; and, then, became yearning, passionate.

April was relaxed, and responded to Jared's passionate kisses ...their bodies were pressed together.

When Jared began to caress April's breast through her clothing, she was shocked into reality. She pulled away, and got up.

"Oh, please, April, don't walk away...I'll behave."

She sat back down on the sofa and fanned herself with her hand, obviously shaken by his thrilling kisses. "Is it me, or is it hot in here?"

"Well, it's not HOT, but it certainly got *WARM*...." he teased.

Glancing at the wall clock, April said, "Jared, it's almost one o'clock! I'd better send you on your way...."

"Wantta do something tomorrow night?"

"Sure, I'd like that. Why don't we go to the Diamond Club and dance?"

"I don't like to dance; but, I guess I can make a sacrifice for you!"

"Thank you, Kind Sir," she said, jokingly, bowing in a comical way. "I'd like to dance with you."

She took his hand, and pulled Jared to his feet. He put his arms around her waist and looked longingly, once more, into her eyes. Her lips parted, anticipating his kiss.

"Well, I guess this is good night, Princess. I don't really want to leave, though."

"Well, Kind Sir, I've got to get some sleep, so I'll be beautiful for you tomorrow night.... so you'll want to dance with me!" she teased.

A slow Elvis song began to play on the stereo. Jared took the initiative and started to move in step with the music, holding April as Elvis sang.

"I think I'll like dancing with YOU!" Jared said, as he kissed her.

April started to dance him towards the door, knowing if she didn't, they would end up back on the couch. "Until tomorrow night, then..." she said, breaking away to open the door.

"Goodnight... Are you sure you want me to go?" he asked wistfully, glancing at the couch.

"Goodnight! See you tomorrow." she said gently, but firmly. Yes, she knew she wanted to kiss him forever; but, she had to maintain her aloofness. She couldn't allow her emotions to control her!

"Are you sure you're safe here?" he said jokingly, looking around the apartment. "Maybe I'd better check for dangerous intruders."

"No, I'll be safe here; that is, after you leave!" she laughed gently as she pushed him out the door. "Goodnight!"

Jared turned around, kissed her quickly and walked into the hallway. "Catch ya later, Princess. When you dream, dream of me!"

"I don't plan to dream tonight. I'm too tired!" Then, jokingly, she added, "But, if I dream about you, it'd be a nightmare."

"No way! There's no way a dream with us in it could be a nightmare. We're a love story all the way."

April smiled, letting him know she agreed. Remembering her recent dreams about her prince, she gently closed the door, and turned the dead-bolt lock.

And, as usual, April's dreams were filled with visions of her prince. She had a burning desire to make love with the prince of her dreams. She awoke several times, shaken by the excitement of making love with the "prince" of her dreams.

When her alarm sounded at six-thirty the next morning, she warned herself to keep her emotions intact. Things were happening too fast...too soon.

CHAPTER FIVE

THE NEXT EVENING - THE 'THIRD' DATE

April meticulously dressed, applied her make-up and every hair was in place when Jared rang the doorbell. She was wearing a red angora sweater and navy blue skirt, with navy blue heels. Her sweater fit snugly at the waist, and had a cowl-neck, tied on one side.

"Wow, April, you look terrific!" Jared said as soon as he saw her.

"Thanks, Jared, so do you." she replied admiring how handsome he was in his cream-colored fisherman's knit sweater and brown dress slacks.

"How about a kiss to start the evening out right?" he suggested.

"Well, this time, you don't have to ask..." In the back of her mind, she thought, this is our *"third"* date. "Since this is our THIRD date, I usually let a guy kiss me on the third date, if he's lucky enough to get a third date!" she joked.

"In that case, I'd like more..." he said boldly, putting his arms around her slim waist and pulling her into his arms. "I feel so lucky."

After a couple of fairly-passionate kisses, April pulled away, "That's enough for now...."

The Diamond Club was crowded; and, they had to wait for a table before they could be served. Since the music was slow and dreamy, April suggested they spend the time on the dance floor.

At first, they danced in the traditional manner with Jared's right hand at April's waist, and his left hand outstretched, holding her right hand. Their bodies were several inches apart, as they swayed to the music.

After a slow dance, they danced to a couple of fast numbers. Then, the pace slowed again...a soft love song. Jared put both his arms around April's waist, and pulled her close as they swayed, in perfect harmony, to the music, and each other's body.

"Oh, April, you're so special. You know, I really like you a lot. It feels so natural to hold you in my arms like this... You're soft and easy to hold. I wish I could hold you like this forever." he whispered in her ear.

April agreed with his words, but decided not to comment. She continued to hold him close while she ran her fingers up the middle of his back seductively. She wanted to hold him forever, too...but, as his wife.

"Oh, Princess, you're driving me crazy." he whispered. "I want you so bad! I can't ever remember wanting anyone like I want you..."

"I know. I want you, too. Look, maybe we'd better get a Coke and cool down..." she suggested.

Jared tried to buy mixed drinks; but, after the bartender checked his ID, he had to settle for Cokes. Since there still wasn't an open table, April suggested they step outside to catch their breath in the cool night air.

The night was clear, and the sky was filled with millions of twinkling stars. At first they said nothing, just stared at the sky.

The Cokes were cold and refreshing; and, although the late-April night was chilly, it wasn't too cold to stand outside without a jacket. April was shaken with desire, and the cool air helped her clear her mind.

"Princess, maybe I shouldn't say this; but, I think I'm falling in love with you. It scares me, in a way." Jared said, suddenly, clearing his throat. "You feel like you belong in my arms. Our bodies were in perfect rhythm when we danced. I always heard that's supposed to be a sign of compatibility or something..."

"Yes, I know; but, we've got to slow down. Things are moving entirely too fast. It's scaring me, too."

"I feel as if we've known each other all our lives, like we were destined to be together. Maybe you're the special woman who's intended for me ... to love forever!" he said, unsure of what he was saying, almost as if it was a revelation he'd just received.

Jared words frightened them; but, they also excited them both beyond belief. He took the glass of Coke from April's hand and sat it on a nearby car. He pulled April into his arms and kissed her, holding her firmly against him - body to body.

"Oh, God, April, I'm on fire with wanting you..." he said huskily.

"Me, too." she said, returning his kiss. Then she abruptly pulled away and stared at him, saying nothing.

"Just hold me... Don't kiss me anymore right now," she instructed, resting her head on his shoulder. Their bodies swayed to the sound of the music, which was emanating from the nightclub.

"Let's get out of here....grab a pizza and go back to your apartment. We'll find a movie on television. I'll behave, I promise."

"Okay, but we <u>are</u> going to watch a movie!" she said firmly.

Jared picked up a pizza and a six-pack of 7-up from Cassano's on the way back to April's apartment. She was surprised that he bought 7-up, because they both normally drank Cokes. She didn't comment.

When they arrived at the apartment, Jared reached under the car seat and pulled out a brown paper bag. At first, April didn't realize what was in the bag; then, she recognized the shape of a bottle .... an alcoholic beverage.

"Jack Daniels goes great with Cassano's pizza!" Jared explained.

"Jared, I don't drink."

"One little drink won't hurt you. You don't have to drink it if you don't like it...."

Being inexperienced with the wiles of alcohol, April had no idea how to keep Jared from bringing the Jack Daniels into her apartment. She didn't want to alienate him, especially since their relationship was progressing so well. After all, he ALMOST told her he loved her at the Diamond Club. She decided not to say anything - to just "wing" it.

Jared turned on the television set, while April got some ice and glasses from the kitchen. She watched as he fixed the drinks, filling each glass almost halfway with liquor, then dropping in a couple ice cubes, filled the rest of the glass with 7-up. He handed one glass to her, and took a sip from his glass. She hesitated, looking at Jared, desperately searching her mind for a solution to her dilemma, wondering if she would be able to handle the situation - under the influence of alcohol.

"You don't have to drink it, if you don't like it, Princess. Here's to us...I'm glad we met." he toasted. Their glasses clinked.

The drink was much stronger than April had expected, and it burned her throat. She gasped and handed the glass back to Jared. "I'm sorry, I can't drink this."

"Get another glass, then. I probably made it too strong. I'm sorry; I'll fix you another one."

When April returned from the kitchen with the glass, filled with ice cubes, she picked up the pizza and sat down on the floor, pretending to watch the news on television, somewhat aloof.

Jared poured part of the contents of April's first drink into the new glass she'd brought him. Then, he filled it to the top with 7-up. He drank the rest of her original drink in one gulp, which really surprised April.

"I'm not much of a drinker. My Dad was an alcoholic; but, I never actually saw him take a drink. My Mom wouldn't allow alcohol in the house when we were growing up." she explained.

"My parents have it around all the time. They said they don't care if I have a drink once in awhile. They'd prefer that I learn to drink at home, rather than on the streets, or driving a car. This bottle came from my house."

April sipped her new drink. "Now, this doesn't taste so bad. How about some pizza?"

The late night movie was "*The Barefoot Contessa.*" April and Jared watched the movie as they ate the pizza and sipped their drinks. April was beginning to feel warm and relaxed from the alcohol.

After they finished eating the pizza, April cleared the mess and sat it aside. Their drinks were almost gone. Jared fixed himself another drink, and sat back down on the floor beside April. Their legs were outstretched in front of them, and they were leaning against the sofa.

"This is supposed to be a good movie. It's okay if I get comfortable, isn't it?" he asked, kicking off his shoes without waiting for a response.

"That depends on how much you're going to take off..." she answered, kiddingly, yet seriously.

"Babe, I'll take off anything you'll let me take off; but, for tonight, I plan to stop with my shoes."

"Okay, then, I'll take mine off, too."

"Princess, I said I'd behave myself. I keep my promises. Don't ever forget that!"

"I'll remember... Let's watch the movie, okay?

He kissed her on the cheek, put his arm around her shoulder, and they cuddled while they watched the movie.

Jared stroked her foot with his big toe. Every time his toe touched her foot, it sent sensuous chills throughout her body. She tingled with desire, surprised that such a simple gesture could thrill her so much.

During the first commercial, Jared turned to look at April. "Am I allowed to kiss you during the commercials?"

"No, commercials are for going to the bathroom..." she joked as she got up. While she was in the bathroom, she checked her make-up and sprayed on some cologne.

"It's my turn, now..." Jared said after April returned to the living room. He disappeared down the hallway.

April took the pizza mess to the kitchen, and got another tray of ice from the freezer. She dropped three ice cubes in her glass and filled it with 7-up.

Jared filled his glass with ice, a little 7-up and a lot of Jack Daniels. She looked at him quizzically.

"Last one, would you like some Jack Daniels?"

"Just a little, please."

He poured about an ounce of Jack Daniels into her glass, and they returned to the living room. They sat back down on the floor and continued to watch the movie, as they sipped their drinks.

In a few minutes, there was another commercial. "Well, we've already been to the bathroom, what shall we do during *THIS* commercial?" he teased, pulling her into his arms.

Before April could answer his question, his mouth came down hard on her soft waiting lips. His tongue probed deeply into her mouth, sending thrills throughout her body, leaving her weak with desire. She could hardly maintain her composure at this, her first French kiss.

The passionate kisses continued; and, with the combination of the Jack Daniels, and the passion they felt, soon they were lying in a prone position, outstretched on the floor, clinched to each other in a body-to-body embrace.

Jared slid his hand under her sweater and fumbled with the fastener on her bra. April was jolted to reality and pushed him away. She sat up, brought her knees to her chin and rested her head on them, shaken by desire.

Jared stroked her back. "I'm sorry, April. I couldn't help myself. I want you so much."

"I think you'd better go. It's not your fault; it's my fault. I shouldn't have let you came back here tonight..."

"Why?"

"You don't understand. You remember what I told you that first night? I *HAVE* to stay pure until my wedding night. I meant that!"

"I don't doubt that you're a virgin, April. I could never hurt you. You're too special to me. I'm falling in love with you. It hurts me to see you cry." he said as he gently, lovingly, kissed away a tear on her cheek.

April could hear her Dad's spiteful words, echoing through her mind.... "You'll disgrace me...end up pregnant with some bastard's kid, not even know who the father is..... You're hot-to-trot....hot-to-trot......hot-to-trot!"

She wanted Jared desperately and their passion was leading them to the natural next step...fulfillment of their passion to lovemaking. She'd never dealt with uncontrollable passion before, and was inexperienced as to how to handle the situation. She had gotten herself in too deep, too soon, in this new relationship.

"Princess, believe me, I could never hurt you, or do anything you didn't want me to do..."

Jared put on his shoes and took April's hands as he pulled her to her feet.

"Give me a goodnight kiss, and I'll leave. I'll give you a call tomorrow. Maybe we can go to a park and roast some hotdogs. It's supposed to be a beautiful spring day tomorrow. How does that sound?"

"Sounds fine, I guess."

Jared put his arms around April and rocked her in his arms, savoring the softness of her angora sweater pressed gently against him. He stroked her back and moaned passionately.

"Oh, April...I'd better go."

"Yes, you'd better. Call me tomorrow morning, okay?"

"Till tomorrow, then, Princess, catch ya' later!"

Jared drove to Frisch's to see who was there. Seeing Tom, he parked in a vacant spot near him. Jared waved, and got into Tom's convertible.

At first they talked about the Reds' game and confirmed they were dating the same women.

Finally, Jared asked, "What are you and Carol doing tomorrow? April and I are going to the park to roast some hot-dogs. Why don't we make it a foursome?"

"Sounds like fun. I'll call Carol in the morning. Unless you hear from me by noon, we'll meet you at Triangle Park at one o'clock."

"Great! Since you're twenty-one, why don't you bring the drinks...beer for us and Cokes for the girls? I'll bring some hot-dogs, buns, potato chips and charcoal. My Dad has a portable hibachi. I'll bring it, too, in case they don't have grills."

"Why don't you bring a softball and bat, too?" Tom suggested. "It'd be fun to play ball, don't you think?"

"Good idea. See you tomorrow!"

Jared got back into his car and waited while Tom backed his car out of the parking space.

As he drove the twelve miles to his house, Jared's thoughts were about April. I'll break down her resistance; he thought, and if the shoes fit, I just might *"buy"* them. She's something else...so pure and innocent, yet wickedly passionate. Just like Tom said, she *IS* a dream girl. Classy around others; but, I'll bet she's an unbridled wildcat behind closed doors. I've known a lot of women... Got my first 'piece' when I was only thirteen years old. I'd love to teach April to be MY wildcat!

CHAPTER SIX

SUNDAY MORNING - A BEAUTIFUL SPRING DAY!

Tom and Carol were sitting on a picnic table under a shady oak tree when Jared and April arrived at the park. They greet each other warmly. Tom showed Jared the cooler filled with beer and soft drinks. Jared smiled, opened a can of beer, and tossed another one to Tom.

"April, would you like something to drink?" he asked. "How about you, Carol?"

"Sure, I'll take a Coke." April answered.

As Jared opened the can of Coke and handed it to April, Carol walked over to the cooler and pulled out a can of beer. She opened it, took a big drink, and said, "Why don't we play some baseball before we eat... you know, to work up an appetite?"

The baseball game was fun as Jared and Tom let April and Carol score six points in their first inning, pretending to fumble the ball. However, when it was *their* turn at bat, they scored ten points before April finally caught a fly ball, giving them their first out. Since the softball was so light, the guys could knock it a great distance.

"Hey, Guys, I protest. This isn't fair odds!" April exclaimed, after running for yet another ball, which Jared had hit so hard, it almost went into the river. "Why don't we play couple-against-couple?"

"Well, Tom, we'd better give in to these pussyfoot ball players!" Jared said, kiddingly, "April and I'll beat the pants off you and Carol..."

"Hum, that's an interesting idea." Carol teased Jared.

They continued to play ball for another hour; then, Tom suggested they stop and fix lunch. This was applauded, and a welcome suggestion to the girls. They were exhausted.

While Jared and Tom grilled the hot-dogs, Carol and April set the table. The atmosphere was relaxed and carefree. April turned on a portable radio, and started to sing to herself. Soon everyone was singing.

April could hardly believe the happiness she felt. It was such a wonderful day. Jared looked absolutely adorable, as he cooked the food, April couldn't keep her eyes off him. When their eyes met, he'd smile at her and wink knowingly, as if he could read her thoughts. It was obvious they both felt the *throngs of domesticity.*

"Tom, I'm glad you introduced me to April." Jared remarked, putting his arm around April. "She's the greatest!"

"That's okay; you can name your first child after me..." Tom teased.

"We might do that," Jared said quietly, kissing April. "We just might do that!"

April's arms and legs were covered with goose bumps at the thought of them having children...that meant making love. She rubbed her arms and looked down, hoping no one noticed her excitement.

After they ate, and the picnic debris was cleared away, Jared suggested they explore the trails in the park. They put everything in the cars, and then walked down the tree-lined walkway, arm-in-arm, feeling like the best of friends.

Since the trails were narrow, they were forced to pair off. Jared held April's hand as they walked along, exploring nature's wonderland. The trees were budding, the squirrels were flitting about in the trees, and birds were singing as they built their nests...all was well with the world.

As they walked along enjoying the nature trails, Jared whispered to April, "Why don't we ask Tom and Carol to come back to your apartment?"

"That's a great idea. This has been a beautiful day. I'm sure we all hate to see it end."

"This is the best day I've had in a long time. We've got to do this more often. Next time, why don't we get the whole gang together? Talk about a baseball game, we could have a 'real' baseball game if we invited all our friends. We could play badminton or volleyball. It'd be a blast!"

Looking back at Tom, Jared suggested, "Hey, Tom, why don't we all go back to April's apartment to plan a big picnic. Invite all our friends to the next one."

At first Tom didn't answer, as he quietly discussed Jared's suggestion with Carol. "Sure, that sounds like fun." he replied.

They jogged back to the cars, started the engines, and drove to April's apartment. When they arrived, April filled the ice bucket; and, Jared fixed everyone a mixed drink, using the Jack Daniels and 7-up from the previous night. April chuckled to herself...."such domesticity."

"Hey, you're pretty handy in the kitchen, Jared." she teased.

"Not only am I good in the kitchen, I'm good in any room... especially the bedroom!" he bragged, kissing her on the neck.

April smiled, pulled away, and walked to the stereo to start some long-play albums.

"Boy, April, you've got it made here!" Carol exclaimed. "I love your apartment. What I wouldn't give to have my own place."

"So would I." Tom said, putting his arms around Carol. "I'd love for you to have your own place, too."

The mood remained friendly, and comfortable, as they danced, and joked around. They planned their picnic to be held on Memorial Day, and decided they'd ask _all_ their respective friends, even though they wouldn't all know each other. It would be a good blend of personalities, it was decided, and anyone could come, as a couple or as a single. It would be a good blend of people.

April had three drinks. When the music slowed to a romantic pace, someone dimmed the lights. Soon both couples were sitting on the sofa, necking.

April felt uneasy when she noticed Tom and Carol's necking had progressed to heavy petting as Tom caressed Carol's breasts and had put his hand between her legs.

Concerned that things might get out of control, she could no longer relax in Jared's arms. His kisses were much too ravenous, and enjoyable. When the music stopped, she was relieved to have an excuse to get up.

"Hey, Guys, I have to turn on the lights so I can see to turn the records over..."

"Okay, we've got to go anyway, April." Tom said, pulling Carol to her feet. "Let's do this again, soon."

"It's been a great day," Jared said, walking to stand beside April. "Being together like this feels comfortable."

"April, watch him! I think he's in love." Tom kidded. Then taking a good look at April, he continued, "Oh, hell, the feeling must be mutual. Looks like she's smitten, too!"

"Oh, come on, could I ever get that lucky?" Jared said, beaming, remembering the challenge they had given each other that night at Frisch's.

"You guys take it easy..." Tom said, looking intently at April to convey a secret message; that he wasn't sure she knew what she was getting into. He still wondered if she could handle the likes of Jared Walker.

As soon as the door closed, Jared, once again, pulled April into his arms, whispering, "Alone at last." He kissed her passionately, longingly. "I want you so bad, April."

She was leaning against the inside of her front door with Jared's body firmly pressed against hers, his hands touching her bare back underneath her clothing. The closeness of his body, the excitement of their kisses, his sensuous hands, soon she was trembling.... sensing their futile frustration. She started to cry.

"What's wrong?" he asked, unsure of the reason for her tears.

"Please don't kiss me anymore. We've got to cool down." she sobbed, wiping tears from her eyes. "Listen, have a seat. I'll be right back."

Jared watched as she walked down the hallway to the bathroom. She washed her face, and repaired her make-up, regaining her composure by putting every hair into place.

When she returned to the living room, Jared was sitting quietly on the sofa. He got up and went to the bathroom, to splash some water on his face. He had definitely had a little too much to drink, and figured he'd be leaving soon because April's mood had become subdued.

While he was in the bathroom, April straightened up the living room and was standing at the kitchen sink, washing their glasses, when Jared walked up behind her. He slid his arms around her waist and kissed the back of her neck. She leaned her head against his chest, and closed her eyes, saying nothing, savoring the closeness they shared.

"Um...you smell so good. What is that cologne?"

"It's called, 'Beloved' by Prince Machiavelli." she answered.

"Beloved, that's exactly what you are..." he said, hugging her, smothering the back of her neck with kisses. "What are we going to do, Princess? I can't stand wanting you, and not having you."

"I can't make love with you...not now. I want you, too, Jared, more than I've wanted anyone in my entire life."

Her statement shocked April. She knew she shouldn't let him know how much she cared. She felt it was much too soon in their relationship.

"Maybe if we double-date for a while. You know, group picnics, go to the movies, or get a pizza with another couple.

Between the two of us, we have a lot of friends. We'll try to avoid being alone." she suggested.

"I'm willing to try anything to keep from losing you." he said.

April turned around, and put her arms around his waist. They shared a simple kiss.

"It's late. I'd better send you packin'," she whispered.

They walked, arm-in-arm, to the front door. Jared put his hands on her shoulders, keeping her at arm's length.

He bowed in a cute gesture and said, using a phony accent, "My Lady, it's been an extreme pleasure spending this day with you. I'll call for you again next week, if it be your wish!"

"Yes, My Lord, it be my wish...." she said jokingly, curtseying.

He kissed her gently on the forehead, turned and opened the door. "Have a good week, Princess. I'll call you sometime this week so we can make plans for a double-date next weekend." he said, reluctantly, smiling and smirking at the same time. "Goodnight, catch ya' later."

She watched him walk away, thinking to herself, someday he's going to be mine...

That night, she dreamt of her Prince, who came charging in on his white stallion to sweep her away to a forever happiness...a happy, loving marriage... a fairy-tale romance.

THE NEXT WEEKEND - DOUBLE DATING

Friday night, after work, Jared and April went to the movies with Paul Miller and Cheryl Henderson, two of his friends. On Saturday night, they went to the Diamond Club with four other couples. When they returned to April's apartment, Jared pulled her into his arms, held her tenderly in his arms, kissed her goodnight, and left, as agreed.

"I'm trying to behave myself," he explained. "You know I really want to make love to you; but, I'm trying to behave."

"I know you are. Thanks for understanding and helping *US* stay in control." she said, returning his kiss.

Sunday morning, Jared asked her to go to his church. April met his parents, and had lunch at their house. Mr. and Mrs. Walker were as nice as April had expected, although she did feel somewhat awkward. She helped Mrs. Walker with the dishes, learning about Jared's antics when he was just a small boy. It was obvious that Jared was their favorite child.

After lunch, April and Jared played pool in the recreation room. Since she had never played, it was easy for Jared to monopolize the table.

About eight o'clock that evening, Jared suggested they drive to Frisch's to get a sandwich.

When they returned to April's apartment, Jared said, "April, it's so natural being with you. You really are special.

You fit right into my family. I could tell my parents liked you."

"Thanks, I liked them, too. I think you're pretty special, too. This has been a great weekend."

"Would it be okay if I stay and talk for a few minutes? I'm not ready to say goodnight."

"Why don't I fix us something to drink and we'll talk." she suggested, going into the kitchen to fix some soft drinks.

"Is there any Jack Daniels left?"

"U-m-m, maybe enough for one drink." April replied, inspecting the bottle. She poured the remaining liquor into a glass, added ice and 7-up. She handed the glass to Jared, turned on the television and sat down beside him on the couch.

Jared stared at April, as if he was seeing her for the first time. She looked so lovely, so virginal, in the pink ruffled dress she had worn to church, sweet and feminine. It was understandable why his parents had taken an instant liking to her. Without saying a word, he touched her hair. It was soft and fluffy. He touched her cheek, it was soft and warm. She smiled at him, knowing he was deep in thought. Thrills raced through their bodies; and, almost simultaneously, they were in each other's arms. Their love was real, so natural.

After a few minutes, April sensed they were at the breaking point...close to losing total control of their emotions. She wanted to ignore the warnings in the back of her mind... "Hot-to-trot" the voice in her mind said. Her Dad's malicious accusations echoed in her mind, stealing her passion, dampening her spirits. Her Dad's prophecies ravaged her mind. She jerked away from Jared and quickly straightened her skirt.

"April, I can't stand this. I need you. If you really care about me, you'd see how much this is hurting me. Don't you know I love you?"

"I know you care, and I care about you. I can't go all the way until I'm married. I just can't. I explained it to you, remember?"

"Oh, yeah, right. Well, I've got to get out of here before I go stark-raving mad!" he said,

Getting up, he turned, looked at April, hoping she was going to beg him to stay. Then, shaking his head, he left, slamming the door behind him. The loud noise caused by the slamming of the door sent chills down April's spine.

She went into the bedroom and threw herself across the bed. She cried herself into a fretful sleep, afraid she'd lost Jared.

Jared was angry as he drove to Frisch's. None of the regular gang was there....and Frisch's was almost deserted.

Ramona Paxton sauntered over to Jared's car, leaned into the driver's window and smiled. Her breasts were about to pop out of the tight blue sweater she was wearing. They were cocked against the window, right at Jared's eye level.

Ramona wasn't well liked by most of the girls in town; but, she was well known as an "*easy touch*" by the guys.

Unbeknownst to Jared, Ramona totally despised April because she was so respected by everyone. Several times in the past, she had purposely pursued a man April was dating. She'd tease them into going out with her, take them directly to lover's lane and *have her way* with them.

She'd fix April! It was her revenge because April was such a goody-two-shoes!

"What's a great lookin' guy like you doin' here all alone?" Ramona purred. "Would you like some company?"

"Sure, why not. Get in."

Ramona walked in front of Jared's car, making certain he noticed her skin-tight shorts and tight sweater. As soon as she got in, she said, running her tongue seductively across her lips, "Why don't you buy me a Coke. I'm mighty thirsty. I'll just do anything for a Coke!"

Jared orders the Cokes, and let Ramona do most of the talking. Her body language told him she was ready, willing, and able to do anything he'd like her to do. Finally, he could no longer resist. "Would you like to take a ride up the hill, Ramona?"

"Any time with you!" she said seductively, stroking his lips with her fingertip.

Jared started the car and drove "up the hill" to the local lover's lane behind Frisch's.

As soon as he'd turned off the engine, Ramona threw herself into his arms and began to tug at his clothes. Jared was so sexually frustrated, and so angry at April, he didn't try to resist...nor, did he try to please Ramona. He used her body to roughly vent his sexual frustrations. Ramona loved his roughness and begged for more.

"Nah, it's late. Let's call it a night."

Ignoring her argument to continue their encounter, Jared started the motor, and quickly drove Ramona back to Frisch's.

Noticing Tom's convertible, Jared dropped Ramona off at her car, and then parked in the space next to Tom.

They talked for a few minutes; then, Tom asked, "What's going on? I saw you with Ramona."

"Just a *momentary* thing. You know how it is, Tom." Jared explained. "Its hell dating a *nice* girl who won't let you do anything but kiss her."

"Hey, Man, I told you, *April's a lady.* Why do you think I said what I did about putting her on a shelf until *I'm ready to claim her* as my wife? I've got to sow some wild oats before I'm ready to settle down. When I'm ready, though, I want April for my wife!"

"Forget it, Man, she's gonna be MY wife!"

"We'll see, Walker." Tom challenged.

As Jared drove home, he thought about April, and the little adventure he'd had with Ramona. In actuality, he didn't want anything to do with Ramona; but, he was about to "burst" with desire from wanting April so badly.

Ramona was simply a sexual release for him; better than a "hand" job. He could continue to see April, on her terms, and pick-up Ramona when he felt the need for sex. Hopefully, April would never find out about his late night dates with Ramona.

CHAPTER SEVEN

B ecause Jared didn't call during the week, April was beside herself with regret. On Friday evening, while she worked the drive-in window at the bank, every moment seemed as if it was an hour long. It was raining, April was having her monthly period, and she was depressed because her dream man hadn't called.

Finally, seven o'clock arrived and she had finished waiting on her last customer. As luck would have it, her window was out of balance; so, she didn't get to leave until after eight.

As she walked to her car, she noticed a rose on the windshield of her car. She removed the waterlogged rose from the windshield wiper and smelled its lovely fragrance. Then, she pulled off the note, which was attached, got into her car and turned on the overhead light.

The waterlogged note read: "April, I'm sorry about Sunday night. Please forgive me. I'll call you later... there's a family get-together tonight. Let's do something tomorrow night, okay? Love ya, Jared."

April clutched the wet note to her breast, smiling. 'LOVE YA!'.....the note was signed 'Love ya!' She trembled with desire and was overwhelmed by the happy feeling that overtook her body. Maybe it wasn't too late, she surmised.

When she arrived at her apartment, she fixed herself a grilled cheese sandwich and opened a can of Campbell's vegetable soup. As she poured herself a glass of skim milk, all she could think about was Jared's note. He loved her!

After she'd tidied her small apartment, she stretched out on the sofa and put her feet up to relieve her menstrual cramps. Soon she was sleeping, dreaming about Jared holding her, loving her forever. In her dream, she had a gold band on the third finger of her left hand. If they were married, finally, they could unleash the wild passion they felt for each other.

April was jolted from her precious dream by the sound of the ringing telephone. She glanced at the clock; it was almost ten-thirty.

"Hello." she mumbled.

"Hi, Beautiful! Are you okay? You sound funny." Jared said.

"Yes, I'm fine. After I got home from work, I fell asleep on the couch. The phone scared me, that's all."

"I'm sorry I woke you."

"That's okay, Jared. By the way, thanks for the rose. It made my day, to say the least."

"You deserve a room full of roses, Lady."

"Why?"

"Because you're so sweet. I've been doing a lot of thinking about us. If you're willing to give me another chance, I'd like to take you out tomorrow and show you how sweet you are, Princess."

"Well, I don't know. What did you have in mind, Kind Sir?" she joked, remember their last goodbye.

"Why don't we dress up....go to an inside theater downtown?"

"Sounds fine. What time?"

"The movie starts at seven and it takes about a half-hour to get downtown. Can you be ready at six?"

"Sure, no problem."

"Well, then, go back to sleep; but, mind you, dream only about me." he instructed. "I'll see you tomorrow. I can't wait to see you again."

April cradled the phone in her hands, daydreaming of her knight. She got up, washed her face and went to bed to dream some more about her knight...charging in on his big white stallion to sweep her away.

SATURDAY NIGHT

Jared arrived a few minutes early with a bouquet of beautiful pink roses intermingled with white daisies.

"Oh, Jared, how thoughtful. They're lovely. How did you know I love daisies?"

"Just a lucky guess."

April was wearing a green Chinese-style dress that hugged her cute figure. She had her hair piled into a French twist, highlighted with a Chinese comb. The dress had splits on each side, which showed her thighs each time she took a step. Although it was the utmost in fashion at that time, April felt self-conscious.

"Is this dress okay to wear downtown?"

"Honey, I love it! You can wear this dress for me anytime. You look so beautiful, I can hardly breathe. I want to hold you forever."

He pulled her into his arms and moved close to her mouth for a kiss. He hesitated and looked deeply into April's eyes. April's breath caught in her throat, anticipating his delicious kiss.

"You're a sight for sore eyes, Princess. It seems like it's been years instead of days since I have seen you."

April ran her finger over his mouth and hesitated as he kissed her, a deep, sweet kiss.

"Let's go, before it gets too warm in here..." she suggested.

Jared and April went downtown to see Elvis' new movie, "It Happened at the World's Fair."

After the movie, Jared drove to the Western Corral and ordered dinner for them: filet mignon, smothered in mushrooms, baked potatoes, salads with Italian dressing,

April smiled when he asked if what he ordered was acceptable. She smiled and remarked... "Sounds great! Our taste in food is identical!"

After they finished eating, Jared drove them back to April's apartment. It was a beautiful night and he put the top down in the convertible, driving slower than usual so he wouldn't mess April's hair. Once they arrived at her apartment, he walked her to the door, kissed her goodnight, and started to walk away. Remembering the previous weekend, he explained, "I'm not going to ask to come in,

Princess. I had a great time tonight. I'll call this week so we can make plans for next weekend."

He gave her a longing look while shaking his head. He took a deep breath and whispered, "Princess, you tear me up!"

"Oh, don't be silly. You can come in for a minute... after all, what if there's a prowler?" she teased.

Jared couldn't believe his ears. He walked into the apartment, smiling, pretending to check out April's apartment. He walked through the living room, kitchen and bathroom, turning on the lights in each room.

When he got to the bedroom door, he hesitated, and then groped for the light switch. The room was pink and feminine, with ruffles and creamy-white eyelet bedspread. As he expected, everything was neat. April walked up behind him..."Is everything okay in here?"

"Yes, I guess so. You know, your bedroom looks exactly like I imagined it would..."

"Oh, no, don't tell me I'm that predictable!"

"No, not at all. I've gotten to know you well enough to know your likes and dislikes. I feel like we've known each other forever." he whispered, putting his arms around her. I've been hearing a lot about soul mates. Could we be soul mates?"

April put her arms around his waist and hugged him while she rested her head on his shoulder. Jared rocked her in his arms, almost as if they were dancing to an imaginary tune. Jared turned her face to his, and kissed her gently.

"April, you're driving me crazy. I want you so bad, I can't stand it. I think about making love to you all the time."

He pulled away and walked into the living room. After pacing around a few minutes, Jared sat down in the side chair, put his elbows on his knees, and buried his face in his hands. April got down on her knees in front of him. She touched his shoulder. She knew she had to be careful how she handled the situation or it would get out of control. Jared grabbed her around the waist and pulled her to him. He held her so tightly she could hardly breathe.

"April, I've got to have you; or, we've got to stop seeing each other."

He smothered her neck with passionate kisses. "If you love me, you'll let me make love to you tonight." he pleaded.

"You don't understand, Jared," she said, abruptly pulling away. "It's just as hard for me."

"I don't think so...."

Jared wiped a tear from his eye, all the while looking intently at April. "Well, I guess I'll see you later. I'll call you....I guess. I'm not sure at this point."

April's mind raced. She wanted him desperately, too. She couldn't stand the thought of losing him. She felt a desperation that couldn't be put into words. Remaining silent, she looked at him.

Although April was crying, she didn't make a sound. Tears streamed down her cheeks and dripped from her chin. She was tempted to surrender; but, how could she? She was having her period.

After a few minutes of silence, Jared got up and walked out of the apartment, quietly closing the door behind him.

April was alone with her thoughts. It would have been so natural to make love with Jared. She would surrender to his demands if he would only say the words .... "Will you marry me?"

After all, he had given her no guarantee he wouldn't love her and leave her...pregnant. Her worst fears would then become a reality. She could hear her Dad boasting, asking for more prayer for his wayward daughter, in the little country church that he rarely attended.

She was torn between the never-ending desire to make love to Jared, and the never-ending fear of her Dad's wrath if his prediction came true.

April went into the bathroom, washed her face, and looked at her image in the mirror. "You couldn't have made love tonight if you'd wanted, Girl. You're having your period. That would have been a terrible experience for your first time."

As she fell into a troubled sleep, she wondered if she'd lost Jared forever. Would he call her again? she wondered. Did her knight in shining armor deserve her admiration? Was he playing games with her emotions just to have his way with her?

Two painful weeks passed without a call from Jared. April's complexion looked pale and shallow. She'd lost all desire for food, and could hardly eat at all. Her friends were concerned about her.

After some strong urging from Sandy, April agreed to get a pizza with a group of coworkers after they all got off work. Sandy and her boyfriend, Rick, sat on one side of the booth; and, April and Marty, one of the bank tellers, sat on the other side, waiting for their pizza.

After they'd eaten their pizza, April noticed Jared's car in the parking lot. She looked around the restaurant, spotting Jared at precisely the same instant he saw her.

April was laughing when Jared saw her. He didn't know she was laughing at a joke Rick had just told them. From all appearances, April was enjoying a fun-filled night with her date, who sat right beside her, very attentively.

Jared stared at April; then, he glanced at Marty, who was sitting so close to her, he appeared to be more than a friend. Hesitating, taking one more look at April, Jared abruptly left the pizza parlor.

April's mood changed immediately. After all, Jared had no way of knowing Marty was NO competition for her affections. He was merely a co worker.

Jared angrily pulled into the gas station at the next corner and dialed Ramona's phone number.

"Hey, Ramona, what's ya doing?"

"Waitin' for you to call, you Big Stud! Wow, my head's swimmin'. Fourth time in two weeks you've called me. I think I'm in love!"

Jared didn't respond. He mumbled into the receiver, "I'll be there in fifteen minutes, okay?"

"I'll be waitin' out front, as usual."

Jared picked her up and drove them to their 'usual' spot at Lover's Lane. Their lovemaking never consisted of much foreplay. They simply got into the back seat and 'screwed'; but, that night, at the moment of climax, Jared said April's name.

Ramona immediately pushed him away and slapped his face angrily. "You guys'll never learn, will ya? Those 'goody-two-shoes' girls never let you do anything but kiss them. April's nothin' but a cock-tease. Haven't you learned that by now?"

"I guess so..." he answered, almost believing it.

"Well, for Christ's sake, from now on when you're fuckin' me, you better be sure I'm the one you're screwin'! I've dated other guys after April got 'em hot and bothered ... cock-teased 'em to tears, and left 'em cold, just like she did you,"

It had hurt Jared to see April enjoying herself with another man. Ramona's words comforted him. "Maybe you're right, Ramona. I'm sorry about saying her name. It won't happen again."

As Jared drove home that night, he decided he'd continue to date Ramona. Maybe he'd misjudged her. After all, he didn't even have to spend any money on her. She'd do anything he asked. Of course, he couldn't take HER home to meet his folks. They thought he was still dating April. They liked her...and kept hinting at a marriage between them.

April became reclusive, rushing home every night after work, hoping for a phone call. She wanted so badly to talk to Jared if only he would call. She would submit to his demands, make love with him. She was miserable with things the way they were. She was consumed with desire for him, not wanting to date anyone else. She didn't think she could ever make love with anyone but Jared.

Sandy tried to persuade her to go out and have some fun. She tried to fix April up with several of Rick's friends. They were interested; but, she wasn't. Soon, she refused all dates.

One evening as they talked in April's apartment, Sandy confessed, "I've wanted to tell you that I went all the way with Rick."

"You did? Did you like it?"

"At first I didn't 'cause it hurt bad – more than I expected; but, once I got over being sore, I really liked it."

"Has it changed your relationship any?"

"It made it better, April. In fact, Rick asked me to marry him. We're planning a Christmas wedding. Will you be one of my bridesmaids? I can hardly wait to be his wife. I love him so much, April. I think we'll be happy."

"I'm happy for you, Sandy. I've decided I'll give in to Jared; that is, if I have a chance. I am really afraid that I've lost him. Like his reputation suggests, I was afraid he'd make love to me and leave me cold. But, I'm going to do it, if he calls. Surely, he'll call, eventually. After all, I think he loves me. He said he thought we are soul-mates, whatever that is. Oh, I hope he'll call."

"You could call him. You're obviously in pain."

"I could never call him...I just can't do it! It's not right for a girl to call a guy!"

"It's a gamble, April; and, you know I hope things work out for you, too. You deserve to be loved. It's fantastic!"

"I can only imagine."

"Listen, let's take a ride to Frisch's and get a sandwich, my treat. We'll only be gone a few minutes. Who knows, he may be there? I'm starved, April. You don't have anything to eat here."

"Oh, okay..." she reluctantly agreed.

While they were waiting for their sandwiches, two school friends drove into Frisch's parking lot. April and Sandy hadn't seen Mike Evans and Frank Beam since graduation.

Reluctantly, April let them get into the back seat of her car so they could talk. It was fun remembering the fun they'd had after the Senior Prom when they went to LeSourdsville Lake, an amusement park. That night, Mike and Sandy convinced Frank and April that the LAST car of the roller coaster was so tame they wouldn't know they were riding it. Since neither Frank nor April liked roller coasters, they refused. Finally, they surrendered to the peer pressure and agreed to ride in the last car....the 'tame' car. However, when the ride ended, they literally kissed the ground, glad to have survived, vowing to never ride another roller coaster.

It was so much fun laughing and reminiscing, April's cheeks hurt from laughing so hard. It was a much needed release of pent-up frustration.

When she turned around to take a drink of her Coke, which was sitting on the dashboard, she noticed Jared's car was parked directly across from hers. He was alone in his car...watching her. The look he gave her communicated that he still cared. He smiled, giving her a look as only HE could. The smile sent waves of thrilling goose bumps through her body.

They stared at each other, saying so much with they eyes. Sandy, Mike and Frank were now oblivious to April. She could only see Jared.

Suddenly, April was distracted....Ramona was getting into Jared's car. She immediately reacted emotionally to Ramona, of all people, getting into his car.

Jared couldn't stand to see the pained expression on April's beautiful face any longer; so, he started the car and quickly left.

Jared automatically drove to "their" spot at lover's lane. Ramona was "purring like a kitten", so full of herself because she had also noticed the pained expression on her arch enemy's face. She was anticipating their lovemaking. She had seen the pained expression on April's face when she got into Jared's car. It had given her a boost of confidence, exciting her as never before.

Ramona tugged at Jared's clothes as soon as he turned off the engine. He pushed her away. She kissed him passionately, from head-to-toe, not missing one spot of his lean body. Finally, consumed with passion, he lost himself in her arms.

As Jared drove Ramona back to Frisch's, he said, "I won't be seeing you again, Ramona."

"Why not? Ain't it good for you, Baby?"

"No, it's nothing like that. It's just, well, I was dating someone else and we broke up. I'd like to continue to see her... try to work things out. It's not fair to either of you to date you both; now, is it?"

"Well, what do you plan to do about this 'bun' I have in the oven, Jared Walker?"

"What in the hell are you talkin' about, Ramona?"

"I'm pregnant—and, it's yours."

"Oh, shit, this can't be happening. I never dreamed...I mean, I thought you were on the pill."

"No, they make me gain weight. You never once asked me, did you? You just got on, had your fun, and left. Now, what are you going to do, Walker?"

"I'll get some money together for you, and find out where you can go to get rid of it." he said, hoping she would agree to his obvious solution.

"No! I'll never do that. You're gonna have'ta marry me and give this kid a name. We don't have to live together if you don't want to...we can get a divorce after it's born, provided you'll agree to pay child support."

"But, I thought you knew this wasn't a permanent thing."

"Well, a baby's pretty permanent."

"How far along are you?"

"About five weeks. I went to the doctor today. Probably happened that first night we were together."

"Give me a few days to think about this. I'll call you." Jared said as he dropped Ramona off at her car, without saying goodbye. Jared looked around the parking lot, searching for April's car. He needed to talk to her...to see if they could start over again. He would wait for her now ... and maybe they could be married. Somehow, he'd work out the problem with Ramona so he could marry his April, he decided.

Jared drove to Tom's house and was surprised to find him home alone. "Hey, Tom, I need to talk. I've got a real problem."

"What now, Walker? You have more problems than anyone I know."

"I saw April tonight. You know, we've not been dating much lately, right? I know she still cares for me; and, I know for a fact that I'm in love with her. I can't wait to call her...see if she'll go out with me again. Hopefully, she'll see me tomorrow night. I've got a lot to say to her ..."

"That doesn't sound like a problem to me. She'll probably go out with you. It's obvious she's crazy about you, you lucky so-and-so."

"That's not the problem! I told Ramona I wasn't going to see her anymore. Guess what, she's pregnant."

"What! You knocked up 'anybody's girl'?"

"Well, she said I did. Tom, what the hell am I going to do? Help me. Do you have any suggestions?"

"Man, you should have made sure she was taking the pill. I make Carol show me her pillbox, or else I reach for the rubbers I keep in the glove box."

"I never dreamed she wasn't on the pill; but, stupid me, I didn't even ask!" She was always so willing to do anything I wanted her to do."

"Well, the ball's in your court, my Friend, did you ask her to have an abortion?"

"Yeah, first thing. She said, 'no way'!"

"Maybe she'll take some money and go away...."

"I wish. I've got a good deal of money in my savings account. I'd give Ramona all of it if I thought she'd do just that. I never want to see her again."

"Somehow, I don't think it'll be that easy, Jared."

"It's worth a try."

"What are you going to do about April?"

"Nothing, right now, I guess. I hope she doesn't find someone else while I'm working out this problem. Ramona wants me to marry her, to give the baby a name; and, then, after the baby's born, we'll get a divorce. She said she'd agree to the divorce provided I'd agree to pay child support. She said we don't have to live together!"

"Would you tell your parents the reason for the marriage?"

"Dad's in his late sixties, you know, and not in the best of health. It would hurt them if they knew the truth. They think I'm still dating April."

"Did they meet her?"

"Yes, wouldn't you know, Man, they love her to death!"

"Dad gave me a big lecture about Walker marriages lasting forever the last time we went to Chicago. If I have to marry Ramona, I'd have to pretend to live with her until the baby's born; then, we can fake marital problems...give them some phony reason for the 'break-up'!"

"Man, I'm glad this is YOUR problem and not mine. You better hope April will wait that long. What you're talking about could take a year. In the meantime, it's open season on April. I'm ready to call it off with Carol. Maybe I'll ask April out. Who knows, maybe she'll fall in love with me!"

"Oh, God, Tom, I'm on fire for wanting April. That's why I picked up Ramona. April's everything I could want in a wife. Ramona is nothing but an easy lay. I really messed up!"

"Well, like I said, I'm glad it's YOUR problem. Good luck, Man. I'll try not to marry April in the meantime. She's MY ideal woman, too. She's a 'forever' woman; and, the man who marries her will be a very lucky man."

"Right! I hope it'll be me!"

CHAPTER EIGHT

During the weekend and the entire next week, Jared picked up the phone several times to call April. Then, he'd lose his nerve and hang up quickly. He had to work out the problem with Ramona before he would be free to work things out with April.

Jared glanced at his parents. They looked old....tired. He couldn't burden them with his problems. It was a problem of his making; and, he couldn't shirk his responsibility to Ramona's unborn child, if it was, in fact, his. He hadn't called her all week.

Saturday morning, Jared called Ramona to see if anything had changed in her situation.

"No, I'm still pregnant, if that's what you're asking. Why haven't you called?"

"I've been busy. Have you given any more thought to an abortion? I have enough money in my savings to pay for it, plus some for your recuperation...until you get back to normal."

"No, way. I told you the other night. No abortion!"

"Well, like I said, I have enough money to support you until the baby's born. I'll continue to support it after it's born, maybe even for the rest of your life, if you'll agree to keep quiet."

"Oh, I see. You want us to go away...disappear. Pretend we never happened, right? I'm going to tell my parents. They'll call your parents. This problem isn't going to just disappear, Jared."

"No, you can't call my parents." he said, frantically, trying to think of a solution. "Well, I have no choice but to grant your wish. We'll get married. You can have the kid; and, then, we'll fake marital problem and split up, right?"

"Sure, sure ... whatever. When are you going to tell your parents?"

"Well, they're not spring chickens. They'll take it hard if they find out about the baby. Will you agree to keep your pregnancy a secret until we're married?"

"Sure, no problem."

"And, you'll agree to split up after the kid's born?"

"Sure."

"What choice do I have?"

"Well, maybe you'd better come over tonight and meet my parents. Then, tomorrow, we'll tell your parents so we can get married before I start to show."

The next two weeks were a nightmare for Jared. He wanted to run straight to the shelter of April's loving arms. He longed to hold her sweet innocent body next to his...to smell her fresh aroma. Ramona had a cheap, superficial odor.

How could he have been so dumb to get himself in this mess, he wondered. If he hadn't been so stupid, he could have been marrying April, loving her...

Jared stuttered through the marriage vows at the Justice of the Peace. He couldn't consummate their marriage until Ramona drove his emotions out of control by going down on him. When they finally made love, Jared again called Ramona, "April."

Ramona slapped him and jerked away. "Your Precious April will never have you now, Jared Walker, because you're mine!"

"Just until the baby comes..." he said, rubbing his face. She had struck him very hard.

"You'll get no divorce until I'm good and ready. I may not agree to the divorce....ever! I've got you now; and I'm not giving you up. So, you'd better learn to like living with me...you're stuck with me!"

Jared closed his eyes. His worst nightmare had come true. He was trapped in a jungle of his own making. A vision of April's lovely face came to his mind. Oh, how he wanted to hold her. Why couldn't it be THEIR wedding night? Why didn't he throw caution to the wind and wait until they were married to make love. Surely the 'shoes' would have fit. A love as strong as theirs could have overcome any obstacle. At least, they would be together.

Jared knew life with Ramona would be difficult. For the present time, he had to endure the hardships. He didn't want to hurt his parents. He'd gotten himself into a mess; and, he had to face his responsibility.

Jared wondered what April was doing...if she'd heard about his marriage.

April was hopeful she'd hear from Jared. It hurt her very deeply seeing Jared and Ramona together. Ramona was nothing but a slut. Everyone knew the truth about her. She had tried to hurt April so many times in the past by chasing after her dates. April recalled when she was dating Ken Sloan, Ramona pursued him. When she was dating Alan Miller, April saw Ramona in the restroom at Frisch's. Ramona bragged she'd been out with Alan. She brazenly walked up to April and almost spit in her face. With one hand on her hip, matter-of-factly, Ramona smirked, "Give that Alan Miller a tumble. He's a much better lover than Ken Sloan!"

April remembered what Ramona had said when she asked her why she always tried to date the man she was dating.

Ramona had replied, with a smirk, "Simply because you get 'em all hot 'n' bothered, then leave 'em cold. I want to be there to smooth their ruffled tail feathers, if you know what I mean. They're very appreciative of my charms at that point. You do me a favor, April, by the way you treat your men. Who do you plan to date next?"

"Ramona, you're gross," April remembered saying to her. "Why would any man want to marry you? You're anybody's girl."

"You'll see.....just wait and see." Ramona had shouted at her. "Someday I'm going to get someone you really care about!"

Ramona's harsh words echoed through April's mind as she recalled the incident....."Someday, I'm going to get someone you REALLY care about!" Although April had laughed at Ramona at the time, she had made good on her threat.

Of course, at that time, April had no idea she'd date someone as special as Jared Walker; or, that Ramona would be able to pull him away from her. April's dreams were filled with visions of Jared riding his white stallion, sweeping her away to forever happiness. Ramona was never in the dream.

Several nights later, April's phone rang. "Hello."

"April? This is Tom. I need to talk to you."

"Okay, Tom, come on over. You know where I live."

Tom arrived at April's apartment a few minutes later, carrying a pizza and a six-pack of beer. April was curious as to why he wanted to see her.

"Let's eat first, and then we'll talk." Tom said mysteriously.

"Okay, but I don't like beer. If you don't mind, I'll fix myself a soft drink."

They enjoyed some friendly, light conversation as they ate the pizza; but, April noticed Tom seemed nervous. She could never recall another incident when he appeared to be anxious.

After his third beer, Tom said, "Um ... I need to tell you something, April, before you hear it from someone else. I'm just going to say it quickly; Jared Walker married Ramona Paxton this weekend. They had to get married, if you know what I mean."

April couldn't speak. She stared at Tom, searching his face for the resemblance of a kidding expression that she hoped to find there. Then, realizing Tom had been nervous because he had to tell her the news, tears welled in her eyes. She made no attempt to brush them away, or hide them from her long-time friend. She stared at Tom, hoping she was having a nightmare. By now, tears were dripping from her chin. She made no attempt to wipe them away, almost as if she was frozen.

"I want to let you know, April. He didn't want to marry her; in fact, just a couple weeks ago, when he saw you at Frisch's, he told me he was going to call you. He wanted to patch things up. He loves you, April; and, if I'm not mistaken, you love him, too. I care too much for you to let you hear the news from someone else!"

Tom put his arms around April and held her as she sobbed uncontrollably. He massaged her trembling back, and held her tightly until her tears had stopped.

"I can't believe he fell into her snare. Ramona, of all people. She told me she'd hurt me, Tom. She's always chased after any guy I was dating, did you know that? She hates me! Now, she's got Jared...the only man I've ever loved."

"Being a man, I understand why it happened. It's rough on guys our age to date girls like you, April. We get so hard-up, excuse the expression, it hurts! We need someone to go to....to, uh, well....you know. Ramona was that girl for Jared ... for all of us."

"Then, how does he know the baby's his?"

"Evidently, she's only been seeing him."

"I can't believe it. I REALLY can't believe it!"

Tom loved holding April in his arms. He got brave, taking advantage of the situation. "To be honest, April," he said, while brushing tears from her cheeks, "You know I've had my eye on you for a long time. Oh, I wanted to put you on a shelf until I was ready to settle down. Now, will you go out with me? I'd like to introduce you to the REAL me. I've loved you for a long time."

"I think the world of you, Tom, but I can't see us together. You're like a brother, not a lover! Jared was the first man I've ever loved. I hoped we'd work out our problems... so we could be together."

Tom knew he should tell April that Jared planned to leave Ramona as soon as the baby was born; but, he decided against it. He left the subject of Jared's marriage as a closed subject between them.

He pulled April's face to his and kissed her passionately. He'd show her he could be her lover.

April pushed him away and walked away from him. "Tom, I've got to think this thing through. I need to be alone so I can cry."

"Well, my shoulder's pretty broad. Have at it...." he suggested, patting his shoulder suggestively.

"I'm sorry, Tom. I need to be alone; but, listen, I'm glad you told me. You're a true friend. It would've hurt a lot more if I'd heard the news from someone else."

"Regardless of whether you believe it or not, I do love you, April. If you'll let me, I'll erase Jared Walker's image from your mind. Will you give me a chance?"

"I'm sorry, I can't .... not now. I need to be alone. I'm sure you understand."

"Promise you'll call me if you need anything. I'll be here in five minutes—morning, noon, or night."

"Thanks, Tom. I appreciate it very much; but, I'll be fine." she reassured him.

Tom shrugged his shoulders and gave her another longing look, trying to convey how different things could be between them. Having no other alternative, he left, closing the door behind him.

As soon as Tom left, April ran to the bedroom and threw herself across her bed, sobbing wildly until she had no more tears. How could Jared marry that awful Ramona? She wondered, Oh, God, Tom said Jared WAS going to call me! He said Jared wanted to work things out with me. Tom said Jared told him he loves me. We were so close to getting back together. Ramona said she'd hurt me; well, she kept her promise. She hurt me in the worst possible way. What did I ever do to her?

Finally, exhausted, April fell into a troubled, nightmare-induced sleep. No dreams came to her that night about her Prince. Was he gone from her forever?

The next morning, April was still upset. She needed time to get over her heartbreak before she could smile at the customers. Since she had several days of vacation remaining, she called and asked her boss to put her on vacation. He agreed.

During the next week, April spent countless hours sitting by the window of her apartment, watching the world go by...people scurried here and there.

She remembered her childhood, and wondered why she couldn't feel loved. Never in her lifetime could she recall her Dad kissing her goodnight, or showing affection in any way. Her Mother was always there when she'd needed something; but, because of her upbringing, she couldn't show affection either.

April couldn't recall being tucked into bed at night as a child, being kissed goodnight, and having someone listen to her prayers. She wondered what she believed about God. She had made a commitment and was baptized when she was a teenager; but, now, God seemed so far away.

April remembered the shame she'd suffered because of her Dad's alcoholism. Since her Mother wouldn't allow alcohol in their home, her Dad was away most of the time. He'd come home drunk and snarl at everyone.

April had always been popular, was well liked by her friends, and was allowed to have parties when she was younger. Her Dad's drinking spoiled most of her parties because he'd come home drunk and throw everyone out of the house, calling her awful names she didn't deserve. So often, she had felt alone, like now. She was alone and felt desperate in this, her hour of need.

Sandy was in love, making plans for a wedding. April couldn't tolerate being around so much happiness. She needed isolation, shelter from the hurt.

The only time she felt peace was when she was alone in her little apartment, with her memories of Jared. She knew she was a "one-man woman" who'd lost THAT man. How could she get past the loss and get on with her life, she wondered.

April took long walks, contemplating her options. Tom and Marty were like brothers. She didn't want to date them.

She scolded herself, "If I'd only had enough self-confidence to call Jared, things might have been different.

Then, we'd be together!" She wouldn't just have her STUPID virginity to keep her company!

The song Jared liked so well, "The Gypsy Cried," was number one on the Hit Parade, and played constantly on the radio. Everywhere April went, she'd hear it playing and she couldn't help but cry...sometimes uncontrollably.

April couldn't get Jared out of her mind. She searched for his face in every crowd. She longed to see his smile. She had gotten into the habit of looking at the drivers of passing cars, searching for him. She had a minor fender-bender when someone who looked like Jared, and who was driving a similar car, distracted her. Somehow, she had to mend her broken heart. She had to get him out of her head.

April met a couple of guys during this lonely period in her life. Desperate, she accepted dates with them; however, when the date ended, she still felt empty, uninterested in a goodnight kiss. Soon they stopped calling.

One Friday night, April met Lonnie Stark at Frisch's when she'd stopped for a sandwich after work. He was nice looking, tall and slim, rugged.

Lonnie had a way of looking at April that sent chills down her spine. Secretly, she feared him but didn't know why. How can someone scare you, as well as excite you, she wondered. Lonnie had mentioned that he knew Tom, and had seen her at Frisch's previously with her friends.

After talking to Lonnie on three different occasions, she accepted his invitation to drive to the Frisch's on North Main Street. She was hesitant at first; but, since she'd talked with him for several hours, and he'd never said or done anything out of line, she agreed, deciding it was just the way he looked at her sometimes that scared her.

Instead of driving to the North Main Frisch's, Lonnie drove straight to the local lover's lane, pulled into a long driveway beside a deserted old farmhouse, turned off the engine and dropped the car keys into his shirt pocket.

"What do you think you're doing, Lonnie?" she asked, "Take me back to Frisch's right now."

"We're gonna have some fun..." he said, as he started to pull at her clothing. It was obvious what he had in mind. She wanted no part of it!

It became crystal clear why she'd felt fearful when Lonnie looked at her. She'd sensed the danger, but chose to ignore it. How ironic, she thought, to herself, I wouldn't give in to Jared's lovemaking charms. I wanted him. Now, I'm going to lose my virginity to a rapist!

April's mind was racing, frantically hoping for a brainstorm, to somehow dissuade him from forcibly raping her. She could see Frisch's lights in the valley below them. She jerked away from Lonnie and started to get out of the car.

"Babe, if you get out of this car, you're dead! I swear, I'll kill you. Now, get out of those clothes!" he demanded gruffly, pulling her arm.

She was desperate, searching for a way to get him to stop pawing at her. Out of total desperation, she whispered, "Lonnie, you're really messin' up a good thing, here. You know, I think you're a doll! Please, you don't have to force me. Will you please stop being so rough with me, and slow down?" she pleaded.

He stopped pulling at her clothes and looked at her. "Would you really go out with me....on a real date? You'd really want to make love to me?"

"Sure, but, it won't be very good right now 'cause I started my period today. Why don't we wait until after my period? Then, we can go out and have a good time." she urged, hoping her bluff would work.

"You'd want to make love to me?"

"Why not? You're a great lookin' guy! But, if you force me tonight, I won't see you again. Why mess up a good thing before it begins?" she lied, praying silently that her plea would work a miracle in the situation.

"Well, then, show me how great it would be. Give me a little preview! How about a passionate kiss? Go on...turn me on. Show me what you got!" he demanded as he roughly kissed her, forcing his tongue down her throat.

April wanted to gag, but pretended to enjoy his hostile kisses. She wanted to vomit, but restrained herself by escaping into a momentary dream of Jared. Lonnie mistook her gagging as passion and grabbed her breast, squeezing it hard.

"Ouch, not so rough...." she begged.

"Well, I had you figured all wrong. Promise you'll go out with me if I'll wait 'til you're off the rag!"

"How could I resist a special guy like you?" she lied.

Lonnie unbuttoned her blouse and unhooked her bra while he watched her face for a reaction. April feigned a smile, as if she wanted him to kiss and fondle her breasts.

Her quickly-thought-up plan seemed to be working. Hopefully, she wouldn't have to prove she was having her period because she had lied. Lonnie's mouth and hands

The Gypsy Cried

on her "virgin" breasts was repulsive to her. This certainly wasn't the way she imagined the first time a man touched her bare breasts.

She gagged again, wanting desperately to push Lonnie away, knowing if she did, he'd rape her for sure, maybe even carry out his threat to kill her. She had to pretend a little longer to enjoy his onslaught so he would be convinced she wanted to see him again.

The only way April could keep herself from vomiting was to pretend Lonnie was Jared as he roughly abused her breasts. She knew Jared would never treat her so roughly; but, she was in a desperate situation. She moaned as if she welcomed his fondling and sucking.

Lonnie finally pulled away from her. She quickly fastened her bra and buttoned her blouse, trying to straighten her clothes.

Lonnie turned on the inside dome light of his car, and took a pen out of the glove compartment. When he opened the glove box, April noticed a handgun. She shuttered, scared that he could change his mind at any moment and use the gun on her.

Using a scrap of paper from his wallet, Lonnie said, "What's your phone number...you know, so I can call you."

"It's 555-5423.... It's unlisted, so don't lose it!' she lied.

"I'll call you in a couple days. We'll have us a ball, a fuck fest. Maybe I'll even spring for a motel room."

She feigned a smile, as if she was looking forward to it. She was relieved when he finally started the car and drove back to Frisch's.

As soon as he pulled into the parking lot, she jumped out of the car and ran to the safety of her own car, locking the doors behind her.

As luck would have it, Tom was at Frisch's and saw her. She started her car and drove around the lot. She quickly parked next to Tom's convertible.

"Hey, Tom, do you know that guy?" she asked, pointing to Lonnie.

"Yeah, we competed against each other a few years ago. It's Lonnie Stark. Why, what's wrong?"

"I'm going home. Will you call me, Tom? I need to talk to you about something that happened."

April immediately left Frisch's. She was so shaken she could hardly drive the few miles to her apartment. As soon as she got home, she pulled off the clothes she was wearing and threw them in the garbage. She felt secure now...in the safety of her little apartment.

She showered, trying to wash the smell and feel of Lonnie Stark from her body, roughly scrubbing her breasts until they were almost raw.

As she was getting out of the shower, the doorbell rang. It never occurred to her until that moment that Lonnie might have figured out she was lying about wanting to see him again and followed her home. She remembered the gun.

April cautiously walked to the front door, not knowing if she should answer.

"WHAM! WHAM!"

Whoever was outside was pounding on the door.

"April, it's me, Tom Wilson. Let me in...."

The Gypsy Cried

With the chain lock still intact, April peered cautiously through the crack of the door.

"What happened, April? Are you okay? Let me in...." Tom insisted.

She opened the door to let Tom in. He put his arms around her, which made her feel safe and secure momentarily.

"April, did Lonnie hurt you?"

"Well, I've talked to him three or four times at Frisch's. When he asked me to take a drive to the North Main Frisch's, I thought it would be okay. Well, he drove straight to lover's lane. Tom, he was going to rape me. He threatened to kill me ... Tom, he had a gun!"

"Did he hurt you? Are you...uh, okay?"

"Well, lucky for me, I lied to him....said I thought he was a doll, and that I actually wanted to make love with him. I lied, told him I was having my period, I talked him into waiting. Oh, God, Tom, it was awful!"

"Are you sure you're okay, April?" Tom asked, holding her in his arms while she cried. He could tell she was naked beneath her terry-cloth robe.

"Yes, but, I feel so dirty...so cheap! I don't think I can ever go to Frisch's again. I'm sorry, Tom, I feel so dirty. I've got to take another shower."

"I'll take care of Lonnie. You don't have to worry about him hurting you again, okay?" If you're sure you'll be okay, I'll see you later, okay?"

"Okay, Tom, but, I don't want you to get hurt. He has a gun."

"It's nice of you to worry about me; but, don't give it a second thought. I beat Lonnie every time we competed against each other in wrestling. He was one of my toughest opponents when we were in school. He went to Franklin High. I can easily take him."

"We could call the police. Let them handle it."

"No, since you said you'd be willing to go out with him again, I'm afraid he'd turn it around. Besides, I don't want you to have to testify against him. I have an old score to settle with Lonnie Stark. Don't you worry....I'll take care of him."

After Tom left, he listened as April locked the door behind him. He drove around until he found Lonnie, and motioned for him to pull his car over to the side of the road.

Tom got out of his car and casually walked over to Lonnie's window. Without saying a word, and with incredible strength, Tom jerked Lonnie through the window of his car.

"Hey, Man, what the hell's the matter with you?" Lonnie asked, trying to get away from Tom.

"April Morgan happens to be my friend, you Jerk! I heard you shook her up pretty bad tonight!" Tom said as he slammed his fist into Lonnie's face, knocking him across the hood of the car. "If I ever hear of you hurting her again, or any girl for that matter, you'll answer to me. Is that clear?"

Lonnie chose not to retaliate against Tom's anger. He was relieved when Tom got back into his car and drove away. He waited a few minutes before he got up to leave, trying to pull himself together. His mouth was bleeding. Tom had knocked out two teeth and broken his nose with his punch.

Tom called April as soon as he got home to make sure she was okay.

"If Lonnie bothers you again, let me know. I took care of him tonight" he boasted.

"Thanks, Tom. He shook me up pretty bad; but, I'm fine now. I don't know what I would've done if I didn't have you for a friend."

"I'd like to be more than a friend. Think about it, okay?"

"Tom, you're a wonderful guy. I wish we could be more than friends. You're been like the 'Rock of Gibraltar' to me. I wish I didn't think of you like a brother. I wish I could love you like I loved Jared Walker; but, unfortunately, you and I are too good 'a friends to be lovers. I'm sorry."

"I still say that might be the right way to start a serious relationship—good friends first; then, lovers. Let me show you how great it could be."

"Maybe someday....who knows?"

"Let me know if you change your mind."

After April hung up the phone, she remembered how adorable Tom looked the day of the picnic. He was wearing cut-off jeans and a T-shirt as he sat on the picnic table drinking his beer. April picked up a pen and wrote a poem to Tom, her friend:

HEY, MISTER!

Hey, Mister, you look mighty nice,
A sittin' there just a' drinkin' that beer,
Would you put your strong arms 'round me,
And, just for a minute, hold me near?

Heck, no, I don't wantta make love,
I'm just'a feelin' kinda down—
I loved him muchly too much,
And now he's up and left this town.

He was more'n I ever hoped for,
He nearly perfected my dreams,
Now, love's too darn much trouble,
Or, that's the way it seems.

Sometimes, I get so lonesome,
Searchin' for love, but findin' pain,
I've loved and lost too many times,
Wantin' sunshine, but findin' rain.

So, like I said, I don't wantta make love,
I just wantta be your friend,
Someone to talk to, have a laugh with,
An' build a trust without end.

So, please, put your strong arms 'round me,
And, just for a minute hold me near,
You don't have to say nothin'
And, NO, I don't wantta beer!

Don't try to take me home tonight,
And, your friend I'll always be,
For maybe tomorra', after the rain,
There'll be time for you and me!

April read and re-read the poem she'd written for Tom. The next day on her lunch hour, she bought a thank you card and sent it to Tom, enclosing her poem.

Tom called to thank her for the poem. He was truly appreciative that she'd spent the time to write him a poem. He convinced her to go out to dinner with him the next Friday night.

When Tom picked her up, April was wearing the ruffled dress she'd worn when she met Jared's parents.

They drove to the "Shangri-la Gardens" for dinner. The food was delicious, the atmosphere was unbeatable, their mood relaxed.

When they returned to April's apartment, Tom pulled her into his arms and kissed her gently, but passionately. The kiss was nice; but, April couldn't return his passion. Unfortunately, she felt nothing but friendship for him.

He kissed her again....

"Tom, you sure know how to kiss. I really wish I felt something when you kiss me. I feel numb, Tom. It's not your fault. Between losing Jared, and the near-rape, I'm empty. I have no feelings left. I'm so sorry. It's not you, Tom. I'm the one with the problem ... I'm so sorry."

"So am I, April. So am I...." he said, as he kissed her on the cheek. Without further comment, he walked to the door and left her apartment.

April watched him leave through the window. How she longed to change things. Why couldn't she have fallen in love with Tom Wilson instead of Jared Walker? she asked herself, wishing things were different.

Somehow, she had to get on with her life...maybe she needed a new circle of friends. She wasn't ready to resume dating. The games and phoniness that were necessary to get someone seemed foolish. Most of her girlfriends were getting married. April was alone. She needed a new friend to go 'man-hunting' with....

April called an old school chum, Linda Putnam. They'd lost touch through the years. After discovering Linda wasn't involved with anyone, April suggested they go to the Diamond Club the next Friday night. Linda readily agreed, anxious, as well, to meet someone new.

As soon as Linda and April sat down at a table, two guys asked them to dance. Linda danced with Greg, the taller of the two men; and, April agreed to dance with Doug, who was shorter than and not as handsome as the other man.

Doug kept her on the dance floor for three dances and made her laugh. The evening moved along smoothly, so when Doug asked for her phone number, April gave it to him without hesitation. She was more sexually attracted to Greg; but, he seemed to like Linda. Doug was nice to her; so, if he called, April decided she would probably go out with him.

The first date with Doug, bowling, was fun. Their next three dates were fun, too. Doug appeared to be a gentleman. April laughed at his quirkiness, his joking mannerism.

After each date, he would walk her to the door, kiss her goodnight, and leave without a hassle. April was glad he made no serious advances...a simple goodnight kiss, and a promise to call was all she needed at that time in her life.

Doug was someone to help her not to feel so lonely. He made no demands of her. He could make her laugh; and, when she laughed, she forgot about Jared, at least momentarily.

CHAPTER NINE

The near-rape scared April, and her date with Tom had been a disappointment to them both; so, when Doug asked if she'd go exclusively with him, she agreed.

Things progressed; and, soon they were engaged. April convinced herself she loved him. After all, he seemed nice... he was asking her to marry him; and, he was willing to wait until their wedding night for her to "prove" her love.

In her mind, she justified it was what she was supposed to do. Her friends were all married, and bragged about their happiness. She was bored with virginity; and, she convinced herself she was ready to experience life. She couldn't think about Jared without bursting into tears ... Doug made her laugh!

By now, April reasoned, Jared's baby had probably been born. She couldn't think about that right now.... It left a bad taste in her mouth.

Doug and April planned a simple church wedding; and, they paid for the entire cost of it. They rented a cute little one-bedroom, furnished apartment to begin their married life so they didn't need to shop for furniture.

The wedding was nice; but the wedding night was a total disaster, to say the least. Doug, who had been nice while they were dating, was extremely rough with her the first time they made love. Instead of the tenderness April had hoped for, Doug was self-satisfying. She had to bite her thumb to keep from screaming as he rammed himself into her. Instead of flowering afterglow, she received accusations.

"Honey, you've not been with many men, but, you're no virgin!" he retorted sarcastically.

His words cut deeply into the crevices of her mind and brought flashbacks of her Dad's painful verbal onslaughts as Doug continued his verbal accusations. She reasoned Jared would never have treated her way Doug was treating her after they made love that first time.

After Doug fell asleep, April curled up with her pillow on her side of the bed and quietly cried herself to sleep. Doug was snoring, oblivious to her tears, her heartbreak.

April escaped from her pain by imagining how wonderful her wedding night would have been if she'd married Jared. She imagined how his shoulder would have felt as they cuddled after making love the first time. April curled her pillow around until it felt like a shoulder....Jared's shoulder.

"Oh, Jared, what have I done?" she whispered to herself and his imaginary shoulder. "Now, I'll never have you; and, I'm stuck in a marriage with a brute who acts like my Dad!"

Doug woke April up three times during the night and roughly made love to her. He had no regard for her satisfaction or comfort; nor, did he care that she was still sore from his previous brutality. She had a high tolerance for pain; but, that night set the pace for their relationship... his self-satisfaction with little concern for her needs. She more or less accepted her plight; and, then, she'd curl up and pretend her pillow was Jared's shoulder so she could escape into a dream world and go to sleep.

Having nothing to compare to their sexual relationship, April was trapped by her marriage commitment. Jared's memory and her "pillow" helped her get through the night—every night.

Their first child, Douglas, Junior, was born one year later. April finally found something she liked....she loved being a mother. She had someone else to love now ..... someone who could ease the pain of her existence, to validate her existence.

The first three years of their marriage were filled with Doug's drinking, bowling, and gambling. There was never enough money—and he was always "horny!"

April got pregnant with their second child. When it came time to give birth, April almost died because of severe complications. Luckily, after many long hours of labor, both she and little Jason survived.

Doug and April now had two sons; but, instead of flowery thank-you's, Doug made wild accusations regarding the baby's paternity. April couldn't understand why he was making such accusations. She had never been untrue to him—it wasn't her nature. She had to admit she was probably untrue to him because of her dreams of Jared, which were nothing but fantasies.

Doug's behavior became even more bizarre. He demanded sex several times a day; and, he continued to make unfounded, wild accusations about who had fathered the baby.

"That bastard has red hair. I know you've been fuckin' around with the god-damn milkman!" he'd shout at her.

April retaliated, "The milkman felt sorry for me because I was pregnant and had a two-year-old to care for. You never left me any money to buy milk; so, he'd give us milk sometimes, that's all. He felt sorry for us!"

"And I bet you were very thankful....what did you give him in return?" he'd accuse her.

"Nothing! I've never thought about being untrue to you. Why do you say these terrible things? The baby belongs to you, Doug."

Most of the time, April was exhausted from caring for their children with little help from Doug. Two months after the baby's birth, April had to be hospitalized because of vaginal hemorrhaging. The doctor was concerned about her health and talked to Doug about getting her some help.

"She's got all the help she needs. She'll be fine." he replied.

"Her iron level is dangerously low and she's suffering from total exhaustion. If something isn't done, I'm afraid she'll have a breakdown." the doctor said.

"Okay, I'll get my sister to come over and stay with us for awhile. Don't worry, Doc, she'll be fine."

Doug never kept his promise to get help for April. She continued to struggle, take care of her children as best she could, often having to leave her housework undone. On those days, she'd beg Doug to help her when he got home from work to no avail.

He'd get angry and stalk out of the house, saying he was going bowling with his friends. He'd come home later, after having too much to drink. He would wake up April and demand sex. If she refused, Doug would rant and rave, up and wn the hallway in a tirade, yelling obscenities until he would wake up the children.

April would calm the children down, and get them back to sleep. Then, she'd drag herself back to bed, or end up sleeping on the sofa. Sleep wouldn't come, though, until she escaped into her fantasyland...dream about her 'prince' – her Jared! Her fantasies saved her from a "hell-hole."

When Doug started to spend most of the time away from their home, April was actually relieved. When he would come home, though, she never knew what to expect.

April wondered where Jared was...... Where was her knight?

SAME TIME PERIOD - FOXHOLE, ConDIAN, VIETNAM

The Vietcong had stopped for a lunch break, so the shooting had momentarily ceased. Jared Walker and the five remaining men in their squad sat down exhausted. Their foxhole was muddier than usual as they swallowed a few K-rations, following by a much-needed cigarette.

Morale was low. One of their squad, Phil, had been killed earlier that morning. Phil and Jared had befriended each other the first day he arrived in Vietnam.

The Marines shook their heads in disbelief every time they thought about Phil. His death was utterly senseless!

Little Vietnamese children would hang around the Marines whenever they could, hoping for a tidbit of food. One little orphan boy, Wong Choy, had become one of their favorite little kids. Wong Choy had disappeared the previous week and the troops feared he had been killed, or injured by shrapnel. They were relieved to see him come running out of the bush that morning, his little arms waving in the air as he ran towards them.

The sound echoed through Jared's mind as he sat in the foxhole smoking his cigarette.

"Pheel......Pheel....." Wong Choy had said...

Phil dropped his rifle and ran to the little boy, so relieved that he was okay. However, unfortunately, the Vietcong had strapped a bomb to Wong Choy's back. When Wong Choy jumped into Phil's arms, they exploded into a fiery nightmare and were killed instantly. There was hardly enough pieces left to put into a body bag.

The Marines, of course, had been warned about such happenings; but, it was hard not to make friends with these little children. The damn war didn't make much sense to them; and, the orphaned children brought a small degree of normalcy into their depressed lives.

"Hey, Walker," one of the men asked, making conversation, "Is there anything you wish you'd done that you didn't do?"

"Nah....I guess not! No, wait...., yes, there's one thing I regret. I dated this really cute girl, April Morgan. Man, she was gorgeous! She was a lady when I took her out; and a sexy little tiger when I got her home. I should've married her!"

"Why didn't you?"

"I was stupid. I thought I had to make it with her before I'd marry her. She kept saying 'NO'. If we'd gotten married and had a kid or two by now, I probably wouldn't be in this hellhole. Wonder what she's doing .... if she ever got married."

"But, didn't you say you were married?"

"Yeah...you're not going to believe this. I married the town slut 'cause she said I knocked her up.....we called her 'anybody's girl'. Hell, she lied. Six months after we got married, I left her. My parents will never forgive me for that. Marriage is a tradition in the Walker family. According to my parents, there's never a good enough reason to get a divorce."

"Did you try to find this girl.....April?"

"Yeah, I did. She'd disappeared. No one knows what happened to her. She's probably married by now, though. I'll die wondering what it was like to make love to her. I tell you this much, I'll never forget her sweet kisses. She's always on my mind. If it wasn't for her, I wouldn't be able to survive over here."

Lunch break was over. The Vietcong had resumed their shooting. As they picked up their weapons, one of the troops said, "Let's win this fuckin' war so Walker can find his dream girl ... and get it on!"

Jared's thoughts turned spiritual during this frightening time in his life. Prior to 'Nam, everything had come easy for him; but, here, he discovered the fragility of life. Lives were snuffed out every second. He wondered if he'd be alive at the end of the day. He was tough, though....trained to do what he had to do in order to stay alive.

The next day, Jared's foxhole was hit with a mortar. Two of the eight men were killed instantly, and the three others were seriously injured, including Jared.

As he waited to be medi-vac'ed to the M.A.S.H. unit, writhing in pain, he prayed silently, hoping God was listening. The last image he'd had of April came to his mind. It was a strong image. She was crying. He scolded himself for messing around with Ramona. He had been so foolish.

"Oh, God, give me a chance to make it up to April." he prayed. Then he lapsed into a coma.

After several months in the hospital, Jared was given an honorable separation from the Marines and sent home to rehabilitate.

At first, he was incapacitated and needed constant care. As the days passed, he grew stronger, determined to recover completely from his leg and spinal injuries. He struggled with the pain when he stood to his feet, forcing his legs to bear his weight, determined to walk again.

The shrapnel, which was embedded near his spine and left leg, would have to remain in his body forever. They were inoperable.

Penny Warren, Jared's nurse, was a divorcee with three children. She was attentive and encouraged Jared to push himself a little further each day of his lengthy recovery. She had a good reputation for helping spinal injury patients. The Walker family paid extra so they could receive her full-time services to care for Jared.

Jared used every available resource to find April during his recuperation. Seemingly, she had vanished from the face of the earth. No one knew what had happened to her. Maybe she had died, got killed in an accident, or something.

Jared wanted desperately to see April. No matter what the circumstances of her life were, he had a desperate need to know she was okay ....just to see her for only a second. If she was married and happy, it was okay; but, somehow, he had to see her again. Where was she?

Finally, after fifteen months of recuperation, still unable to find April, Jared succumbed to Penny's charms. Three months later, they were married.

A year later, Penny gave birth to a beautiful baby girl, Kristie; however, their marriage was in serious trouble. No matter what Jared did, he couldn't please Penny. She wanted more than his ample income could provide. She nagged constantly, wanting him to cash in his trust fund—to give her the money.

Jared suspected there were other men in Penny's life; but, he had no proof—just a gut feeling.

One rainy afternoon, a migraine headache caused him to leave his assistant in charge of the store so he could go home to rest. Penny's three children were at school, and Kristie would probably be taking a nap, so Jared knew he could lie down for a few minutes.

When he arrived home, there was a strange car in the driveway....a black Cadillac. He didn't say anything when he entered the house, anticipating company in the living room; but, no one was there. The house was quiet. Suddenly he heard Penny squeal delightfully. The sound had come from their bedroom.

Jared opened the bedroom door and discovered Penny, naked, in bed with a large black man. Jared had never been prejudiced and some of his best friends in the Marine Corps had been black; but, when he saw his wife with another man, it infuriated him. He jerked her off the bed.

"What the hell's going on, Penny?"

"He's doing what you won't....satisfy me!" she sneered.

"God-damn it, Penny, in our bed? A black man? With my baby asleep in the other room! What the hell's the matter with you?" he asked angrily.

Penny laughed at him as she slowly pulled on a robe. She motioned for the other man to leave. He quickly grabbed his clothes and ran naked to his car.

"You think you're hot stuff! You're nothing. You're not man enough for me, that's for sure!" Penny sneered at Jared.

"Then get your things and get out. I'll give you your freedom, and take care of Kristie." he said as he grabbed a suitcase from the closet and started to pack her things.

"No, way, 'Jose'! If anyone leaves, it'll be you!"

"Then, I'm taking Kristie!"

"You take that baby out of this house, I'll kill you!" Penny yelled, as she pulled a gun out of the nightstand drawer and cocked the trigger, aiming it directly at Jared.

Jared stopped in his tracks.....he'd faced many a gun in his life and sensed she was serious. His life was in danger.

"Go ahead, Penny, pull the trigger. My life's not worth much without my baby!" I've really fucked-up my life. I sure can pick wives—the worst ones!"

"Well, you're no prize, either. I thought you were filthy rich! I didn't know you were a damn miser."

Jared jerked her clothes out of the suitcase and threw them on the bed, packing his things instead. Penny stood in the doorway with the gun still cocked and aimed at him.

When he finished packing, Jared picked up his car keys left without further comment. He didn't know if Penny would shoot him in the back or not. He knew he had to get out of the house before someone got hurt.

"I'll see you in court, Prick!" she shouted after him. "I'll put you in the god-damn poor house!"

SAME TIME PERIOD, APRIL'S LIFE

April was recovering from double pneumonia. Her health hadn't been the same since the birth of the baby. Doug was drinking heavily and stayed out several nights a week. He was "out" that evening.

April felt weak and went to bed as soon as she had the boys bathed, had listened to their prayers, and tucked them into bed. Her chest hurt so badly, she could hardly breathe. When she saw the doctor that morning, he said he'd have to hospitalize her if her lung congestion hadn't improved by the next morning.

Although the doctor considered her condition to be life threatening, April had refused hospitalization and talked the doctor into giving her one more day. He reluctantly agreed and prescribed the largest dosage of antibiotic he could administer by tablet, each costing over a dollar!

It was after three o'clock when Doug came home that night, drunk as usual. He roughly woke up April from a sound sleep by fondling her breasts, kissing her snobbishly. She pushed him away.

"Please leave me alone, Doug, I'm sick."

"What good are you?" he sneered, "You're always sick." He pulled off his clothes and got into bed.

April turned her back to him and hugged her pillow, trying to go back to sleep.

"Well, I'm not doing without tonight, Woman!" he said as he jerked April over on the bed, pinning her arms beneath her. "I'm gonna get what a husband's supposed to get! You're not going to put me off again!"

"Doug, I don't put you off. We did it this morning, remember? Please, I'm so sick...the doctor said if I'm not better tomorrow, I have to be hospitalized. For God's sake, leave me alone....I have double pneumonia. I need to sleep so I can get better."

"Not tonight!" he said, forcing himself brutally upon her.

"Doug, stop it...you're hurting me!" she cried.

"Not 'til I'm good and ready...you're my wife! I deserve this...it's mine!"

April struggled. Doug slapped her hard across the face. Tears streamed down her cheeks; and, she resisted no more. She let him have his way, knowing it wouldn't take long for him to get finished.

Finally, he rolled off her and moved to his side of the bed. By the time April managed to drag herself to the bathroom, he was snoring.

April closed the bathroom door and cried, "Oh, God, why have you forsaken me? Why must I live such a horrible life?"

She ran a tub of hot water and soaked her aching muscles in the bathtub for almost an hour, crying, remembering the pain of Doug's rape. Would she report it? No, probably not, because a wife couldn't testify against her husband. It would only make things worse for herself. She escaped momentarily to the pleasantness of a dream about Jared. Life would have been so different if they were married, she thought, I know it! "If I find him again," she whispered, "I'll never tell him "no" again ..... for any reason!"

As was typical, the next morning, Doug couldn't remember anything that had happened the previous night.

He acted as if everything was fine and didn't understand why April was giving him the "cold" shoulder. She wouldn't even fix his coffee.

Still sick from the pneumonia and heartbroken because of Doug's cruel treatment, April calmly, silently, gave the boys their breakfast and took them outside to play. She was weak. She could hardly stand to her feet. Since there was no one to take care of the children, she knew, somehow, she HAD to get well!

She sat outside on the porch to watch the boys play, hoping the sunshine would help her to feel stronger. She wondered what would happen to the children if she gave into the pneumonia and just allowed herself to die....which was what she wanted to do. She was miserable; her children were the only reason to go on.

April had become Doug's love slave. She had heard him brag to his friends that he was the "king" of his castle; and, April was his "slave!" Him, help around the house? How absurd! According to him, housework was woman's work. He'd never changed a diaper, fixed a bottle, or lifted a finger to help around the house. He didn't even know how to work the washing machine!

Since childhood, April had dreamed of a handsome prince charging up on a white stallion to sweep her away to forever happiness, crowning her to be his princess.....not a slave. Unfortunately, she had a distorted view of marriage. She'd never seen a happy one. Is marriage supposed to be like this? she wondered.

Luckily, the antibiotic worked, and slowly, April regained her strength. She could once again take a breath without experiencing chest pain.

A few days later, April noticed Little Doug was pale and listless. He kept staring at his mother strangely. The next day, he was vomiting blood, as well as passing it through his bowels. April rushed him to the hospital. The pediatrician was concerned because Little Doug's bowels seemed to be blocked, and he was bleeding internally.

"April, is everything okay at home... I mean, between you and Doug?" the doctor asked, trying to discover why Little Doug was so sick.

"No, not really. Why?"

"This condition is sometimes caused by an ulcer. I'd hate to put this little fellow through the tests it would take to confirm my suspicions. We may, however, be forced to operate if his bowels don't move on their own today...."

"An ulcer!? A four-year-old with an ulcer! I've never heard of such a thing...."

"So, again, I ask....how's everything at home?"

"Terrible, Doctor. I don't know how I can continue to live with Doug; but, if I leave him, how will we make it?"

"There are programs which can help you make the transition, April. If Little Doug has an ulcer that is caused by the problems in the home, I suggest you make some changes. In the meantime, I'll begin treatment for an ulcer to see if his condition improves. I've scheduled an enema for him this afternoon. I'll closely monitor his vital signs. Just as a precaution, I need you to sign a surgical release in case we have to rush him in for emergency surgery."

Luckily, Little Doug's condition improved after the ulcer treatment began, and his bowels started to function on their own. He was discharged three days later.

Since Little Doug's had lost a great deal of weight during his illness, April took special care to prepare nutritious meals, including lots of fruits, vegetables and fiber.

One afternoon while Little Doug watched "Sesame Street" on television and Jason was napping, he looked at his Mother and remarked, "Mommy, I saw Daddy hurt you the other night. I'd had a bad dream and came to your room. Is my Daddy going away?"

Suddenly, in that brutalizing moment the puzzle pieces painfully fit together. April couldn't stay married to Doug any longer. It was one thing for her to be hurt; but, it was an entirely different matter when her children suffered.

Doug had never been a good husband. Although he made plenty of money in his job, he had never properly provided for them. He would only pay the bills when he had no other choice. Currently, they were in default on their mortgage payments; and, they were threatening to foreclose if they didn't receive three payments by the end of the week.

When they received the notice from the mortgage company, Doug threw it down on the table and sneered, "When hell freezes over..."

April wondered where Doug's paycheck went. His job for the local government provided more than enough money to supply the family's needs. Where in the world did the money go? she wondered. Her thoughts were interrupted by the ringing telephone.

"Is this April....Doug's wife?" the voice said after she said hello.

"Yes, who's this?"

"Well, you don't know me. I've seen you a few times when you've picked Doug up at work. What I wouldn't give to have a beautiful wife like you, and two rugged boys."

"Who is this?" she demanded, ready to hang up the phone.

"Ma'm....excuse me for buttin' in; but, he doesn't deserve you. He's not doin' right by ya. He brags all the time about other women, saying he spends his money on wine, women and song. He's a loser, Lady, and you deserve better..."

"Who is this...please tell me your name."

"I'm someone who'd like to be wearing his shoes. I'm just one of several people who thinks you're gettin' a raw deal, having to stay with the likes of him. You can listen and take heed; or, you can continue to live with that low-life scum!"

"I find this call hard to believe, Mister. Please tell me who you are. I'd like details. How many women? How's he spending his money? Do you know that? He's not paying the bills!"

"I'll just say this, Ma'm ...he's not bowling all those nights when he tells you he is...."

"Well, I'm not sure about your motive for calling me. How do I know you're tellin' me the truth? Men stick together, don't they? What's in this for you?"

"Well, who knows, maybe someday, if you lose that creep, we could be friends. I'm a lonely man. I'd like to get to know you better. I think you're very pretty...."

"You don't have to be lonely; there are a lot of single women who'd like to meet a nice man. I'm still pretty leery about your motives. How do I know you're tellin' me the truth?"

"Well, I've said too much. Really, I meant you no harm. I thought you should know.... A pretty woman like you should be treated like a queen..."

"How do I know you're telling me the truth?"

"Follow him some night when he says he's going bowling. You'll find out the truth...." the line went dead.

April was shaken by the call. Was it an obscene call, she wondered. The man seemed sincere.

Later that night and against her better judgment, April got her next door neighbor to watch the boys for a few minutes so she could go to the bowling alley and "check" on Doug's activities. After all, it was a "bowling" night.

April quickly drove to the bowling alley that was located only three miles from their house. She parked in the shadows and waited, wondering if she should go inside.... thinking about what she would say to Doug if he saw her to explain why she was there....

Suddenly, Doug came out the front door with his arm around a willowy blonde. They were laughing. April could hear Doug's boisterous voice. He was laughing ....."I didn't lie to her. I told her I was going to the bowling alley. Well, I DID go to the bowling alley. I just didn't STAY there... What she doesn't know won't hurt her!"

The woman laughed at his remark as he helped her into the car.

April continued her surveillance and followed them to an apartment complex. She watched them enter the building, and observed the lights coming on in one of the units.

After determining which apartment Doug and the woman had gone into, April nervously walked to the lobby of the building to read the names on the mailbox and was shocked to discover the apartment was listed in Doug's name. No wonder he wasn't paying their bills; he had his own apartment!

April drove home and calmly bathed the boys, listened to their prayers and tucked them into bed. Then, she meticulously packed Doug's clothes and put them on the front porch with a note attached.

She left the porch light on so he'd be able to read the contents of her note, which simply stated that she knew about the apartment...so, since he had a place to go....go there. He was no longer welcome in her home.

April felt as if a two-ton weight has been lifted from her frail shoulders as she put the chain-lock on both doors, double-bolted the locks and went to bed. So, five years of marriage was going to end like this.....at least she had her precious boys, she justified. Doug doesn't care about them....any of them!

If Doug came home that night, April didn't hear him. The bags she'd packed were gone the next morning.

That afternoon April made an appointment with an attorney; and, divorce proceedings were filed and papers served to Doug at work a few days later....on their sixth wedding anniversary.

For the sake of the boys, April would somehow pull her life together. Little Doug would start school in the fall. She was able to get her job back at the bank; and, although it was tough financially, she eked out a meager life for them.

Life, as a divorcee, was difficult, to say the least. There was never enough money. Most of the time, Doug refused to pay the court-ordered child support; and, he rarely picked the boys up for their court-appointed visits. Their house had to be sold, and the profit used to pay bills.

The marriage ended without a final shouting match. The courts did April's shouting for her. When Doug didn't pay the child support, April had to sign papers to have him put into jail. Soon, he learned that in order to stay out of jail, he had to pay the support.

April found an old house she could rent for seventy-five dollars a month. She was able to get the boys enrolled into a head-start program. Life as a single parent was difficult, but somehow, April reached deeply into herself to find the strength to persevere because of the boys....her reason for living. She learned, as long as they have each other, nothing can make her lose her footing in life. She's tough. She is a survivor!

Sex, what was sex? So far, she wasn't impressed by sex! She was repulsed by the idea. She had no interest in dating, especially since the sexual revolution brought about promiscuous times and dictated a man's expectation of having sex, sometimes even on the first date! April concentrated on raising the boys and tried to forget about herself for the time being.

When she thought about love, or lovemaking, Jared was the only man she thought about. She wondered where he was; but, except to look in the local telephone book for his name, she made no attempt to find him. There was a listing for Jared's parents; but, she decided against calling them. She lacked enough confidence to make the phone call that could have changed her life.

CHAPTER TEN

. . . .

Jared filed for a divorce; and, after much groveling with Penny, the final settlement papers were signed.

Several nights later, Jared stopped by the house that he'd signed over to Penny as part of their final settlement. She wasn't home; but, the children were scattered throughout the neighborhood. Kristie was playing in the street in front of the house, unattended. She was dirty, hungry, and seemingly unkempt.

Jared stayed at the house until Penny came home. When she arrived, she looked as cheap as the hookers he'd seen in Chicago. She was surprised to find him waiting for her.

"Where in the hell have you been, Penny?"

"What's it to you? Where are my kids?"

"I have no idea where your kids are; but, MY daughter has been fed, bathed and put to bed. Penny, she was playing in the street! She was starving. There's NO food in the refrigerator. I fed her some cereal. What the hell's going on around here? I pay you plenty of money. What do you do with the child support?"

"What's it to ya'! It's none of your damn business what I do, when I do it, or who I do it with."

"We're going back to court on this one. My daughter won't do without. My God, Penny, she was playing in the street at ten o'clock at night...with no one looking after her!"

"I'll talk to the kids when they get home. They were supposed to baby-sit tonight."

"Well, I've been here for three hours, and I haven't seen them." he said.

"Look, Jared, this doesn't concern you. You left, remember! You were too stingy to take care of your family..."

"That's a lie and you know it! I've always taken care of you and your kids, as well as provided for our baby. Those brats of yours have gotten plenty from me, you know they have!"

"No judge will give you Kristie! I've checked it out already. The courts think the best place for a baby is with its mother; besides, you agreed I could have custody. Now, get the hell out of my house..."

"Yeah, well, this used to be MY house, and Kristie's my child."

"Well, then, come back to YOUR house and take care of YOUR daughter. You're not taking her away from me. If you want her, you have to move back in. I'll quit my job at the Go-Go Club..... The Club pays better than nursing; and, I have a lot more fun. Things weren't so bad between us, were they?"

"You repulse me. I never want to live with you again; but, I swear, if I ever find things like I found them tonight, I'll take Kristie away. You'll never find her!"

"Don't threaten me, Jared Walker. I'll have your ass in jail before you catch your breath. You know I'm dating the Chief of Police. He's crazy about me....he'll do anything I ask him to do!" she bragged.

"Don't try to threaten me either. If I were to move back into this house, like you suggested, how would HE fit into your plan? If I would come back, it would be for Kristie. She's all I have in the world."

"Oh, you're breaking my heart!" Penny sneered as she pretended to wipe her eyes in a sarcastic manner. "I'll ask no questions and I'll tell no lies. Our divorce is final. I have no intention of breaking up with Roy. We'd pretend to be together for Kristie's sake. You can come and go as you please; but, I'd expect you to pay the household bills, and still pay the court-ordered child support."

Jared shook his head, threw up his hands in exasperation, and left. That night, at his condo, in the wee hours of the morning, he couldn't sleep. He was so troubled; his daughter was the only thing he had in his life, besides his parents.

By six o'clock the next morning, Jared had decided to move back into the house of the woman who disgusted him so he would be certain Kristie was properly cared for. He vowed, though, he'd never remarry Penny; nor, would he sleep with her, at any time!

When he moved back into the house the next day, he wondered where April was.....he hoped wherever she was, she was happy.

The loneliness was more than April could stand. The old house she was renting was infested with roaches. She had to pick them out of their food before they ate, and brush them out of their beds at night. She wondered if the strange bites on the boys' legs were roach bites although she'd never heard of roaches biting people; but, the infestation in the old house was massive.

April felt she was trapped in a financial hell. It was a constant struggle to get support from Doug; and, her salary at the bank provided only the bare necessities.

When April was selected by the president of the bank to be his private secretary, she was ecstatic and jumped at the opportunity. It would mean more responsibility; but, it would also mean more income. She was carrying too much responsibility, trying to maneuver too many stressful problems in her personal life....to be everything to her children, mother, father, nurse maid, maid, cook, caretaker....and she felt she wasn't doing a good job at any of them. The children were her life...she wanted to succeed.

One rainy night, loneliness got the best of April. Jared had been on her mind all day. Earlier that day, curiosity got the best of her and she went to one of Jared's sporting goods stores on her lunch hour to see if she could find him to no avail. Not knowing his personal situation, she was afraid to ask a clerk if he was working. She surmised that, more than likely, he had his own office somewhere in the three-story building.

Recently, there was an article in the newspaper about the chain of stores. Jared had been named to manage the entire chain. His office could be anywhere in the continental United States; besides, the article indicated Jared was married with four children. April had no way of knowing three of them were his step-children, or that his marriage was in trouble.

Desperate for news about Jared, April picked up the telephone book and looked through the listings for Walkers, hoping to locate Jared. She had to know he was okay. Unable to find a listing for him, she quickly dialed his parent's number, using every ounce of available nerve. She was afraid, and trembled as the phone rang.

"Hello," the voice said. April assumed it was Mrs. Walker.

"Hello, Mrs. Walker?"

"Yes, who's this?"

"I don't know if you remember me. This is April....it used to be Morgan. Jared and I dated several years ago."

At first, there was silence. "Oh, yes, April. Of course, I remember you. How are you, My Dear?"

"I'm fine, thanks. I'm calling to see how Jared's getting along. I'd like to get some of the old gang together for a reunion party. Does Jared still live in town?"

"Yes, in fact, he was here just a little while ago. You know, we almost lost him in Vietnam?"

"No, I didn't know! Is he okay?"

"Yes, he's fine now. It was touch and go for awhile. His first marriage didn't work out like we'd hoped; but, he's re-married. They have a precious little girl and bought a new house, a few miles from us. But, tell me, My Dear, how are you?"

"I'm fine as well. I got married, too; but, it didn't work out either. I have two little boys. So, needless to say, I'm raising my children alone. I'm the President's Secretary at the First National Bank. It's a rough life, but, all in all, I'm fine, we're fine."

"You know, April, as I remember, Jared was very fond of you. I always thought you'd be my daughter-in-law. I'm sorry to hear about your divorce; but, I'm sure you'll find someone to share your life with. I do recall you were a lovely girl. Jared and Penny separated for awhile; but, they're trying to work out their problems. Do you want me to let him know you called?"

"No, please don't mention it. Now that I think about it, it's a stupid idea, trying to get the old gang together. We're all so busy, with our own lives."

"Well, you take care of yourself, April. Bring your boys by someday. Carl and I would love to see you."

"Maybe I will....someday. Bye, bye for now. Take care of yourselves."

"Goodbye, Dear."

April knew she'd told a little white lie about her motives for calling; but, somehow, she also knew Mrs. Walker understood. How sweet of her to say she thought I would be her daughter-in-law, April thought. It was nice of her to invite them over; but, in my heart, I know I can't intrude, she reasoned.

Hum..... Jared was separated for awhile. I should have called him then. Who knows what might have happened then......Oh, well, if it's meant to be, it will be! He could have called me! He evidently doesn't care....not really. I'm sure he never thinks about me, April told herself.

Somehow, I'll pick up the tiny shreds of my life, patch them together, and get on with my life....for my boys' sake. They deserve the best life I can give them.

What can I do, she wondered, to generate more income? I make some of the boys' clothes and most of mine. I count my pennies and spend my money wisely. This new position at the bank requires that I dress well; so, I hand-tailor most of my business suits. I only have three basic suits with several interchangeable blouses, a couple pairs of good heels. I radiate a successful image; but, in reality, I'm the picture of poverty. I'm sure no one knows how tough we have it financially. Somehow, I'll survive until a new door opens....she surmised.

Two months later, Charlie Miller, a tall, divorced real estate investor, and a good friend of the president of the bank, was so impressed with April's secretarial expertise; he offered her a job as his executive secretary in a one-girl office, at more than double her present salary. Without giving it a second thought, April accepted his offer.

When Charlie discovered April's living conditions, he found her a house, rent-free, without roaches.

He explained, "The house is scheduled for demolition when the new highway is finished; but, that's several months away. All you have to do is keep the grass cut until the construction crew moves in. I warn you, though, it's been vacant for over a year, so it's pretty rustic. I'll be glad to help you whip it into shape."

"I can't tell you how much I appreciate this, Charlie. I'm not accustomed to living like I am now. I'm not afraid of hard work. This little house will give me a chance to get on my feet." she said as they walked around the small three-bedroom home, which contained a stove, refrigerator, washer and dryer. "I can't thank you enough. This is great!"

With the help of Charlie and a few friends, April had the house spotless three days after their move. She loved living in the country.

Within weeks, April had planted a vegetable garden. Since there was an apple tree and two peach trees on the property, needless to say, she took advantage of the fresh fruit, making a cobbler for her boys at least once a week. She also took one to Charlie at the office.

April was very grateful to Charlie for allowing them to live in the house, rent-free; so, when he asked her out, she accepted without reservation.

During the next few months, Charlie showed April the finer things life had to offer. They attended the ballet and opera. They ate at the finest restaurants.

Little Doug and Jason relished Charlie's attention, too. He taught them to play ball, took them to see the Cincinnati Reds' games; and, introduced them to several of the major league players. They spent many hours at local amusement parks.

Christmas with Charlie was thrilling as they ripped open the many presents he brought them. His gift for April was a beautiful diamond ring, and a marriage proposal. They were married immediately.

Charlie taught April how to experience the joy of lovemaking, and showed her how fantastic sexual love can be, even though they were never able to experience simultaneous climax.

April worshipped Charlie; he was her savior. On their wedding night, she was the happiest girl in the world. Finally, she had found the love she'd been searching for and felt she was where she belonged....in Charlie's arms. His arms were different than Jared's but they were a close second best to fulfilling her dreams.

Charlie and April were extremely happy the first year of their marriage. They bought a nice brownstone; and, after finding a suitable replacement for herself at the office, April quit her job so she could be a full-time wife and mother – something she had always wanted.

On the night of their first anniversary, Charlie came home late. He'd been drinking. April, at first, laughed it off; but, that night, when he turned his back on her in bed, she was confused. They relished their loving time, and rarely missed a night. That night was special....being it was their first anniversary!

Although April was disappointed, she tried not to make much of the incident. However, when there were more repetitious occurrences, she didn't know what to think. Charlie would come home late, with alcohol on his breath, offering no explanation. Then, she'd receive the cold shoulder in bed.

April was heartbroken....devastated. Her dream of happiness was again shattered. For the first time in a long time, April had to revert to her imaginary shoulder pillow, and Jared's memory, in order to sleep.

April took special care to prepare Charlie's favorite meals, and went out of her way to dress the way he liked. She wore the cologne he'd given her, and strived to be patient and understanding, thinking he was going through a midlife crisis.

Finally, one night, she could remain silent no longer: "Charlie, have I done something wrong? Have I hurt you somehow? Things aren't normal between us. Is everything okay at the office?"

"Sure, everything's fine at the office. The new secretary's not as skilled as you are; but, she's acceptable."

"Then, what's wrong?"

"Well, I guess we do need to talk. I may regret what I'm about to say for the rest of my life; but, April, I'm sorry if I'm hurtin' you. You're a good wife....much better than I deserve. I care about your children....they seem like my own, treat me like a Dad. You're super to my children, too; and, they like you a lot. But, Honey, we made a mistake."

"A mistake?"

"I don't want to be married anymore. I feel trapped by the responsibility of your children, my children ...that's six children all together."

"But everything's going so well. Until our Anniversary a few weeks ago, I was very happy."

"I know, I was, too. You haven't done anything wrong, April. We just got married too soon after my divorce. I wasn't ready."

"I didn't push for marriage."

"I know, I thought it was what I wanted."

"Oh, no, Charlie, surely we can work this out. I know you love me....I worship you!"

"Maybe that's the problem...you worship me. I feel like a caged eagle—trapped by my environment. Like I said, I'll probably regret this for the rest of my life; but, I want out."

"Why don't you give us a month.....if you feel the same way after 30 days, I'll agree to a quiet divorce. I don't know how in the world I'll ever explain it to the kids. They love you to death!"

"Okay, I guess I can give it a month. Who knows, maybe I'll change my mind," he said, taking her in his arms. "We've always had the best part of our relationship right here in this room. Oh, April, I do care about you!" he whispered, tears welling in his eyes as he held her close. Charlie tenderly made love to April; and, she hoped for a complete reconciliation.

During the next thirty days, April did everything she could think of to make Charlie happy. Everything she did, though, seemed to drive him further away. At the end of the month, she knew their marriage was over.

April tried to find the words to explain to the boys why they were renting an apartment. She accepted a position as an office manager for a self-made millionaire, James Jones, a demanding, older man, who was happily married.

Charlie helped April move into her new apartment and told her how sorry he was that things hadn't worked out. With a tear in his eye, he took her in his arms and tenderly made love to her—the sweetest of their relationship. She knew Charlie loved her. It was hard to understand why they were separating.

The deep rejection she felt cushioned the low self-esteem she'd shelved. It had been years since she'd thought about her Dad's accusations. The brief period of marital bliss allowed her to shove them deep into the crevices of her mind. Suddenly, they came flooding back into her existence. She became deeply depressed.

"Will ANY man ever love me?" she asked herself. "How can I expect a man to love me—really love me—if my own father didn't love me? I'm a misfit, a castoff.... unwanted. I need desperately to be loved. I lost Jared because I wouldn't make love to him. I was afraid to be the woman he needed... the woman I wanted to be because my Dad had me afraid to take that next step in our relationship. I made a stupid mistake and rebounded from Jared to Doug. There was no comparison between the two men; and, now, Charlie! Well, I wanted things to work out so much, I smothered him.... he couldn't breathe. I must have driven him away!"

April's new employer was extremely demanding; and, she received no personal satisfaction from performing the mundane secretarial duties, which mostly consisted of listening to him brag about his accomplishments. He also suffered from severe mood swings.

Mr. Jones traveled extensively, sometimes for weeks at a time, so April was alone in the office a great deal. Because of his temperament, April was glad Mr. Jones was only in the office a few hours each week; however, when he was out of town, he'd call several times a day. If she didn't answer the phone on the first ring, he'd be angry with her. She would put off going to the restroom until after he called so she wouldn't miss his call. This schedule, however, caused her to spend too much time in the office alone, trapped by her negative thoughts.

On the day her disillusionment from Charlie was final, they both had to appear in court. April cried throughout the entire proceeding. The judge asked her several times if she was certain she wanted the divorce. She nodded through her tears, knowing she had no choice.

After the hearing, Charlie took April out for a pleasant lunch. On a whim, they checked into a hotel and laughingly made love. Charlie told April he'd love her forever.

April still didn't understand why they couldn't be together. "Why don't we pick-up where we left off before we got married? You know, go out on dates, remain friends and lovers, without a marriage contract." she suggested.

"No, Honey, I'm sorry. It's too late."

"Too late?"

"Yes, don't ask me to explain."

"Is there someone else....?"

"Please, I asked you not to make me explain. Someday, you'll understand." he promised, as he lovingly kissed her goodbye.

"Will you be in any trouble with your boss for taking the day off?" Charlie asked.

"No, I told him I was taking a day's vacation. He doesn't expect me back in the office today. Honey, are you sure we can't work things out. I love you...and I know you love me."

Nothing she said made a difference. Finally, all she could do was to sit on the edge of the bed and cry. Charlie dressed and left, without further comment. He could no longer resist her charms. He had to leave while he was still able to leave. It wasn't really what he wanted either; but, he had plans that couldn't wait.

Later that night, Charlie sat quietly in the bedroom he'd shared with April, writing a letter. He methodically folded the note and propped it up on the phone. Then, remembering April's tears, he closed his eyes. Without expression, he put a gun into his mouth and pulled the trigger before he could change his mind. Death was instantaneous.

The sheriff broke the news to April and handed her a copy of Charlie's goodbye note. She was unable to read it because of the tears in her eyes. She asked the sheriff to read the note:

"Darling, April, I'll always love you. I'm so sorry I hurt you. What I failed to tell you is the doctor told me a couple months ago I only have about six months to live—cancer. I didn't want you and the kids to watch me waste away to nothing. I'll not put myself through that suffering, nor will I expose you, and all the children, to it. Goodbye, My Love."

When Charlie's will was read, he'd left everything to his children; however, he put a note of explanation to April. "I know you'll survive, Darling. I'm proud of your strength. Be happy. You deserve it, Baby..."

April was devastated by Charlie's suicide. She was so angry with him; she changed her name back to Phillips. Charlie was worth millions. She was struggling for every penny. How could he do that to her!

April came dangerously close to having a complete mental breakdown. Mr. Jones didn't at all understand through this period of time, and constantly threatened to replace her. She couldn't face another rejection; so, somehow, she HAD to pull herself together....again! Would she ever find happiness? she wondered.

One evening, while the children were with their grandmother, the deep-seeded depression got the best of April. She couldn't face her lonely future another day. Crying, she went into the bathroom and turned on the hot water faucet and reached for a razor blade. Charlie did it ... maybe she should do it, too.

While holding her wrists under the hot faucet, she ran the blade across her tiny wrist. To her amazement, the blade didn't cut. She threw the razor blade in the trash can and reached for a new one. The new one wouldn't pierce the skin either. She sliced back and forth several times; but, the blade would not penetrate her skin.

"Boy, I'm really a mess. I can't even commit suicide!" she cried.

April collapsed on the bathroom floor where she sat for almost an hour, crying, trying to make sense of her life, to sort out the fragments. She'd known too much negativism, too much pain. She needed something good to happen.

Then, she realized that if she'd succeeded with her suicide, the boys would have found her. How could she have been so selfish? she wondered. It would have ruined their young lives! They were her only hope for future happiness.

If necessary, she'll live her life through her children. For their sake, she'll pull herself together and get some professional help to deal with the problems that were haunting her. An analyst could help her sort through the problems.

She would pull herself up "by her bootstraps," she decided, and take life "one-day-at-a-time." One way or another, she'd make it—for the boys' sake. They were the only good that had come from her life.... her justification for being born....her only purpose in life! She was hopeful for the first time in months.

When April got up from the bathroom floor, she accidentally cut herself with the razor blade she was holding. "How strange," she whispered, actually speaking to the blade, "You cut my finger now; but, an hour ago, you wouldn't cut my wrist. How strange."

April took a mild sedative and drifted into a dream-filled sleep. Jared entered her dreams once again, riding his white stallion, riding her direction....

THE NEXT MORNING:

April's friend, Betty Lou, called early the next morning.

"Hi, April, is everything okay? I've been worried about you lately. In fact, for some reason, I had you on my mind really strong last night."

"Yeah, I'm fine. The boys stayed with my Mother last night, so I decided to sleep in this morning. I haven't been sleeping very well..." she said, recalling her attempted suicide.

"Well, hey, get your butt outta that bed and get gorgeous! I'll be over to pick you up in about twenty minutes. There's a sports spectacular at the new mall today. You know, jocks ....athletes, baseball players, football players, race car drivers. In other words, Girl, MEN. Get beautiful so we can go stare at their muscular biceps."

"Oh, I don't feel like shopping today, Betty Lou. I want to stay in bed and rest."

"Poppycock! I'll be there in twenty minutes. You'd better look gorgeous!"

April managed to drag herself out of bed and stumble to the bathroom. She washed her face, put on some make-up, combed her curly hair, and pulled on her favorite pair of jeans and a light blue knit sweater. By the time Betty Lou pulled into the driveway, April was having a cup of coffee.

When April and Betty Lou got to the mall, it was crowded. They walked around, looking at the displays that were scattered everywhere. At first they kidded each other about the different men they saw....

"Wow, this is a single girl's heaven!" Betty Lou exclaimed. "Smell that testosterone."

April laughed at her remark. Then, she suddenly stopped walking, as if she was paralyzed. Her mouth dropped open in disbelief.

"What's wrong, April?" Betty Lou asked.

April didn't answer. She was aware of nothing except the man who stood in front of her....JARED WALKER! Of course, she thought, his sporting goods stores would have a display. There HE was....in full display!

She stood quietly; her eyes were drinking in every detail of the magnificent sight which stood directly in front of her. The years had been kind to Jared. He looked wonderful, an Adonis. April was glad she'd taken care to apply her make-up, and style her hair. She had to talk to him!

As soon as Jared saw her standing in front of his display, he recognized her and his face lit up. He smiled and immediately excused himself from the customer he was talking with. As he approached April, his eyes relished in her beauty. For them, no one else existed on the planet at that moment in time, almost as if they were suspended in a time warp.

"Boy, I can't believe my eyes. April, you look fantastic! You're certainly a sight for sore eyes."

"So are you! How long has it been?"

"Too long....much too long. I've searched for you so many times, but no one knew where you were. You vanished. I was afraid something had happened to you....an accident or something!"

"No, I've never left the area."

"Now that I've found you, I don't want to lose you again.... ever! Can I buy you some lunch?"

"Sure, Jared, that would be nice and turning to Betty Lou, April introduced them. They spoke to each other; however, Jared didn't take his eyes off April. The feeling was mutual.

"Betty Lou, would you mind if Jared and I get some lunch?"

Betty Lou didn't say anything. She was trying to find out who the handsome stranger was. She'd never seen April smile the way she was smiling....

"Well, I...uh, guess you could join us, if you'd like to." Jared stuttered....hoping Betty Lou would refuse.

"No, I've got some window shopping to do," Betty Lou said, winking at April. "You guys go ahead. I'll see you in an hour or so. I'll meet you back here, okay?"

"Good ... thanks, Betty Lou. I'll see you then." April said knowingly, a secret signal between them.

Jared took April's hand and they strolled down the aisle of the large mall. Jared walked close and finally slipped his arm around her slim waist.

"I'm so happy to see you, April. Where have you been all my life?" he joked.

"Well, let's see, I've been right here. I got married, had two boys. The marriage didn't work out; so, after six years, we were divorced. Then, I got married again; but, it only lasted a year. We split up a couple months ago. The day our divorce was final, he committed suicide. So, needless to say, life's been tough!"

"Oh, God, April, I'm so sorry to hear things haven't worked out for you. They haven't for me either. I stupidly married Ramona, thinking I had to; but, she lied to me. We were divorced after six months. I tried to find you. No one knew where you were."

"I guess I was getting married. We just had a small church wedding...didn't make a big announcement or anything. I'd made a new circle of friends, I guess; but, I was still in the area."

"After the divorce, I joined the Marines, to keep from being drafted, thinking it would keep me out of Vietnam; but....as luck would have it, that's exactly where I ended up. After I was wounded, I came home to recuperate. I tried to find you then, too. No luck!"

"I was still right here.....in Dayton."

"A year or so after that, I got married again and we had a little girl. The marriage went sour; so, we're divorced. We're living in the same house; but, I swear, April, we're not married. I don't sleep with her."

"Our lives sound somewhat similar, don't they....tragic!"

"My last marriage was a total waste, except for Kristie, my little girl. No matter what I did, though, I couldn't satisfy my ex-wife, Penny. No matter how much money I gave her, it was never enough. One day I came home early and caught her in our bed with a black man. That's when I moved out...filed for divorce."

"Then how did you end up living in the same house?"

"Because of Kristie, my daughter. Penny was working in a go-go joint, neglecting the baby. My little girl's the only thing in the world that means anything to me...that is, until today, when I saw you. It's good to see you, Honey. You may not believe this, but I've missed you so much."

"Sounds like we've both been through a lot, Jared."

"Let's put an end to the tragedy in our lives. April, I want to see you again. It's like we've never been apart. You're always on my mind. Will you please go out with me tonight? We'll go dancing. I remember how much you like to dance."

"Oh, I don't know, Jared. If you're still living with your wife, would it be right?"

"Remember she's my EX-wife. The only thing we have in common is our daughter. Penny's dating the Chief of Police. Please, April, lately I've been so depressed, I wasn't sure I could face another day...that is, until today, when I saw you." he pleaded.

"I've been depressed, too. I shouldn't tell you this; but, at the hardest times in my life, I've escaped to the memories of you holding me, kissing me. Because of these memories, I could face the next day."

"I can't believe it....me, too!" he replied. Thinking of you, remembering your kisses, helped me survive Vietnam.

After they left the restaurant, Jared grabbed April and pulled her into his arms, savoring the feel of her body against his.

"Oh, God, April, you feel so good, it's amazing. Like I said, I'd never survived Vietnam if it hadn't been for thinking about you. Please, go dancing with me tonight."

"Okay, I shouldn't tell you this, Jared, but, not too long ago, I made myself a promise that I'd never say 'NO' to you again. So, in view of that promise, I'll go out with you tonight, provided you're telling me the truth about your ex-wife. Your marriage is over, is that right? You are divorced?"

"Yes, I'm divorced; and, boy, am I glad, now that I've found you again. I don't feel anything for Penny. We live in the same house so I can be sure my daughter isn't abused; but, we sleep in separate rooms. Penny dates openly. I come and go as I please."

Jared pulled April into his arms again and held her tenderly. "I can't stand it, Honey; I need to hold you for a few minutes. It's been so long."

They held each other gently, caringly, rocking each other in their arms. Their eyes were closed as they savored their joy at seeing each other again. Jared kissed April longingly, passionately, oblivious to the crowded mall. The kiss left them breathless. A couple teenage boys walked by and whistled, "Hey, Man, get a room ..." they retorted. April and Jared ignored them.

"I'll see you tonight at seven o'clock, okay? Since I don't know your address, will you meet me at the Holiday Lounge?"

"No, I don't want to meet you someplace. That sounds sleazy. Come to my apartment. It's just down the street from the mall .... 345 Cherry Hill Drive."

"I'll see you at seven. I can't wait! Right now, I have to get back to my customers; but, my mind won't be on business today. All I can think about is seeing you again, April."

Almost as if it was planned, Betty Lou returned. They smiled at Jared and waved as they walked away.

April quickly told Betty Lou about their conversation, how unhappy they'd both been.

"I saw him kiss you ... Wow, you two look great together!" Betty Lou exclaimed.

"Oh, God, I can't believe it. I've never really gotten over him. Tonight's going to be very special."

"What about the kids?"

"Ut, oh, you're right. I'll have to get a sitter."

"No, you don't. Let them spend the night at my house. I'll take them to a movie, get a pizza or something."

"Really? You'd do that for me? Thanks!"

"I don't have any plans tonight. It'd be my pleasure."

"Well, then, it's been so long since I bought anything new, will you help me find a new outfit?"

Betty Lou helped April shop, excited for her. She found a blue ruffled dress, which accented her svelte figure. They agreed the dress was perfect for dancing.

As they drove back to April's apartment, Betty Lou said, "Boy, April, you're lucky to have a date with him tonight. Now, aren't you glad I made you go to the mall today?"

"I sure am. Oh, Betty Lou, we were teenage sweethearts. We've been through a lot, both had two unhappy marriages. He said he's been so depressed lately; and, so have I. I probably shouldn't tell you this, Betty Lou, but I was so depressed last night, I tried to kill myself. Isn't it amazing? At the lowest point in our lives, Jared and I found each other again? Love's in bloom for the second time for us. After all these years, it's like we're still the best of friends, so much in love."

"Since the boys are staying at my house, go for it! Your kids like me; they'll be delighted that they get to spend two nights away from home. That way, you can come by for them tomorrow ....whenever you're ready. Who knows what the night has in store for you!" Betty Lou teased.

"Normally, I'd never let them be away from me two nights in a row; but, this is a very special night! I appreciate you doing this."

"No problem. It's my pleasure. You haven't stopped smiling since you saw him. You look much better with a smile on your face. Like I said, I've been really worried about you lately. I want you to be happy. Maybe tonight, you can find that happiness."

When the boys got home, April fixed them some grilled cheese sandwiches and warmed up some homemade vegetable soup. She and Betty Lou quickly did the dishes before she put the boys in the car.

"We'll have a great time, won't we, Boys?" Betty Lou said, then, looking at April, "Now, you have yourself a great time tonight... you deserve it!"

As April dressed for her date, she remembered the times she'd gotten ready for dates with Jared so many years ago. It took her just a few minutes to style every hair into place, and make sure her makeup was perfect. She felt confident when she looked at her image in the mirror. She would "knock his socks" off! She decided, knowing it would be a life-changing evening. Something they'd never forget. Something they had both needed and longed for ... for so long.

The doorbell rang. Taking a final glance in the mirror, she walked to the door, opened it, and the sight of Jared Walker took her breath away.....

CHAPTER ELEVEN

THEIR DATE LATER THAT NIGHT - FINALLY!

"God, April, you look like a million bucks!" Jared said after April opened the door to let him in. "It's so wonderful to see you again.... can I hold you in my arms, please?!"

April and Jared had tears in their eyes when the embrace ended.

"I'm glad to see you, too."

"Let's go have a couple drinks...and a couple dances, okay?"

"Sure, sounds great."

At the Holiday Lounge, the music was loud and the action was fast. April and Jared tried to talk; but, the music was too loud for the small lounge.

Their excitement at finding each other again was evident. Dancing filled them with desire; and their passion, if anything, had increased over the years; only now, she didn't have to say "no." After all, times had changed. It was now acceptable for two people who loved each other as much as she and Jared did to go to bed, without being married, she reasoned, however, she was still somewhat moralistic.

April was aware of Jared's every movement, every breath he took, as she snuggled against him on the dance floor. By the time their first slow dance ended, they were trembling.

After they'd finished their third drink, Jared whispered, "Honey, let's go someplace where we can be alone...."

April wanted Jared desperately. A lingering, longing desire deep within her psyche fogged her sense of reasoning, and the years of yearning magnified into an uncontrollable wave of passion.

She looked at Jared questioningly, knowing what he had in mind. The look in his eyes told her everything she needed to know. He felt the same desire...the same passion. She smiled, picked up her purse, and they left the lounge, convincing herself she could do this thing....

Jared pulled April into his arms and kissed her passionately as soon as they were outside. They sensed their years of longing to know the intimate details of their long-lost love were about to end.

They got into Jared's El-Camino and drove to a motel on the outskirts of town. April snuggled next to him, debating in her mind if she was doing the right thing. After all, she had never been to a motel with a man who wasn't her husband. She was a little apprehensive.

While Jared registered, April continued to struggle with her conscience. Could she really do this, she wondered.

"Room 154, Honey, our lucky number!" Jared said as he got back into the truck. He drove to their room located on the other side of the motel.

As soon as he unlocked the door to the room, Jared pulled April into his arms, very excited at the prospect that finally they would be able to make love. The years in Vietnam and the unhappiness he'd known with other women had taken their toll on his emotions. The sweet memory of April was always in the back of his mind. This was a dream coming true for him, a fruition badly needed by them both.

April pulled away. "What would you think if I told you I'm losing my nerve?" she asked tearfully, afraid of his reaction.

"Oh, is April still a virgin?" Jared teased, pulling her into his arms again. "April, don't you know I'm so glad to see you I don't care if we make love or not."

"You don't?"

"Sure, don't get me wrong. I desperately want to make love to you; but, I'm so happy to see you again, to be alone with you, to be able to hold you in my arms again, it's okay if we don't make love tonight. It's been so long since we've seen each other. We've both been through a lot. Hey, honest, no problem. Let's just hold each other...."

"God, Jared, I've never been to a motel with anyone except my husband when I was married. The idea scares me. I want to be with you; but, well, I need some time before..."

"Tell you what, April; I saw a Coke machine down the hall. I've got some Jack Daniels in the truck. Sit down and relax. I'll get the stuff and fix us a drink. We'll listen to some music on the stereo, dance and talk. Now that we have found each other again, we've got so many years to catch up on, don't we? You don't have to do anything you don't want to do, I promise. Have I ever broken a promise to you?"

"No, I don't think you've broken a promise. It's a good suggestion. Let's give it a try."

After turning on the stereo, April sat down in a chair in the corner. When Jared returned with the whiskey, ice and sodas, she watched him fix the drinks.

"You haven't changed at all, Jared. You look the same as you did ten years ago." she said. "Remember fixing the same drinks at my old apartment?"

"Thanks, April. Yes, I remember clearly as if it was yesterday. If anything, you're more beautiful." he said, "I'm never seen anyone who looks more beautiful than you do right now. I've never gotten over you, you know. There were nights in Vietnam when your memory was the only thing that helped me carry on the fight. Sometimes I wanted to stand up in front of one of the 'friendly-fire' rifles and end it all; but, the memory of your sweetness, your freshness, your innocence, helped me to survive. I swore I'd find you when I got back."

"Friendly-Fire?"

"The shots they fired over our bodies at night so the enemy wouldn't sneak up and knife us while we were sleeping...."

"Oh, yes, I think I heard about that. Well, when you got back, why didn't you find me? I needed you, Jared."

"I tried. There was no trace of you. I searched for over a year before I settled for less than I deserved and married my nurse. I wanted only you, I settled for less. I'll never settle for less again. I've tried desperately to make my marriage work... she's not YOU!"

Jared kissed April when he handed her a drink. Then, he pulled another chair next to hers and they propped their feet on the bed next to them so they could relax, just talk.

"Before you take a drink, I want to make a toast...to you, April, the woman I should have married...my soul mate, the woman who should have been the mother of my child...the only woman I've ever really loved!"

Tears welled in April's blue eyes as their glasses clinked. "I've never stopped loving you either, Jared. You should have been the father of my boys. It would've been great! We would have made our marriage work, wouldn't we?"

"I don't doubt it for a minute. Instead, we've only seen tragedy. Hopefully, it's not too late to find happiness ... together!" he said.

A soft romantic love song, "Behind Closed Doors" by Charlie Rich, began to play on the stereo. Jared pulled April to her feet so they could dance.

"Oh, Honey, it would've been better than great if we'd been married. I remember how badly I wanted you. You were a lady when we were in public; and, you became a ravenous tiger when we were behind closed doors. You drove me crazy with desire..."

April hugged Jared and ran her hands across his back as they danced. Their bodies conformed in perfect harmony as they danced, as if they were one body.

It was wonderful being in each other's arms again, they danced and talked for over an hour, sharing their hopes, and relating their tragic experiences for the past ten years. They felt each other's pain and heartaches, and bragged endlessly about their adorable children.

"I've always wondered, April, did you keep your promise?"

"What promise?"

"Did you make it? Were you a virgin when you got married?"

"That, My Love, is none of your business, is it? What do you think?"

Jared hesitated and stared deeply into April's eyes...."I would guess you did!"

She nodded, and then said, "Yeah, but it hurt like hell! I'd never go through that again," she said, with a chuckle. "I thought about leaving him on our wedding night. There was no tenderness. And then, guess what, he accused me of not being a virgin because I didn't scream. He was so rough with me I almost bit my thumb off to keep from screaming; but, then, to accuse me of not being pure was too much. It hurt me deeply. God, Jared, it feels great to finally tell someone about it!"

"You must've been married to a real cad! If I'd been the lucky one to have you first, it wouldn't have been like that!" He said, wiping a tear from his eye. "I wish it had been me, April."

"Me, too." she whispered. "The only way I could sleep that night was to curl my pillow around until it felt like your shoulder. I fell asleep on my wedding night, thinking about you!"

"How long were you together? Why did you split up?"

"We were together about six years. After I almost died having our second child, he started to drink heavily. He stayed away from home a lot. One night, in a drunken rage, he raped me. I had been sick and the doctor was threatening to put me in the hospital..."

"Why?"

"Because I had double pneumonia. Unfortunately, my oldest son, Dougie, heard his father hurt me in the middle of the night. The emotional trauma was too much for him; so, HE ended up in the hospital instead of me. It was one thing for Doug to hurt me; but, when he hurt the children, it was unforgivable. I left him."

"How cruel. Are you okay now?"

"I'm okay NOW....I'm with you.

Holding April gently, Jared whispered...."Honey, let's pretend we got married today. Let's pretend we're finally alone, getting ready to make love, for the first time."

His mouth came down hard on hers and their passion became undeniable. Soon Jared was removing April's dress. He unhooked her bra, lifted her into the air, and kissed her aroused nipples as they continued to dance. She wrapped her legs around him.

"Oh, God, Honey, I've wanted to do this for so long..."

April quickly pulled Jared's sweater off so they could dance, bare chest to bare breast. It was a long-awaited embrace ...their bare chests pressed together. It was heavenly as they stroked each other's bare back and kissed as they danced.

The kisses became intense and Jared undressed April from the waist down. She didn't stop him. She fumbled with the button on his jeans. It wouldn't come unfastened. Jared stepped back and stripped to his underwear while she watched.

The bulge in his underwear was prominent. April stripped away his under shorts and stared at the size of his erection.

"Wow, nothing I've seen in Playgirl Magazine compares with this...I'm not sure I can handle this!"

"In a way, it's a curse. Some girls can't handle it! But, I can't believe you didn't know I was this big. Remember when we used to make out on your sofa? I'd get so turned on I thought I was going to burst. Didn't you notice then?"

"I was so young and innocent, Jared." she replied as she brushed a curly lock of his hair out of his eyes and pulled him against her. "I was very shy and naive...."

"Remember, this is our 'honeymoon', Darling; and, we're finally able to make love..." he whispered, continuing the fantasy.

"Let's take this nice and slow...." she said, with a growl in her throat. Jared smiled, remembering that she became a tiger behind closed doors. He was finally with his little wildcat, his tiger, his dream coming true.

Jared kissed her slowly and passionately, savoring their first coupling. He brought her to the brink of passion before he tried to penetrate her body. Very gently, so he wouldn't hurt her, he drove every inch of his love machine into her welcoming body. She moaned with delight.

"Oh, Jared, I've never known anything to feel so great! Don't stop....as I live and breathe, I've never known anything like this!"

April was ecstatic. Jared had awakened an unbelievable, ravenous passion within her in their first mating. She finally knew what the "big deal" was all about...two bodies acting as one. When they climaxed, a multitude of 'fireworks' exploded inside the small motel room.

After their passion cooled, they lay quietly, kissing and caressing each other, unable to restrain themselves from touching each other's bodies.

"God, April, I'm overwhelmed. I knew it would be great between us; but, never in my wildest dreams did I imagine it would be this fantastic! There are no words in the dictionary to describe how wonderful I feel..."

"Me, too! Mere words are inadequate to express this feeling."

"Did I hurt you? I've never known a better fit, Honey. This tells us we were truly MEANT for each other...." he whispered.

April smiled in agreement. "God, Jared, Charlie taught me how to climax; but, we were never able to attain mutual satisfaction...nothing like this!"

Within minutes, they were aroused and made love again, ending with the same glorious fireworks.

After resting a few minutes, Jared got up to light a cigarette. He inhaled deeply, looked at April and said, "I guess I've made love with every woman I've wanted except you. None of them came close to what we found tonight. You're great, April ....for a virgin!" They both laughed. "I don't want to make love to anyone but you for the rest of my life."

"Well, Jared, I have to confess. Over half the territory you covered was 'untouched' by man; if you know what I mean. You know, 'virgin territory'!" she kidded him, touching his penis.

"Oh, come on, April. You've been married twice. I'm sure you've been around 'cause you know what you're doing when you make love. I don't know if I believe you or not; but, you flatter me! WE are a perfect fit, don't you think? Sometimes, it's a real problem, finding a girl who can handle this thing! It's a curse!"

"Don't curse him...Jared Walker! He made me the happiest girl in the world." she kidded. "I never dreamed it'd be so great!"

Jared kissed her and tenderly pinched her nose. "I'm going to take a fast shower. Relax, Honey, I'll be right back. Don't you dare leave!" he commanded jokingly.

April lay on the bed, joyfully thinking about their lovemaking. She could hear Jared whistling in the shower. Smiling to herself, she got off the bed, opened the bathroom door, pulled back the shower curtain and stepped into the shower with Jared. At first, he was surprised; then, smiling, he pulled her into his arms.

"Tell you what, you wash my back and I'll wash yours....

The shower was almost as fantastic as their lovemaking. Lovingly, sexily, caressing each other's soapy bodies caused them to renew their passion. They couldn't get toweled off fast enough to get back to bed...back to the ravenous ecstasy of each other's arms.

Finally, exhausted, Jared whispered, "Can you stay all night?"

"No, I'd better not! The boys'll probably call early in the morning. I should be home when they call."

After a couple more kisses, they started to get dressed, reluctant to leave their "honeymoon" suite. That would mean they had to pick up their mundane lives again.

Passion once again overtook them. They grabbed each other hungrily and fell back into bed, in a seemingly, never-ending embrace. They couldn't get enough of each other's bodies, each other's lips.

"Please, April, stay with me! Sleep in my arms. I've imagined you sleeping with your head on my shoulder for so many years. I want to see if it feels as great as I imagined it would. I'll call the desk for a wake-up call. We'll end our date by having breakfast together. I'd love to wake up with you in my arms....to see how beautiful you look in the morning. I can't stand the thought of taking you home right now..." he pleaded.

"Jared, I don't think I can EVER tell you 'no' again..."

"Good!" Jared said, as he picked up the phone to call the desk. He asked for a six o'clock wake-up call.

As soon as he hung up the phone, he pulled April close to him. She snuggled in his arms, her head resting on his shoulder.

Just as they were about to fall asleep, Jared whispered a prayer, "Oh, God, I love this woman so much! It feels like we're married. Allow us to always love each other as much as we do now...."

April smiled and snuggled closer to Jared. "Jared, I love you, too. I can't imagine loving anyone as much as I love you..."

"Let's work things out soon so we can be together forever. We can be a real family...your boys and my little girl. It'll be exactly the way it should have been ten years ago. I'll never want anyone but you, April. You FEEL like my wife, finally safe in my arms where you belong. As far as I'm concerned, we're married!"

They peacefully fell asleep with April's head resting on Jared's shoulder, which, ironically, felt exactly as they'd both imagined through the years. There was so much joy in their hearts, they were about to burst from sheer happiness.

During the night, Jared gently fondled April's nipples until he awoke her to a renewed, insatiable passion. They once again lost themselves in an amorous delight.

Afterwards, they lay awake, curled in each other's arms, talking softly, making future plans to be together.

"Oh, April, I couldn't believe it when I saw you at the mall. When I looked at you, you were surrounded by clouds! I was aware of nothing but you. You were so beautiful, I couldn't believe my eyes."

"So were you. I wasn't aware of anything except your face when you looked at me. I thought I was dreaming. I was afraid you wouldn't recognize me after all these years. The look on your face when you saw me said it all. And, to think, I almost didn't go to the Mall. Betty Lou insisted."

"I'm glad she did. I'll have to thank her the next time I see her...." he joked, letting April know he expected there would be another time.

"I was so depressed, Honey. Friday night, I tried to kill myself. Charlie, my second husband, killed himself the day our divorce was final. He didn't tell me he had cancer. Why didn't he tell me, Jared? Promise me you'll always tell me everything. No secrets between us, please. You can say anything to me; and, as long as you say it with honesty and love, I'll understand ....whatever it is, I promise."

"I can't imagine wanting anyone else but you as long as I live. We have to work things out so we can be together. I need you to sleep in my arms every night for the rest of my life. I'm so glad you didn't commit suicide."

"Me, too, Honey. I'll love you 'til the day I die. You'll be on my mind when I take my last breath. God intervened in my suicide...He must have. The razor blade wouldn't cut my wrist. Later, I cut my finger with the same razor blade....see!" she said, showing him her finger in the dim light emanating from the bathroom.

"Thank you, God, for intervening; and, for what we've found in each other." Jared prayed, kissing her injured finger. "You were created for me, April. We were meant to be together.... we're already married in God's eyes.

"Yes, I think so, too."

It was after six-thirty when they finally left the motel the next morning. "Hey, let's go to our old hangout, Frisch's, for breakfast. It seems appropriate." Jared suggested.

"Great idea!"

Breakfast was delicious. They were oblivious to anyone in the restaurant as they enjoyed breakfast, hanging onto every word the other had to say. They lingered, holding hands, and continued to talk over three cups of coffee.

After Jared drove April home, he turned off the motor and took her hand affectionately, saying, "Let's promise, right now, to never lose touch with each other again—no matter what! Somehow, we'll work things out so we can be together. You WILL be mine, I promise. I always keep my promises."

"Okay, Jared. Thanks for a beautiful 'wedding' night. I'll never forget it, no matter what happens in the future. You know what, I feel like a bride...I'm even sore!" she teased.

"Maybe it won't be too long before we can take a real honeymoon. Your children should've been mine; Kristie should have been yours. I believe that with all my heart. We'll become a family. You need my ring on this finger...." he said as he kissed the third finger of her left hand tenderly. "April Walker sounds like a good name, doesn't it? Someday, I swear, if you'll have that name, I'll put my ring on this finger."

"Oh, I hope so, Jared. My boys will love you simply because I love you. They're special little boys."

"It's because they have such a special mother. Kristie'll adore you, too."

Once they'd gotten inside April's apartment, Jared pulled her into his arms and hugged her tightly.

"Don't you want to check out the apartment...make sure it's safe?" she teased, remembering the way he checked the apartment after a date ten years previously.

Jared walked around the well-kept apartment. Even the boys' rooms were clean.

"Well, I guess you're safe. I don't see any intruders." he teased.

"Thank you, Kind Sir!"

When they got to her bedroom, she put her arms around him and whispered...."Will you make love to me again before you leave...in my bed? Tonight, I want to be able to smell you on the sheets..."

Jared smiled...."Boy, Woman, you've 'bout worn me out. Kiss me and let's see what happens." he challenged.

April made the growling sound deep in her throat... the sound that Jared loved. It sent thrills through his body; and, as expected, they shared a slow, sweet, gentle lovemaking in April's bed. Jared held April as if she was a priceless piece of porcelain. He never wanted to break her heart and told her so...

"God, April, it's like I'm having a dream. We've got to be together real soon. I already miss you...."

Jared got dressed to go. April pulled on a robe so she could walk him to the door.

Kissing her sweetly, he said, "I'll call you. Soon, we'll be together, Princess."

April watched from the window as he backed his El-Camino out of the parking space. He saw her standing in the window and waved.

They were so happy, their hearts were about to burst with joy. Could they finally be together? That thought was prevalent in both their minds.

CHAPTER TWELVE

A fter April arrived home from work the next Monday evening, a florist delivered a dozen long-stemmed red roses. She knew immediately Jared had sent the flowers. The card read: "Pledging my love forever. Your Secret Admirer." Her life had suddenly been transformed from being "stormy" into a happier "sunshine" time of life. April felt happy and it showed in her rosy cheeks.

April and Jared dated every weekend for the next few weeks, and their love grew stronger. They yearned to be together every possible moment they could manage.

She didn't feel it would be proper if Jared moved in with her because of the morality question. After all, she had to think about her boys. What would they think if their Mom lived with a man without the sanctity of marriage? Besides, April couldn't forget Jared was still living in his ex-wife's house. She felt she couldn't live with Jared without the benefit of marriage; but, she wanted to know they would be compatible if they lived together.

"Honey, my Mom wants to take the boys to Florida for a two-week vacation next month. Can we spend those two weeks together? Do you think you can arrange it without causing a major catastrophe?" she asked Jared.

"Oh, sure, no problem. I'd love it! It'd be wonderful to sleep with you every night, to eat with you, to make love to you EVERY night! It would be a dream come true for us both, don't you think? There's no reason why I can't stay with you during that time? After all, I'm not married! I'll tell Penny I'm taking a vacation. She knows I'm seeing someone."

April and Jared were ecstatic during the first week of their "vacation;" but, during the second week, he started to receive phone calls from his angry ex-wife.

Penny Walker talked to April several times and quirked that she was happy Jared FINALLY had someone in his life. April couldn't figure out why Penny's words sent chills down her spine ....maybe because she had a malicious, vindictive tone in Penny Walker's voice. She confirmed to April that they were, indeed, divorced, and they lived together only because of the child.

When April told Jared about the strange conversation with Penny, he assured her she had no reason to be upset. The phone calls stopped.

On Thursday night, Jared stopped by Penny's house. Kristie was dirty, hungry, and alone.

He grabbed some of Kristie's clothing from the closet and took her to his parents' house. He explained the situation to them....the unkempt condition of Penny's house, the fact that there was no food in the refrigerator, the fact Kristie had been in the house alone. She had been left to fend for herself, which was totally impossible for a three-year old child.

After Jared left his parent's house, he went back to the house to wait for Penny's return, quickly calling to let April know he'd be late and explained the reason.

When Penny finally came home, she was with the black man who drove the Cadillac. Penny jumped out of the car as soon as she saw Jared's El-Camino. They glared at each other without saying anything. Then, Penny yelled at Jared, "You're out sluttin' around every night with that whore! I'm not doing anything you're not doing!!!"

"Keep April out of this; but, for the record, she's not a whore...she's a lady! We've loved each other since we were twenty years old. I'd marry her in a minute. The only reason I'm here is 'cause I found Kristie alone in this filthy house. She was hungry, dirty, and had no supervision. This is a clear case of child abuse, Penny. I'm taking her away from you!"

"Try it, Mister! If you try, I'll kill that whore you're screwin' around with! You know I'll do it, Jared Walker. With my connections at the police station, and my experience as a nurse, everyone will think it's an accident. Then, you'll never see your 'precious slut' again!"

"I'll know you did it ... and I'll tell about your threat!"

"No proof....after all, brakes go out every day. I know where she lives. She has two boys. I'll make sure they're in the car, too!"

"I'll still tell the police about your threats. You'll burn before and AFTER you go to hell, Penny!"

"And, you'll NEVER see your daughter again...you bastard!'

"You mean, YOU'LL never see her again. I'll take her away with April. We'll build a family. Kristie'll have a GOOD mother, then!"

"I swear, if you don't get MY daughter and bring her back to the house tonight, I'll kill April and her brats! You'll never see Kristie again. You know I can do it. It'll look like an accident. They won't believe YOU; after all, I'm the one with connections in the sheriff's office."

"You mean you're the police chief's whore—anybody's girl!"

Penny slapped Jared. "Shut your god-damn mouth and get that piece-of-junk truck out of my driveway. I'll give you until Saturday morning to get your ass back in this house; or, I swear, soon, you won't have your goddamn April! She'll be D-O-A!"

"If I come back, I'll have Kristie with me; but, we won't be back tonight.....maybe Sunday afternoon. I detest the sight of you, Penny. Now, you and your black stud have a ball; that is, until Sunday. We'll be back on Sunday!" Jared shouted as he got into his truck. He squealed his tires and spread gravel as he pulled out of the driveway.

He took a deep breath and glanced at his watch. It was midnight. He felt a heavy sadness as he drove to April's apartment. God, how he loved her...how could he work it out so they could be together?

Jared wondered if Penny could make good on her threat to kill April and the boys. He knew his ex-wife was a mean, vindictive woman, who was, in fact, capable of making it happen. He didn't dare take a chance; so, until Jared could come up with an alternate plan, he had no choice but to go back to the house he'd shared with his ex-wife. Although it was the last thing he wanted to do, he'd play along with her evil living arrangement for Kristie's sake until he could get her away from Penny.

He'd move April and the boys to a safe location first, far away from Penny before he would do anything more to upset her. He'd allow things to cool down before he made his move.

Jared wondered how he'd explain everything to April.... his sweet April. He decided not to say anything to her until his plans were set.

Jared and April spent a loving weekend together; but, she knew he was troubled. "Jared, is everything okay?"

"Not really...." he hesitated. "How would you feel about moving to California? I'll put my brother-in-law in charge of the stores in this district and take over the management of our California division. It's much larger than this district so you wouldn't have to work. We'll get married and become a family. Maybe we could even have a baby, who knows...."

"Wow! I don't know. I'd hate to move so far away from my Mother; but, of course, I'd go anywhere with you. Do you think my ex-husband would pitch a fit? Do I need his permission?"

"We'll find answers to these questions....one at a time. The important thing is, we'll be together!"

"Oh, Jared, it would be great; but, I can't have anymore children. I almost died when Jason was born. They tied my tubes because of the serious complications. You know what, I cried when they put me under the anesthetic because it meant I could never have your child. Even then, in my heart, I hoped we'd get back together someday, that I could have your child."

Jared pulled her into his arms to comfort her. "It's okay. You can be Kristie's mother; and, I'll be the father to your boys. We'll make it work. It may be possible to have another child. We'll see an expert. They're doing a lot with artificial insemination these days."

"I would love to have your baby, Honey. I want to work things out so we can be together. I know we'll be happy."

"I'll start the paperwork tomorrow for the transfer to the West Coast Division. I have another brother, Paul, who lives in Los Angeles. Although he's been overseeing the business, he's asked me to come out so they can take a vacation. I'll go out first, get us a house, and send for you and the boys. I'll take Kristie with me. Paul's wife, Sally, will take care of her until you and the boys get there."

"Okay, I'll give notice to my landlord. When should I let my boss know?"

"Not yet. I'll let you know. It'll probably take several months to get everything set up. These two weeks have given us a preview of how wonderful our life will be when we're together; but, let me caution you, April, don't say anything to anyone yet. I don't want Penny to find out about our plans. She could make a lot of trouble for us if she finds out. Promise you'll stay quiet about our plans for now."

"Okay...but, I don't understand. You and Penny aren't married."

"No, we're NOT married; but, trust me on this. Oh, another thing, I want you to get an unlisted phone number so Penny won't bug you after I leave. I'm not going to give her any idea what we're doing....or where we're going. My parents can't stand her; so, they won't say a word."

"But, she has no claim on you...."

"I know that; but, you don't know her. She's a real shrew, Honey. If she finds out where we are, we'll never find happiness. It'll work out, you'll see. We have stores all over the country. She'll never suspect California 'cause she thinks I hate Los Angeles. I'll see my attorney tomorrow."

"Why?"

"Well, I didn't want to spoil our weekend; but, when I stopped by the house the other night, Kristie was alone. Like I told you, she was dirty, hungry, and had no babysitter. Honey, there wasn't any food and the house was a wreck; so, I took her to my parents house. She's still there."

"Does Penny know where Kristie is?"

"Yes, I went back to the house and waited for her to come home. She came in with her black stud about eleven o'clock. I have no idea where her children were....probably running the streets."

"Are you sure you can't be charged with kidnapping?"

"No way. I'll hire a private detective tomorrow and get evidence against her, including pictures, if possible. April, this is a chance for us to be together. By the time Penny figures everything out, we'll be married and living in sunny California."

"But, I don't understand.....why do we have to be so secretive?"

"Don't ask. Just trust me. Remember, you said you'd never tell me 'no' again!"

"Touché!"

"After today, Honey, I can't see you very much. I want Penny to think we've stopped seeing each other. I'll call you every day from work; and, I'll dream about holding you like this every night. Give me time to work it out so we can be together ....for the rest of our lives, Princess."

April snuggled against him, welcoming his embrace. She agreed to wait, to remain silent, although she didn't understand why the urgency or the need for secrecy; however, she trusted Jared's judgment.

After kissing April goodbye on Sunday morning, Jared picked Kristie up at his parents' house and drove to the house he shared with his ex-wife. He refused to start an argument with her. He looked at her, matter-of-factly, and said, "It's over between April and me; so, I guess, if it's okay, I'll continue to live here, Penny. This doesn't mean anything's going to happen between us, though. The sight of you repulses me. I'm only here because of Kristie. You can do anything you want, with anybody you want, but not in front of my daughter."

Penny Walker agreed, with a satisfied smirk.

Jared put the balance of his plan into action, saw his attorney and hired a private detective to watch Penny. The evidence he received from his detective the first two-weeks was very incriminating. While Jared worked during the day, his ex-wife had sexual orgies with groups of men. She didn't bother to get a sitter for Kristie.

In one of the detective's photos, Penny was in the bedroom with two men while Kristie played in the backyard. Kristie could actually be seen playing in the backyard through the bedroom window. Penny was so involved with her tryst; she didn't notice the detective, or the camera flash.

Jared's attorney couldn't believe his eyes when he saw the detective's pictures. He felt Jared had an excellent case of child abuse, and filed the petition for Jared to receive total custody of Kristie.

Unfortunately, the judge saw the case differently, and threw it out of court, refusing to reopen the custody matter, stating it had been resolved and settled previously.

When Jared explained the court's decision to April, he was heartbroken. "April, I'm going to leave for California a week from Monday. Kristie's going with me even if I have to take her without Penny's permission. I'll have my attorney file the appeal after we're gone."

"Jared, couldn't that be construed as kidnapping? You don't have legal custody. They'll force your parents to tell them where you went; and, when they catch you, you'll go to jail. If you're in jail, we'll never be together! Isn't there another way to work this out?"

"God, April, what can we do? I love you so much it hurts. It's driving me crazy not being with you. We're already married in God's eyes. I need you....you're my wife in every sense of the word but legal; but, I need Kristie, too."

"I need you, too, Jared. The only time I feel secure is when we're together. I need security, the security of your love. Why don't you move to California alone; but, have your detective continue to watch Penny. Surely, after you're gone, she'll let her guard down and mess up even more. You'll have enough evidence, the courts will be forced to grant you custody; and, you won't have to face criminal charges."

"I can't leave Kristie alone with her, not even for a few days."

"Go to California, get us a house. I'll be there two weeks later. We'll be together; then, we'll work out a plan to get custody of Kristie. Surely, the courts will decide she's better off with us.....a normal family household."

"It's worth a try, I guess. Before I leave though, April, I've got to be with you. Can you get a couple days vacation so we can spend some time together during the day? Penny'll think I'm at work. It has to be during the day so she won't get suspicious. Trust me, she can't find out we're leaving until we're married."

April arranged for two days' vacation. The time they spent together was heavenly and they made love endlessly. The separation they were facing was devastating to them both; and, they were depressed when the time came for Jared to say goodbye, their time together had slipped away.

"I'll call you when I find a house. It'll probably be a couple weeks because housing is tight in L.A."

"Go, Honey, find us a place! I'll be waiting by the phone for your call. I've already started packing; but, whatever you do, don't lose my phone number. It's unlisted now."

"It's etched in my brain. I'll never forget it!"

"I still don't understand why we have to 'sneak' around; but, I trust your judgment."

When Jared hugged April for the last time, she begged him not to leave without her. He could sense she was near hysteria. Never had he known such love....tears ran down her lovely face and dripped from her trembling chin.

"Don't wait too long to send for us. Goodbye, Jared." she stammered, barely able to speak.

"Never say goodbye, April....just say, 'catch ya' later.' Goodbye sounds too final. There's no way this is final. It's only a temporary separation, I promise. Soon, we'll be together."

"Catch ya' later, then, Jared." she said, trying to smile through her tears.

"I love you, April. I REALLY love you. I've dedicated a special song to you this afternoon on W-P-L-P. It's a song I could only dedicate to you. I mean every word."

He grabbed her and crushed her body to his in a final embrace. She felt limp in his arms....like a rag doll. They were both crying.

"I've got to leave you, My Darling, catch ya' later."

The sound of the door closing was deafening to her. He was gone. April fell to the floor, on her knees, sobbing. She heard him start his truck. She stared through the window until he had disappeared down the road. She knew if for some reason he didn't send for her, her life would never be the same. She was hopelessly in love with him.

Once she'd gotten her emotions under control, April turned the stereo to W-P-L-P. After a couple songs, the disc jockey said, "This is a special...and I do mean special.... request for a very special lady from the love of her life. See you in California, Princess!"

Engelbert Humperdinck began to sing "After the Lovin'" as April listened carefully to every word. Chills ran up her spine, and goose bumps prickled her skin. She couldn't sit still. The song continued..."So I sing you to sleep, after the lovin'..... I'm still in love with you...."

"Oh, Jared, I love you, too." she said to the radio. "Please keep your promise."

Saturday morning, April received a bouquet of beautiful red roses from her "Secret Admirer" with a note...."Before these roses are withered, you'll hear from me."

CHAPTER THIRTEEN

THREE DAYS LATER

It had been an extremely difficult day for April; so, she was relieved when she finally got the kids bathed and tucked into their beds. While she was washing the dinner dishes, the phone rang.

"Hello." she answered quickly so it wouldn't wake the boys.

"Is this the 'Best in the West?'" Jared asked.

"You bet your boots, Partner! Are you in California?"

"Yes, but I miss you. It was a good trip....long, but I didn't have any problems. I'll find us a house as soon as I can 'cause I can't wait for you to get here. You'll love my brother, Paul, and his wife, Sally. I told them about you. They can't wait to meet ya. They're glad we've found each other again."

"Oh, Jared, I miss you, too..." she said as tears pooled in her yes. Wait a second...I'm about to cry. I don't want to cry. I want to talk to you. I love you so much; and, I loved the song you dedicated to me when you left. What a thoughtful thing to do!"

"That'll be OUR song forever, April, no matter what. I can't imagine loving anyone but you as long as I live."

"Thanks for your thoughtfulness and the beautiful flowers. By the way, they're still beautiful."

"You're most welcome, My Love. Do you and the boys want to fly out, or would you rather drive?"

"Oh, I don't know... What do you think? Should I bring the furniture?"

"No, let's start fresh. Hell, I'm wealthy! Let's buy everything new. You can decorate our home anyway you like. Just bring your clothes. Hopefully, I'll call you before your roses are withered to let you know when you can come."

"What do you want me to do with my furniture?"

"Give it away, or sell it....whatever you want; but, remember, keep quiet about the move. I don't want Penny to find out about us until we're married."

"Okay, I guess; but, I don't really understand. This feels so sneaky; and, we don't have any reason to be sneakin' around. We're both single."

"I'll explain when you get here."

"Why don't we drive out so the boys can see this beautiful country? It might be their only chance to see the desert."

"Good! If you drive, it'll be harder to trace you. Is your car mechanically sound? Do you think it'll make the trip okay?"

"I think so, Jared. I'll just bring our clothes and donate everything else to a mission. Material things aren't important ....being together's what matters, right?"

"Right! Do you think Doug will give you any trouble about taking the boys out of Ohio?"

"No, I've already checked with my attorney. Since I have total custody of the boys, I'm free to move provided I let Doug know our address. He only lives six miles away; but, he doesn't see them very often right now. I'll tell him once I know the moving date."

"I'll rent a post office box so you'll have a forwarding address, okay?"

"That's a great idea. I can't wait to see you, Jared."

"It'll be great, Princess. I miss you so much it hurts; but, listen, I've gotta run. I'll catch ya' later!"

"Catch YOU later, Babe!" she replied, smiling.

THREE WEEKS LATER

The mission was waiting for April's phone call. Their clothes and basic essentials were packed. She had given away the odds and ends she'd accumulated over the years; and, April had given her boss a tentative notice. The only thing she was waiting for was a phone call. Why hadn't Jared called, she wondered.

Her once-beautiful roses were withered and smelled rotten. April threw them into the garbage. Her thoughts were obsessed with why she hadn't heard from Jared. "After the Lovin'" played on the radio constantly. Every time she heard it, she cried.

Almost on key, the phone rang.

"Hello." she said hopefully.

"April, this is Jared..." he said sadly. "I've got some bad news for you. Penny showed up last week with the furniture. I don't know how she tracked me down; but, unfortunately, she did."

"What am I supposed to do now? Can't I come out anyway? We'll work it out."

"There's something I didn't tell you, Hon. Penny threatened to kill you and the boys before I came to California. I didn't tell you because I didn't want to worry you. She said I'd never see Kristie again. I know her, April. She's a vindictive bitch. That's the reason I led her to believe we'd broken up."

"I'm not afraid of her."

"Well, you should be....she knows how to kill someone and make it look like an accident. She makes me so angry, I want to kill HER! It breaks my heart, Princess. I can't sleep, remembering our last day together. I need to hold you in my arms."

"Me, too."

"I have to stay in California a couple more weeks because Paul and Sally went to Europe for a much deserved vacation. They were expecting to meet you when they got back; but, now, I guess you'd better not come out, at least, not yet."

"Jared....I can't believe it! My heart's breaking....I can't talk to you right now. Goodbye....."

"Oh, Darling, please, don't say goodbye. I need to hear your voice. I can't stand not being with you. Part of me is missing when you're not around."

"My heart's broken into a thousand tiny pieces. I don't know if it can be patched, Jared. I miss you, too. It's hard for me, too, not being with you. We compliment and complete each other; but, right now, I can't talk anymore. I've got to cry. Goodbye, call me later, okay?"

"Only if you don't say 'Goodbye.' I'll call you, April .....I promise." He stopped talking because the line went dead.

Jared relaxed the receiver. "I'll catch ya' later, April. Somehow, I'll catch ya' later, I promise." he said as he surrendered to the pain deep in his heart..... He sobbed, almost uncontrollably.

The next two weeks were the hardest April had ever faced. Jared chose for them not to be together again. What hold could Penny possibly have on him, she wondered, after all, they're not married? Jared said he wants to marry me....I want to marry him. Will my heart mend this time?

April wouldn't allow herself to think about Jared. She took life one-day-at-a-time; but, except for her precious children, her life was empty.

Her bed was empty and cold. Sleep would come only after she'd cuddled her pillow and imagined it was Jared's shoulder. She sprinkled his cologne on the pillowcase to add imagery to her fantasy; but, her pillow was a poor substitute. She had felt safe and secure in Jared's arms. Now, there were no fireworks, only emptiness....severe, devastating loneliness.

April's boss gladly allowed her to keep her job. She persuaded her landlord to remain in their apartment. She called the mission and apologized for not giving them her furniture. She sent them a donation.

Weeks passed with no word from Jared. April had resigned herself to not hearing from him.

One day at a time, she started to mend; after all, she was a survivor. If her dad could see her now, he wouldn't believe her emotional strength. She's not a fat, little girl who's hot-to-trot! She's an adult who survives life's obstacles. She's a "winner"....even if it's only a front for the boys' sake. They were her reason to live.

April was drawn to a rundown shack on the outskirts of town. The simple, weather-beaten cabin intrigued her. Finally, unable to contain her curiosity; she had to find out who lived in the tiny run-down house.

Before she lost her nerve, April nervously stepped onto the front porch and knocked on the door. There was no answer. April was almost relieved because she didn't know how she was going to explain why she had knocked.

Just as she was about to leave, an old woman opened the door. She said nothing, just looked at April and smiled. The old woman, which looked to be about eighty years old, didn't have a tooth in her mouth. Her gray hair was askew, sticking straight up in every direction. Her glasses were so thick it made the woman's eyes look gigantic. She was dressed modestly in the pink faded housedress, brown cotton stockings held up with elastic garters, and sloppy, gray-wool slippers. A tattered blue apron hung around her ample waist.

Since April didn't know why she'd been drawn to the house, she couldn't explain the reason for the knock. When the silence became uncomfortable, she stammered, "I don't know why I'm here. For several weeks, I've been drawn, like a magnet, to this house; but, I don't know why."

"I know, My Dear. I's been waitin' fer yous. Come in, soon ye'll understand why you've come 'ere."

April was frightened; but, her curiosity was the stronger of her emotions. Maybe she should turn and run away from the old house, from the strange old woman who seemed to know her.

"I'm a gypsy fortune teller. I's knowed yous' comin' fer quite som' time. Be'n 'waitin' for ye to knock. Sit down...I's has som'thin' to tell ya." The old woman said, pointing towards a chair in the corner.

April was numb. She couldn't speak. She sat down quietly in an old, tattered chair in the corner, next to an old worn sofa. The old woman pulled up a kitchen chair and sat down across from April. April felt as if she was trapped by the ample-sized woman.

After staring at April for several minutes, she took her hand. "I's knowed you be'n deeply hurt, My Dear. I's also knowed ye loves a young man wit all yer 'eart and soul. I tells ye, he loves ye dearly, too; but, there's some evil forces keepin' youse two 'part, ain't it true?"

April nodded her head, unable to speak, mystified by the old woman's words.

"But, he's not married, ain't that right?"

"No, he's not married." April replied. She decided she wasn't going to volunteer any additional information until she found out why she was so intrigued by the old woman's words.

"But he loves ya', My Dear, 'n', God wants youse two to be together. Youse two are meant to be ta'gether....forever. He's got a little girl. Ain't' that right?"

"Yes, that's true."

"He's broken'earted right now, ain't that right? His child's mama's forcin' herself 'pon him, makin' 'erself part o' his life. She hates ya', My Dear. She'll do anythin' ta hurt ye, to keep youse two 'part."

"Yes, I suppose that's true."

"He wants ta be wit ya'. He wants ye chil'en to be his'n. Youse two can be a real family. Ye'll be happy if that other woman will leave ye 'lone, right? My Dear, be patient wit' him. Give him time to work t'ings out. Youse two'll be together someday if ye'll be patient wit' him. But, I caution ye, youse two kin only find 'appiness in the woods by the seashore. Ye'll find happiness only there...."

"How do you know these things?"

"God's given me a gift. He's sent hunderds o' people to me humble door over the years. I's tell 'um what's in me heart. It makes me happy when he send someone me way. Honey, yer man wants ye. He intends to have ya. He needs ye to be patient and wait. He loves ya very much....wit' all his 'eart."

Tears started to roll down the old gypsy's weathered cheeks. April couldn't speak. She opened her mouth but the words caught in her throat. She sensed sincerity in the old woman's eyes. Her tears were real.

"Do you know our names?" April asked.

"No, I's only knows ye 'earts. He loves ye, My Dear, he wants ye to wait fer him 'til he can work out dis t'ing. Now, ye must leave. I feel weak from tellin' youse all dez t'ings."

"Do you have any idea how long I'll have to wait?"

"Can't say; but, keep yerself busy. Youse been wantin' to write 'bout yer love fer 'long time. Write 'bout ye love... it's a mighty, God-given love. Write youse story. It'll be published, and you'll make many dollars from de book;

but, mind ye, don't youse sell ye rights to the book. Youse'll make millions ...ye young man'll be mighty proud o' ye!"

The old woman got up and shuffled away, as she wiped the tears from her eyes on the corner of the dingy apron she was wearing. April watched, deep in thought, as the old woman disappeared into another room.

April sat alone, thinking, for a few minutes, as if she was frozen to the chair, unable to move. Then, taking a last look around the modest room, she got up quietly, pulled a twenty dollar bill from her purse and laid it on the table. She walked outside without looking back, got into her car and drove away.

April was still stunned by the old woman's words when she got back to her apartment. She pulled a notebook out of the desk and tried to write down exactly what the old woman had said. Then, she remembers Jared's favorite song when they first met..... "The Gypsy Cried." He had mentioned that he didn't necessarily like the words; but, he loved the melody.

Could there be a connection, April wondered, trying to remember the words to the song.

After a few minutes, April was inspired to write a poem:

WILL THE MOUNTAINS GET IN THE WAY?

Romeo, if I could send a mental message
Clear across the U.S.A.,
Would you receive it, Darling,
Or, would the mountains get in the way?

I need to hear the sound of your voice,
I need to hear you say,
Everything to reassure me,
That we'll be together someday.

Can we hold hands and laugh
In the sunshine by the sea?
Forever, forever, My Romeo,
Where we'll be free to be?

I went to see a gypsy,
Just to see what she would say,
She said we belonged together,
God had intended it that way!

She said, "Together, we'll find happiness,
Provided I'll take enough time,
To learn your good points and bad points,
And learn you're not handing me a 'line.'

To trust, to wait, no matter how long,
To fulfill God's destiny...
Oh, Patience! Oh, God, please,
Don't let this loneliness get to me!

CHAPTER FOURTEEN

April was devastated because she wasn't able to be with Jared in California. She fell into a deep emotional chasm.... severe depression. She couldn't sleep during the night, and numbly managed to get through the day, without caring or noticing what was happening around her. She was observing others as they lived life to the fullest, instead of living it herself. It was much worse than when she was a teenager.

She longed for Jared's touch. It was easier before she knew how wonderful it was to make love with him. The gypsy's words, and her boys, were the only glimmer of hope she had. Finally, unable to cope with her emotions any longer, she sought help with her depression.

April's psychologist, Mark Everson, was a very handsome and sympathetic man. He understood her loss. Step by step, he helped her patch the scar tissue in her heart.

Soon, she was laughing; and, since she hadn't heard from Jared, she decided it was time to try to find someone with whom she could build a life. Her boys needed a father; and, she needed a husband.

At the end of April's final session, Mark said, "I would normally never ask a patient for a date; but, since your treatment's ending today, would you have dinner with me?"

"Sure, I think it would be good for YOU to spend a little money on me for a change...." she kidded him, remembering how expensive his sessions had been.

"How about Saturday night?"

"Sure....you have the address."

"Is seven o'clock okay?"

"Perfect."

"I'll see you then, April."

Their dinner was pleasant and their conversation light as their relationship progressed to friendship instead of doctor-patient. When the evening ended at April's front door, Mark kissed April lightly on the cheek.

"This was fun, April. Let's do it again...."

"I can't think of any reason why not; after all, you're my best friend. You know everything about me."

"But, you don't know much about me, April. You're truly a fascinating woman. You should have been a psychologist. All my education doesn't compare with what you've learned from life. You have the ability to help people because you have a certain way of grasping reality—hitting the nail right on the head—zeroing in on the problem in record time. I would cherish your friendship now that I'm no longer your analyst."

Mark and April became friends over the next three months ... they went to symphonies, ballets, ate in the best restaurants, and attended book readings...highbrow stuff. April was confused by their relationship because Mark never asked to do more than kiss her goodnight after a date. Since Jared was seemingly out of her life once again, she wanted more from their relationship and felt she was ready for it to become physical.

When Mark called the next evening, April suggested, "Hey, Mark, I'm a good cook. Why don't I fix dinner for you tomorrow night?"

"That sounds nice."

"Well, you've been so nice to take me to all the fancy restaurants, concerts, ballets....I really liked the ballet; but, it's time I do something for you, don't you think?"

"I'm honored that you'd like to cook for me; but, your friendship's all I need, April. You're sweet...see you tomorrow night about seven...."

"Okay!"

After the conversation ended, April sat for several minutes, thinking about everything. After all, she thought to herself, it's the "sexual" revolution. Sex is usually expected after a few dates.

She and Mark had been dating for several months. Their platonic relationship confused her immensely as Mark had never given her a passionate kiss. She wondered if he was gay.

April prepared "Jared's" favorite dinner for her date with Mark the next day.

The Gypsy Cried

As she fussed around the kitchen, making the lasagna, she had flashbacks of her dates with Jared—remembering their lovemaking. She wondered why hadn't heard from him; after all, he had promised. He said he ALWAYS keeps his promises!

Oh, well, she thought, it's time to move on to a fresh relationship. It's been too long since I made love; but, tonight, with Mark's help, maybe I'll rectify that situation. Maybe he can wipe the memories of Jared completely out of my mind. My heart was broken when he let Penny back into his life after promising we'd be together.

The sound of the doorbell jolted April back to reality... her date with Mark. She answered the door, smiling, feeling exhilarated.

Mark looked around the apartment. "Boy, April, you went to a lot of trouble to make everything special for me tonight. It's been a long time since anyone cared enough to cook dinner for me. That's Bach on the stereo? You know it's my favorite. I'm touched. The burning candles which provide the lighting in the living room is simply lovely. How romantic!"

"Thanks, Mark. I wanted to do something special. Tonight is special.... You look great!" she remarked.

Mark was tall and blonde, with a yuppie-styled haircut and manicured mustache and goatee. He was wearing brown dress slacks, a white oxford cloth shirt, and a beige golf sweater.

The salad was crisp and the salad dressing perfectly blended. The lasagna was superb, and the wine was light and dry....a perfect meal for a perfect evening.

They quickly cleared the table and put the dishes in hot water in the sink. Mark poured them another glass of wine as April served her homemade cherry cheesecake.

The mood was light as they went into the living room to enjoy their dessert, still listening to the music from the stereo.

"Mark, do you like to dance?" she asked.

"Yes, I do. I don't dance very often, though. I might be a little rusty."

"Ah...hum." April joked and motioned in her own form of sign language that she wanted to dance with him.

Mark put his arm around her slim waist, took her hand, and they swayed to the smooth sounds of the music. He remained rigid, staunch. April couldn't get close to him.

When the dance was over, she politely thanked him for the dance and sat down. It wasn't happening between them....there were no sparks.

The silence was uncomfortable as they sat side-by-side on the sofa. Mark put his arm around April and pulled her close.

"Thanks for a great evening, April; but, it's getting late. Guess I'd better go...."

Mark kissed April gently and pulled away. April threw her arms around him and kissed him passionately. Mark was surprised and pulled away, looking at her questioningly.

"Don't I turn you on, Mark?"

"No, we're friends. I don't want to spoil that."

"Do you think being romantically involved will spoil our friendship?"

"No, not necessarily."

"Then, what's the problem?"

"Well...." he hesitated, searching for words. "The problem's not with you. I'm the one with the problem. I have to take medication to control a physical problem. It's rendered me impotent. I couldn't make love to you if I wanted." he explained sadly. "I should have told you long ago."

"Well, at least you're finally telling me. I thought I was the one with the problem. I was feeling unattractive, I guess. I'm sorry I put you in the position of having to explain, Mark. Please forgive me. I value your friendship....I thought maybe we could be more than friends." she explained.

"Don't apologize for being normal; and, don't ever fall back into that old trap of feeling unattractive. You're a truly remarkable woman...strikingly beautiful. I'm sorry your Father gave you an inferiority complex. I'm sorry Jared left you. You deserve the best. I am honored that you're sexually attracted to me. Your sexual aggressiveness pleased me. If I could, I'd love to make love with you. It saddens me that I can't be your lover."

"We can still be friends, right?"

"I treasure your friendship. If I thought you'd have me, I'd marry you in a minute. Could you settle for a life without sex?"

"Well, sex isn't everything in a marriage, is it?"

"No, but it's pretty important.....something we couldn't enjoy. I'm afraid it would create enormously-stressful problems between us in the future...after you realized we'd be sleeping in the same bed every night but couldn't make love. Stress can kill a marriage in record time."

"I guess you're right; but, we might be able to work something out...." she said, still hopeful.

"There's another problem, April. I don't like children. If we were to marry, you'd have to give your children to your ex-husband. I won't be a stepfather. I could handle being with your children 'cause your mother has them one night a week....the night we go out."

"Mark, I can't believe what I'm hearing. You know everything about my past; and, you know how much my children mean to me. You know what kind of person my ex-husband is...he only spends a couple hours a month with the boys. They would be devastated if I sent them to live with him. It would be the worst kind of rejection. I could never do that....NEVER!"

"Think about it, April. You've had a hard life. You'd never have to work again. You'd have a beautiful home... drive a new car, shop in the best shops throughout the world. I travel a great deal, you know that. If you'd give my proposal serious consideration, I'd take you around the world for a honeymoon."

"You go straight to hell, Mark. Boy, what a fool I am. I hoped tonight would be special; but, instead, I see you as you really are. You have more problems than I do. Physician, heal thyself! Your money would be a poor substitute for my boys. Now, get the hell out of here. I don't ever want to see you again!"

Mark didn't say anything. He quietly walked to the door and opened it. As he pulled the door closed, he whispered, "Call me if you need a FRIEND, April. I'll always be there for you...."

April was too angry to cry. Why can't I find someone to REALLY love me? My Dad must've put a curse on me." she said to herself as she pulled a photo album from the bookcase. She quickly flipped through the pages until she came to her baby pictures.

"Look at that, you were an adorable baby!" she said to her picture. "Your Dad was an idiot! He's the one with the problem, not you. God blessed you with two beautiful children who think you're the greatest person in the world. I AM A GREAT PERSON!" she shouted. "Jared may be the only man I'll ever love; but, I'm trying to get over him, once-and-for-all, so I can get on with my life. God-willing, I'll find a special man who'll adore me. He's somewhere out there, searching for me, too. I miss him. I miss the love we could have between us. I miss his arms around me every night. If Jared's not willing to keep his promises, I'll find someone who will...."

April sat down and made a list of attributes her perfect man had to possess. She read and re-read the list, thinking Jared was the only man she'd ever known who could fulfill the requirements on her list.

"I miss the love we could have. I miss his arms around me every night. I won't let it get me down, though. Maybe it's time to leave this depressing town. Mom's talking about retiring to Florida." She said as she looked in the mirror... "Florida is supposed to be a great place to live. No more snow and ice! We could move to Florida, too. We deserve a fresh start."

The next morning when April's mom brought the boys home, she said, "How would you boys like to move to Florida with Grandma?"

"We'd love it, Mama!" They said, jumping for joy. "But, you'd move, too, wouldn't you? You've never been to Florida. You never went with us on vacation."

"Yes, we'll all move. We'll sell everything so we'll have enough money for the trip. Are you willing to get rid of all your things? To start fresh?"

"Yeah, let's go! Let's move to Florida! We'll live real close to Mickey Mouse....YEAH!" The boys said as they ran outside to tell their friends.

April and her Mother continued to discuss her idea, and made plans for the proposed move. The decision had been made.... they'd move in ONE month!

Everyone worked hard to get ready for the move. They had a big "garage" sale, selling their beds last. They kept only their clothing, a portable color television set, the stereo, the basic pots and pans, dishes and linens. The boys were allowed to keep three of their favorite toys.

With the proceeds of the sale, April was able to raise over seventeen hundred dollars. She gave her boss a two-week notice, and was given an additional five hundred dollars from her co-workers at a good-luck party, held in her honor, on her last day at work.

April drove to Florida alone, leaving the boys with their grandmother. This would enable April time to get a job and a place to live. It was decided the boys would join her before school started.

Since her resume was impressive, and her references were excellent, April had a job just four days after she arrived in Florida.

Then, she rented a small two-bedroom house near the woods, with a big backyard. She bought three new beds, and picked up some second-hand living room and dining room furniture. The boys arrived in mid-August.

Three months later, when April's Mother arrived, she and the boys were ready for her. Although she stayed with them at first, shortly after she arrived, April's mother bought a small country home for forty thousand dollars a few miles down the road from them.

Once they'd settled in, loneliness returned. April was able to shelve her emotions because of the move; but, she usually had friends to spend time with but her co-workers at her new job seemed aloof. She missed Jared but refused to allow herself to think about him... to remember their lovemaking.

April agreed to go out with a group of her co-workers the next Friday night to have some fun. They went bar-hopping and dancing. Since there were three women and two men, April felt like a fifth wheel.

She excused herself to go to the restroom. When she returned to the table, her friends had left. She was left in the bar alone, except for a few hundred strangers.

April checked her purse....she only had a dollar left in her wallet, and her uncashed paycheck. She used her change to try to call someone to pick her up. Since her Mother couldn't see to drive at night, she didn't call her. Besides, she didn't want to worry her mother.

Since they had been to several places that night, April wasn't sure of the location of the bar. She called a taxi and was told they didn't service that area. Panic began to set in!

Scared, realizing her predicament, April sat down at the bar.

"What'll it be, Miss?" the bartender asked.

"Make it ice water...."

The bartender could tell from her nervous expression that something was wrong. Normally, he couldn't permit her to sit at the bar unless she ordered a drink; but, the hour was late and the crowd had thinned out. She seemed like a little waif.

"Is something wrong?" he asked.

"Yeah, you might say that... What's your name?"

"Sam."

"Well, Sam, it's like this....I came here a couple hours ago with four of my co-workers. I went to the restroom and when I came back, they were gone. I can't believe they left me alone here. I've only been in Florida a short time; and, I think it's a long way home. I only have a dollar. The taxi service said they don't serve this area."

"Tough break, Kid." Sam pretended to care.

"Normally, I wouldn't tell a stranger my problem, Sam; but, I'm starting to worry. I've called everyone I know, used all my change, trying to get a ride. No one answered. 'WELCOME TO FLORIDA!'" she said, as she toasted herself with the glass of ice water Sam had placed in front of her.

"A great lookin' woman like you shouldn't have a problem gettin' home. I'm sure some guy would be glad to accommodate you...take you home."

"Well, you don't see anyone asking, do you?" she said, looking around. "Besides, from the looks of who's left, I'd be safer walking home."

"Well, ask one of them for a ride...."

"No, thanks. Point me in the direction of Tarpon Springs, Sam. I'll walk."

"Due west, Miss...." he said, laughing, pointing in the direction. "It'll be quite a walk, though."

April walked outside. The night was warm and dark. The few cars that were left in the parking lot had lovers in them. April shivered....she was scared.

She went back into the bar and sat back down at the bar.

"Change your mind, Miss?" Sam asked with a smirkish smile.

"Do you think the police will help me, Sam?"

"I doubt it...cops don't provide taxi services..."

Her heart sank. Sam noticed her hands were trembling when she picked up her glass of ice water, which was still sitting on the bar.

"Listen, Missy, if you don't mind hangin' around till I get my work done, I'll drive you home. What did you say your name was?"

"April. Can I help you with your work? It's the least I can do...." she surmised, relief evident on her face.

"Sure, there's a sinkful of dirty dishes..." he said, pointing to the small sink, which was overflowing with dirty glasses....

April washed and polished the glasses, and put them in the rack for the next day. She swept the floor while Sam placed the chairs on top of the tables.

It was after three thirty in the morning when Sam finally turned out the lights and locked the door. April was exhausted.

Sam ushered April to the door of his black pickup truck, opened it and helped her maneuver the high step to get into the cab. He slammed the door behind her and got in on the other side.

After starting the motor, he drove in a westerly direction, saying nothing.

April's mind was racing. She'd be glad to get home.... home to a safe weekend. She'd never go out with her co-workers again, she decided. In the back of her mind, she was rehearsing what she'd say to them on Monday morning. What a horrible thing to do to someone...leaving them stranded in nowhere-land, with no way to get home!

April was a little leery of the burly stranger who was driving her home. What choice did she have but to accept his offer to drive her home, she reasoned. It was a dark night. She couldn't very well have walked.

Sam kept picking up a bottle that he kept on the seat between them. He kept looking at April, and tried to make conversation a couple times. Handing her the bottle....he said, "Here, this'll calm your nerves, Missy."

"My nerves are fine, Sam, thank you. I can't wait to get home... I'm exhausted!"

"It wouldn't hurt you to be nice to me.... Tarpon Springs isn't on my way home. I'm doing you a favor."

"Remember, I did the dishes and helped you clean the floor. I'm going to give you the dollar I have in my purse for your gas. Believe me, Sam, I appreciate you giving me a ride home. I don't know what I'd have done otherwise...."

"You're a snooty little thing, ain't ya? I bet you've never been properly kissed .... or know how a real man can make you feel, Missy."

"If you don't mind, Sam, my name is April. I just want to get home. My boys will be worried about me..." she lied, knowing they were at her Mother's house.

Sam glared at her. He suddenly pulled the truck into a deserted roadside park and turned off the motor, making a grab for April.

Before he could grab her, she jerked open the door and jumped out of the truck. She ran as fast as she could; but, since she couldn't see in the dark, she tripped and fell, falling headfirst into a pile of garbage bags, next to a park bench. She quickly pulled herself to her feet, ignoring the sharp pain in her knees. She had to get as far away from Sam as she possibly could....as fast as she could.

"Oh, Jared, where are you when I need you? Why aren't you here to protect me...you said you'd always be there for me. Where are you now?" she cried frantically, blubbering to herself.

Sam caught up with April and hit her on the back of the head, sending her flying, face down, in the gravel, barely missing a barbecue pit.

April struggled and kicked at Sam, trying as best she could to get away from him but, because of his massive strength, he was able to pin her to the ground, tearing at her clothing.

Once he had her freed of all restrictive clothing, he brutally forced himself into her. April screamed in terror as he savagely sodomized her, and then raped her vaginally.

When she screamed, Sam hit April hard with his fist, jerking her arms so fiercely she thought they were going to break.

After Sam had finished with April, he stood to his feet and kicked her in the stomach. Then, grabbing her arms, he jerked her to her feet, and hit her several times with his fist. As April lost consciousness, she moaned, "Oh, Jared, where are you?"

When April regained consciousness, she immediately remembered what had happened, and began to swing her arms at an imaginary shadow, thinking her abductor was still with her.

Then she lay still, listening, wondering if Sam was still there, if anyone was around. After she decided she was alone, she started to cry uncontrollably. She hoped her attacker was, in fact, gone. She hoped he wasn't waiting for her in the darkness.

April could hardly move because of the injuries she'd suffered. She tried to cover her nakedness with her torn clothing to no avail. She lay on the damp ground and cried until the first break of daylight appeared.

Looking around, she recognized the little park. She'd brought the boys there once or twice for a picnic.

She saw a car's headlights approaching, off in a distance. She dragged herself to the edge of the road so she could flag down the car. Every muscle in her body ached. Although her arms hurt, April decided they weren't broken. Blood was running down her legs from her genital area. Her eyes were almost swollen shut. Her stomach hurt so badly, she couldn't stand to her feet.

She tried to move faster so she wouldn't miss the car. Using every ounce of available strength, she managed to reach the edge of the road just as the car reached the park. She waved her arms to stop the car, which contained an

The Gypsy Cried

elderly couple on their way to an early breakfast. Luckily, they stopped.

It was obvious what had happened. They asked no questions. The man jumped out of the car and grabbed a blanket from the back seat and wrapped it around April.

The man and woman gently helped April get into the back seat of their car, and then quickly drove her to the hospital.

Before she disappeared into the emergency room, April tried to thank them for their kindness. The hospital called the police. The elderly couple waited so they could tell the police where they'd found April.

April was indigent. The rape exam was horrendous … collecting tissue samples, cleaning and clipping her fingernails, hair samples, vaginal smears, photographs….a seemingly endless humiliation.

The next three days were a mass of confusion as April slipped from consciousness into the blackness of a drug-derived sleep. She preferred the darkness to the horror of consciousness.

April tried to answer the policeman's questions the best she could, and gave him a complete description of Sam.

On the fourth day, as April waited to be released from the hospital, a detective came to her room.

"Well, April, Sam was a fictitious name. He's only worked at the bar for three weeks. When we tried to track him down using the information on his employment application, which by the way was all fictitious, we were able to trace him to Arizona. Then, we hit a brick wall. No leads."He cleaned out the cash register at the lounge and took some alcohol as well."

"Nothing at all....you need to catch him so he can't do this to anyone else...." she whispered.

"From what we can tell, he's used at least a dozen aliases, and has a record in three states. He's been arrested five times for aggravated rape; but, he was released each time for lack of evidence. The witnesses were afraid to testify against him. I'm afraid we've done all we can right now. His trail vanished in Arizona."

"Well, if he's in Arizona, he can't hurt me anymore can he? As long as I know he's gone...as far as I know, he doesn't know who I am. He didn't bother my purse. My identification was still in my wallet, right? My paycheck? I'm lucky to be alive."

"Yes, you are. We found your purse and it still had your paycheck. He simply left you for dead."

April went back to work three weeks later. Her right eye was still slightly gray from a deep contusion.

The co-workers who'd left her kept apologizing; but, April found it hard to forgive them.

When she confronted them, April shouted, "How could you drive off and leave me there...so far from home. I can't forgive you....ever!"

They reimbursed her for the wages she lost while she was out of work, hoping she wouldn't file suit against them. The hospital bills were paid by her company's insurance plan.

Unable to continue to work with them, April was offered a position as a secretary for a large manufacturing firm in Tampa. She immediately accepted.

CHAPTER FIFTEEN

April struggled with the physical problems that were the result of the brutal rape. Needless to say, life wasn't a "big party" for her. She felt empty and hungry to know real love...the kind of love she'd read about in the Bible when she was a young girl. In her lifetime, she'd known too much heartbreak.

The rape left her feeling dirty, violated, and unworthy of a decent man's love, reverting back to her low self esteem as a child. Since it had also caused severe vaginal nerve damage, she was diagnosed as being a nymphomaniac... always needing sexual satisfaction. She was repulsed by the idea of sex!

Do I want anyone in my life? she wondered. Can I ever let another man touch me? She was so upset she had to be sedated in order to sleep.

Since she'd allow no one into her life, she could only cry.... "Jared, where are you? Why didn't you keep your promise?"

The doctor told April she needed cryosurgery to repair some internal vaginal damage. Against the doctor's wishes,

April insisted the surgery be performed in his office rather than in a hospital. However, during the surgery, the pain was so intense, April fainted.

"It hurt more than I expected, Doctor..." April explained after the nurse revived her with smelling salts.

"That's why I wanted to do this in the hospital under anesthesia. You insisted on office surgery. I was afraid it would be pretty rough on you, April."

"After what I went through at the hospital after I was raped, I couldn't stand the thought of going back there."

"Are you sure you'll be okay to drive home? Did someone come with you?"

"No, your nurse didn't tell me to bring someone."

"Well, she should have. Can you call someone?"

"Not now. I'll have to wait here until I'm able to drive."

April had to wait in the doctor's office for almost two hours before she was strong enough to drive her car. About halfway home, she started to feel woozy.

Noticing an old country church with a big steeple, she pulled into their parking lot to rest for a few minutes before she continued the drive home.

Since it was Wednesday, many people had gathered at the church for a prayer meeting.

Feeling light-headed and dizzy, April parked her car and leaned her head on the headrest. She closed her eyes, listening as the congregation sang inside the church.

The singing soothed April's pain. She allowed the peaceful spirit from the music to flow into her. She slowly got out of the car and walked inside the church. Every step was painful.

April sat down in the last pew as the minister introduced a special speaker....”who will lead you into renewed commitment...” the minister said.

April laid her head on the pew in front of her as she listened to the speaker talk about Jesus Christ.

“Can you imagine the pain Jesus must have felt as he hung on the cross? How the nails must have felt as they dug into his hands. Every breath he took was torment as the nails pulled when he inhaled. The weight of his body was excruciating.”

April listened, imagining the pain Jesus must have felt. Her pain was nothing compared to HIS pain.

“Did YOU drive those nails into Jesus’ hands?” the speaker asked. “Close your eyes and imagine how it must have felt to hang on that cross, the weight of your body pulling at the nails every time you took a breath! Do you feel sorrow? A sinner who refuses to answer the call of Christ is driving nails into those sinless hands by refusing to accept Him as their personal savior. Jesus suffered and died for YOU...and He wants to carry your burdens...feel your pain....because he suffered the worst pain of all.... FOR YOU!” he shouted, pointing his finger.

April looked up. She thought the speaker was pointing his finger directly at her.

She had an instantaneous flashback of the brutal rape, and the pain she’d experienced. She thought about the pain she was having as a result of the cryosurgery she’d had that afternoon. And, yet, Jesus’ pain was greater. Why didn’t she call out HIS name the night of the rape instead of Jared’s name? she wondered. Jared had never REALLY been there for her; but, Jesus was always there, loving her, forgiving her for her multitude of sins. She realized she HAD, in fact, been 'driving nails' into Jesus' precious hands because of her lack of faith.

"I want everyone to get out of their seats and come to the altar to kneel in reverence to Jesus and the price He paid for us." The evangelist demanded. "Tell Jesus what's in your heart. Let Him carry your burdens....your pain."

April struggled to move into the aisle. She felt as if she had to kneel. Her body was racked with pain and heart felt faint however, the driving need to get to the altar was greater than her pain.

Struggling with every step, April fell to her knees when she reached the altar as the entire congregation realized what was happening and knelt in prayer.

April surrendered her pain and anguish to Jesus. As she prayed, she felt the pain leave her body....pain from her past hurts were being washed away. She felt clean and fresh for the first time since the attack. She was reborn... pure as a virgin! She cried and stood to her feet, assisted by the evangelist. Her body was totally free of pain. It was a miracle!

"Thank you, Jesus," she prayed aloud. "I do believe you are the Son of God...and that you died on the cross for me. You washed away all my many sins; and, I feel white as snow—pure in Your sight, Lord. Thank You for saving me, for dying on the cross for me. Thank You, Jesus, for causing me to stop here tonight, for taking away my pain, and healing my hurts. It's a true miracle. Thank You, Jesus!"

The congregation of the small church gathered around her and many hugged her as she told them what had happened. Many people cried with her as she told her story, and praised God.

After that life-changing experience, it was easy for April to pull her life together for the Glory of God, and her precious "gifts,"—her children! Her heart had been broken into a million tiny pieces; but, when she asked Jesus into her heart, He used the best "super glue" known to man. His Super Glue lasts forever! she surmised.

April now had an insatiable hunger to read the Bible every day. She never neglected her children; but, after she had them tucked into their beds at night, she escaped to her room to read the Word.

Sleep came easily now...a nice restful sleep. Money was still a problem; but, God never failed to provide their needs. They didn't have everything they WANTED...but they certainly had everything they needed. Often, April would run out of money with several days remaining until payday, and very little food in the cabinet. Either someone from church would invite them to dinner; or, she would receive money from an unexpected source, such as an insurance refund, that would see her through until payday. April gladly tithed her income—the first check she wrote each payday.

April became an active member of the little country church, sang in the choir, taught Sunday School, and led the Singles' ministry. She made friends, and felt peace for the first time in her life. She did not know what was happening in Jared's life, or even where he was, but she prayed for him every day.

When she talked about Jesus, her face would light up with excitement. Jesus was her BEST friend. He knew everything about her...and still loved her! April's family became involved in the church; and, she proudly watched as her sons were baptized.

During April's "quiet" time each morning and evening, she would pray for the "Wings of Protection" around her loved ones, including Jared. Of course, she prayed for specific prayer need for those she cared about; and, she saw God answer many prayers and work miracles in her friends' lives every day.

April also prayed for Jared's salvation; after all, when it was time to go "home," she wanted him to be with her in heaven. She asked to forgive Sam, the bartender, for hurting her, which was something she thought she could never do. She also prayed for his salvation.

Several months later, the phone rang in the middle of the night. April struggled with the receiver; but, she was finally able to get it to her ear. She blurted out..."Hello!"

"Hello...Is this April?"

"Yes, who's this?"

"You mean you don't recognize my voice? I know it's been a long time since we talked; but, I thought you'd never forget my voice. It's Jared Walker!"

"Well, this is a surprise. What's wrong? Do you know it's three o'clock in the morning?"

"I'm sorry to call so late; but, it's been so long since I saw you. I needed to hear your voice, April. How have you been?"

"Fine, I guess. And you?"

"I'm not doin' so well; but, I feel better being able to talk to you, Honey. I still love you, you know; and, I think about you all the time."

"Jared, have you been drinking?"

"Jus' a couple little Jack Daniels. He's my best friend... and my only friend, except for you." he slurred.

"I'll always be your friend, Jared. Now, what's wrong?"

"My life's pure hell, Princess. I can't go on like this any longer. I need to see you."

"Jared, it's been so long since I heard from you...."

"Let's rectify that! I have a deal I'm working on in Tampa. Do you think, maybe, if I come to Tampa, I can see you?"

"Sure, I'd love to see you. Where are you living now? The last time we talked, you were in California..."

"I've lived in the Fort Lauderdale area for about two years now. We opened another chain of stores in the Palm Beach-Boca Raton area. I came over here to get them organized. We're negotiating a deal for the Tampa-St.Pete area now."

"That's great. Business must be good."

"Oh, you wouldn't believe how good! Why did you move to Florida?"

"My Mother retired and wanted to move here. I was the only one of her four children who is single; so, since the boys really love Florida, we decided to move with her. She lives just a few miles from our house. I never want to move back to 'Cold Country' if you know what I mean!"

"Me, neither! Do you have someone special in your life? You're not m-m-married or anything, are you?" he stammered.

"No, but, I've become very religious. My life's been pretty rough, too; but, through the Grace of God, I'm happier now than I've ever been." she explained.

"I'm glad you're not married; and, I'm happy you found God. God and I have an understanding. He always takes care of me..."

"Yes, but, do you REALLY believe? Beyond a shadow of a doubt? Do you KNOW you'll go to heaven when you die?" she asked.

"God takes care of me...that's all I can say. I want to see you, April." he said, hoping to change the subject.

"How in the world did you find me after all these years?" she asked curiously.

"I had to hire a damn detective. You vanished again. I was about to give up when I got a clue you'd moved to Florida. I'm glad I could track you down."

"Well, Jared, you never called back after you told me Penny had moved to California."

"I know...I'm sorry. My life's been hell!"

"Well, Jared, it's late. Call me when you have your plans set; and, I'll be happy to see you."

Two weeks later, Jared called April late one Friday evening as she was about to go to bed.

"Tell you what, April; it's a four-hour drive to Tampa from Boca Raton, right? Why don't I leave about eight o'clock in the morning? That way, we can spend the weekend together before my appointment on Monday."

"Call me when you get into town." she instructed.

"Maybe we can have dinner or something. It'll be great to see you again, April. I'd love to be with you right now... right there in your bed..."

"Enough of that, Jared. Let's get some sleep, okay?"

"How can I possibly sleep after talking to you, and thinking about seeing you again? I can't wait to see you tomorrow, Princess. Catch ya' later...."

"Bye, Jared..." she said.

The line went dead.

April hung up the phone and immediately prayed for Jared. She could tell by his voice that he'd had quite a lot to drink. "Lord, help him as only You can..." she prayed. Soon she was peacefully sleeping.

Jared poured the last of the Jack Daniels down his throat and tossed the bottle across the bed. He'd had too much to drink; but, everything would be fine when he saw his April again. He'd hold her in his arms and make love to her. It had been a long time since he'd made love with anyone. Being able to hold April in his arms again would put everything into perspective.... all would be right with the world again. He could go on. Somehow, she'll help him put his "ducks in a row." He needed her level-headedness.

Penny had been especially hateful lately; and, now, she'd taken Kristie away on vacation. Jared was alone.... terribly alone, except for his best friend, Jack Daniels. He opened another bottle and poured some down his throat...

Jared finally fell into a drunken sleep, forgetting to set the alarm for the next morning. It was almost noon when he awoke. At first, he didn't remember his conversation with April; then, seeing the note by the phone on the nightstand, it came back to him. He should be in Tampa, not Boca Raton.

He quickly dialed April's phone number....

"Hello."

The Gypsy Cried

"Hi, April. You're not going to believe this; but, I forgot to set the alarm last night. I just woke up! I'll leave as soon as I take a quick shower and shave. I should be there about four-thirty or five this afternoon, okay? Will you go out to dinner with me tonight? I have reservations at the Hyatt Regency. I'll call you when I get to the hotel."

"Jared, promise you won't drink and drive, okay? I'm concerned about you. I could tell you'd had quite a bit to drink last night. Are you sure you'll be able to drive that far?"

"Yeah, I'm fine; but, you're sweet to worry about me. I'll always love you, Princess."

"I guess I'll always love you, too, Jared. Please drive carefully."

"See ya' later....I mean, catch ya' later."

April decided to wear her black dress with the white organdy collar. She wanted to look sweet and choir-like when she saw Jared.

It was five-thirty when Jared called. "Well, I have a beautiful room, and they have a nice restaurant downstairs. Would you mind coming here for dinner, April? Tampa's a nice town; but, I don't know my way around. How far is Tarpon Springs from Tampa?"

"About an hour's drive, depending on traffic. I imagine traffic will be light this afternoon. Sure, I guess I can drive to the Hyatt. It's one of my favorite places."

"Oh, really?"

"Now.....now, let me explain. I've planned several company functions at the Hyatt. They were very successful, and the food was great!"

"I'm gonna lie down for a few minutes, Hon. My room number is 303. I'll see you when you get here, okay?" Jared said.

"I'll leave in about ten minutes. See ya'!"

As she drove to Tampa, April remembered the love they'd shared....the good times and some bad times. She remembered how they'd found each other again at the mall after ten years of separation.

Perhaps this reunion would be as dynamic as that one; but, in her heart, she knew she couldn't jump into bed with him no matter how badly she wanted him. She lives for Jesus now. She had to control her emotions for HIM. Ironic, she thought, when we were twenty years old, I felt I had to stay in control because of my Dad's premonitions and accusations.

April parked the car and walked the short block to the Hyatt. The entrance, with all the small twinkling lights was a sight to behold. She was excited by the prospect of seeing Jared again; but, she was also apprehensive. Could she control her emotions, she wondered.

April quietly prayed as she entered the elevator, "Lord, I trust you completely. Help me do as you would have me do tonight. I give you this night. Thank you for whatever's going to happen...."

The elevator stopped on the third floor of the large hotel. April found Room 303 and knocked. The door opened slowly.

As soon as Jared saw her, he smiled. "Hello, Beautiful! It's great to see you again. You look fantastic!"

"You look great, too, Jared; but, where did all those gray hairs come from?" she teased.

"I don't know. Don't you like them?"

"To be honest, you look wonderful! Gray hair makes a man look distinguished; and, the way your temples have streaks of gray, makes you look absolutely gorgeous."

"I'm glad you said that. How long has it been since we saw each other?"

"About ten years, I think. You look the same except the gray hair in your temples makes you even more handsome."

"You're a sight for sore eyes, Princess. I dream about seeing you again, just like this. You're still a very beautiful woman. Come here, Woman.....my Woman, let me hold you in my arms, just for a minute."

They embraced and stroked each other's back during the long hug. Then, Jared turned her face towards him and kissed April, gently at first, then, with more passion.

"I've wanted to hold you like this for so long, April. I've missed you. You have no way of knowing; but, not a day goes by that I don't think about you."

"Me, too. I feel the same about you...." she whispered.

"Let's spend the night catching up on what's been happening in our lives. If you don't mind, I thought we'd eat in the room. I took the liberty of ordering dinner." he said as he led her to a beautifully-set table, which included a magnum of chilled wine, flowers and candles.

"Let's have some wine and talk before dinner arrives," he suggested.

April watched Jared pour the wine and light the candles. After handing her a glass of wine, he walked across the room and dimmed the light, transforming the room into a romantic dream.

Jared was still a very handsome man. The gray streaks in his hair enhanced his rugged masculinity. He'd gained a little weight; but, he looked magnificent.

April could sense the deep passion smoldering inside her. No other man she'd ever known came close to causing so much passion. She wondered if he felt the same.

Dinner was pleasant as they took turns talking about the past events of their lives. Jared mainly discussed his business and how it had grown, and news about his daughter, Kristie.

Finally, April told Jared about the rape, and being left for dead. As she talked, she was able to release the painful experience, and was relieved to vent the last of the repressed anger she held inside.

When she started to cry, Jared held her gently in his arms. They were both in tears when she'd finished talking about the horrendous event.

Then, April told him about the small country church, and the miracle she witnessed when she knelt at the altar to pray. They continued to hold each other, kissing away the tears. Soon, they were lying on the bed, their bodies pressed together, kissing passionately.

April regained control of her emotions and pulled away abruptly, getting off the bed.

"I'll always want you, Jared; but, not like this....I can't make love to you unless we're married. I feel strongly about that. I need to make love to you, to erase away the pain of the rape, to experience gentle lovemaking again. I remember how wonderful it was between us. I'll never forget it; but, if we're not married, it's a sin. I can't sin without thinking about the consequences."

"Only three more years, Honey. I'm asking you to wait just three more years. Please say you'll marry me; and, allow the engagement to last three years. I'll buy you an engagement ring. I'm not married; but, I don't think it can work for us until my daughter's out of school. Penny won't leave us alone until Kristie's on her own; then, she'll have no hold on us."

"I can't understand why she can control anything you do. If you were married, maybe I'd understand; but, you're not married. Today, couples get a divorce and share custody of their children. Why couldn't that happen for you?"

"Believe me, I've tried. She'll never give us a moment's peace, Honey. You don't know her."

"Yes, but we'd be together. I dream about the day when we can get married; but, please, don't put pressure on me to sleep with you tonight. I can't make love to you again until I'm your wife. I'm not punishing you or anything. I just think it would be a mistake for me ...for both of us."

"Making love to you could NEVER be a mistake, April; but, I'm willing to wait provided there will be a next time for us. Will you marry me in three years?"

"I can't give you an absolute answer. I have no objection; I'm afraid to get my hopes up, that's all. We've tried to be together in the past. It never happened. Why not? Especially since we both want it...."

"As soon as Kristie's grown, Penny will no longer have a hold on me. There's so much I could tell you about the horrible times we've had together. I don't feel anything for her except hate. I feel nothing for you but love. Somehow, someday, if you're willing to wait, we'll be together. Please say you'll think about it...."

"Yes, I'll think about it, and I'll pray about it. We've always loved each other. If it's God's will, we WILL be together, someday, Jared."

"Let's dance. Just one dance, April." he suggested.

Jared walked to the intercom to tune the stereo to a local station. A soft and dreamy song, "If" started to play as he pulled April into his arms and snuggled her close.

Their bodies moved in perfect harmony. When the dance ended, they had a feeling of fulfillment and satisfaction, even though they hadn't made love. It was miraculous.

Jared kissed April tenderly. The kiss broke and they stared deeply into each other's eyes. April noticed the deep, weathered lines around his eyes, which added character to his handsome face. There was no doubt....April knew he still loved her.

"You know, Princess. I don't see a gray hair on your head, and you don't have a wrinkle on your face. Are you sure we're the same age?" he teased.

"You're one month older than I am, Jared, and you know it. Are you outdoors a lot?"

"Every weekend, if possible. I go out in my boat with Kristie. The Florida sun does strange things to a person's face...like cause wrinkles! You look like you're thirty years old, April, not forty!"

"Thanks, Darling. That's quite a compliment and greatly appreciated at my age."

"Will you stay with me tonight? I promise you I won't make love to you. I'll hold you in my arms all night. I'll be a gentleman. You can trust me."

"I'd better not. I may be the one to lose control…"

"Would that be so bad?"

"It would be bad for me right now, Jared. I hope you understand. I'm not rejecting you. I'm just afraid, what with the rape and everything, that things might not be as wonderful as we remember. I don't know how I'll feel when I make love again."

"Please don't make love with anyone else but me, April, for the rest of your life. I want to be your husband. Stay here with me tonight. We'll stay awake all night and talk. I need to be with you, hold you in my arms. I'm so starved for common, ordinary affection." he pleaded.

"It's already midnight, and I have an hour's drive ahead of me. I'd better leave. Why don't you come with me?"

"Tell you what, Princess. I don't want you to drive home alone at this time of night. I'll call the lobby and see if they have another room available. I'll put it on my bill. That way, you won't feel bad about staying. Your boys are old enough to stay by themselves, right? What do you say?"

"Okay, on one condition…..go to church with me tomorrow morning. I have to sing in the choir; and, I'm singing a solo. I should be practicing right now; but, it's my favorite Christian song. I know it frontwards and backwards."

"I guess I can handle that!"

"Okay, then, make that phone call. I can wear this dress to church. Can you loan me a robe or something?"

"I can do better than that! But, first things first, let me get you a room."

Jared picked up the phone and called the front desk. They told him the adjourning room was available. "Good, send the Bell Captain up with the key, and charge the bill to me. Thanks."

Within five minutes, there was a tap at the door. It was the Bell Captain with the key. Jared handed him a five dollar bill and took the key. He walked next door, opened the door, and then returned to his room using the connecting door to his suite.

"Now, we have two rooms, Princess. Let's see, you said something about needing a robe." Jared said as he walked to the dresser. He opened the drawer and pulled out a beautiful satin box.

"I bought this for you in California a couple years ago. It reminded me of you. I hope you like it, Honey."

April opened the box and found a beautiful, blue-ruffled silk negligee. She could tell by the label that it was expensive.

"Jared, it's lovely. I've never had anything like this in my entire life."

"When you're my wife, I'll shower you with nice gifts."

"Spoil me rotten and you'll be sorry." she kidded.

"I'll never be sorry for buying you pretty things. You deserve it! I'll bet you've received very few nice presents in your life."

"Well, I guess you're right about that; but, it's not something I expect. This is gorgeous, Jared. Thanks for thinking about me...."

"I can't wait to see you in it. Is the size okay?"

"I'm sure it'll be fine. If I model it for you, do you promise to behave yourself?"

"Scouts honor!" he said, saluting in a kidding way.

"I'll wear it tonight; and, then, I'll put it away until our wedding night. If you like, you'll have my permission to tear it off me then."

"No, that sounds too brutal. I'll gently remove it as I kiss you, all over your body...." he whispered, kissing her neck.

April disappeared into her room with the negligee in hand. When she returned, Jared had fixed them both a drink and was stretched out on the bed.

"Well...." she said, twirling around.

Jared watched her twirl for him. "You look like a dream come true...MY dream. Let's dance again. When we dance, I can hold you close. I need to feel you in my arms....It's been so long."

They danced, body to body, locked in an embrace. Jared was true to his word and didn't push April to make love with him. The night was spent talking, while Jared drank almost a fifth of Jack Daniels.

"Why do you drink so much, Jared?"

"Because I don't have you in my life. I need you, April. You believe me, don't you?"

"If you say it, I guess I believe you; but, I'm concerned. You're drinking so much...."

"Well, April, some really frightening things happened to me in Vietnam. Sometimes I wake up screaming, thinking I'm still there. Then, I realize you're not in my bed. My memories of you, and my determination to find you after I finally got home, was all I had to hang onto. Your memory has always been very intense in my life. It has helped me get through many nightmares since that horrible ordeal overseas. The only way I can get the visions out of my head is by drinking. I'd spend every penny I have if the nightmares would go away..."

"Jared, please stop drinking and talk to me. Let me help you..." she pleaded.

"I'll stop drinking when we get married. Then, when I have a nightmare, I'll be able to reach for you and drive the nightmare away. You'll see....we'll be happy, Princess. After we're married, I'll never let anything like alcohol cause a problem for us."

"Come on...." April said, taking Jared's glass. "Let's curl up and go to sleep."

Soon they were sleeping peacefully with April curled up on Jared's shoulder. The desire to make love was strong between them; but, Jared kept his promise to behave. It was wonderful to sleep in each other's arms. It felt right.

Jared's mumbling during the night awakened April. He was drenched in perspiration. She gently caressed his chest, realizing he was probably having another Vietnam flashback.

Suddenly Jared sat up and screamed. He jumped out of bed and dove to the floor. April could tell by the way he held his hands that he was holding an imaginary rifle.

April whispered Jared's name. The dim light from the bathroom helped Jared realize he was dreaming. Seeing April, he sat down on the edge of the bed, put his head in his hands and cried.

"Talk to me, Honey. Maybe your nightmares will go away if you tell me about them. Why were you so scared?"

At first, he just shook his head. Then, after April insisted, Jared said, "Little kids were always hanging around the barracks, begging for a scrap of bread. Honey, they were so cute. We desperately needed to feel normal. The war was hard; and, we never knew which one of us would be blown to bits next."

"Go on...." she urged.

"It was nothing for me to kill fifty people in a day, many of them young boys or girls. We were under orders to fire at anything that moved. Sometimes, we killed our own men!"

"I understand how terrible it must have been. Go on...."

"My best friend, Phil, befriended one of these little orphan kids. He'd save him a few scraps of food, and buy him cheap toys. One day, the little kid came running out of the bushes and jumped into Phil's arms. They both exploded, right before my eyes."

"What happened, Jared?"

"The damn Vietcong had strapped a bomb on his back. Phil and the little kid died instantly. I'll never be able to erase the memory of seeing their bodies fly apart."

"You poor thing..."

"It's a relief to finally be able to tell someone about it. It's one of the worst things I experienced while I was there; but, everyday, we wondered who would be next. I wondered when it was MY turn. It was hell! Sometimes, I hoped I would be next so I wouldn't have to kill anymore, or see more of my friends get slaughtered in the senseless war."

April held Jared gently, massaging his back as he talked. "Go ahead and cry, Jared. Get it out of your system. It's not a crime to cry. It sounds like you have a lifetime of tears bottled up inside you."

Jared stretched out beside April, holding her tightly. He whispered..."April, I love you more than you can imagine. Do you believe me?"

"Yes, Jared, I know you love me. I love you, too. Maybe, God willing, we can be together soon. We can help each other heal. We've known too much pain in our lives...and not enough love."

"You've got that right, Honey."

"Did you suffer from these nightmares ten years ago when we were together?"

"No, it seems as if they get worse as each year goes by. Maybe it's because nothing good ever happens to me since you're not in my life...."

April held Jared in her arms until he fell asleep. The rest of the night, he slept peacefully in her arms.

The next morning as April showered and put on her make-up, Jared ordered breakfast. Breakfast was pleasant; and, soon, they were driving to April's church. She introduced him to her friends; and, they made him feel welcome.

During the service, Jared was brought to tears by April's beautiful solo, "There is Coming a Day."

After she finished singing, she excused herself from the choir and went to sit with Jared rather than returning to the choir loft.

The minister delivered a powerful message about Jesus, and the gift of His salvation. April noticed Jared was trembling during the service. When the altar call was made, Jared quietly slipped out of the pew and left the church. April prayed for him silently and, then, followed him to the car. He was crying.

"Honey, talk to me...tell me what you're feeling." she asked gently.

"I can't believe in something I can't see, April..." he replied.

"I'm praying for you to believe, to make a commitment to God while there's still time. From what I understand, when we surrender our lives to Jesus and REALLY believe, our sins are forgiven, wiped away; and, we will spend eternity in heaven. Hell IS a reality. The worst day you've ever spent on this earth will be the BEST day you'll spend in hell. Jesus is calling you to commitment. He wants to redeem you, forever, no matter what! He loves you more than I love you...and that's a lot!"

"I can't think about it right now. Let's go, okay?"

"Okay, but one final word on the subject. I've been praying for you to spend eternity with me; especially, since we've not been able to be together on earth. You can't do it for me. You must truly believe in Jesus. Jesus didn't promise us a rose garden, he promised to save us, to walk with us, to never leave us, if we will only believe in Him....."

"I can't talk about this right now..." he said again. His voice cracked.

April changed the subject and drove them back to her house. She prepared lunch, Jared's favorite meal, lasagna.

"You continue to amaze me, Princess. My Mother is a full-blooded Italian. Like I told you years ago, her lasagna isn't this good...."

"My pleasure, Kind Sir."

"Boy, if that doesn't bring back memories, PRINCESS!"

They spent the next three hours talking, laughing and dancing. As April sat next to Jared, listening to him talk, she realized how lonely he was; and, all too soon, the afternoon had slipped away.

"The boys will be home soon. Would you like to see them?"

"I'm afraid if I see them again, I'll never want to leave. I've always thought of them as MY boys. You'd never know it though, I've never sent them a gift, or called them. I've failed you guys miserably. April, I'm sorry. I've never even asked you if you have enough money."

"God has always taken care of us, Jared. I forgive you for the times I needed you and you weren't there. But, if you don't want to see the boys, I understand. They'll be home soon, though, so we'd better leave. I'll leave them a note. They're almost grown; they can take care of themselves. They've been on a camping trip with some friends from church this weekend. They'll be tired."

The drive back to the Hyatt was pleasant. When they arrived, Jared asked April to come up for a while.

"I'm really tired. I need to get back and get ready for next week. You know, laundry and all that stuff. Tomorrow is a workday! I'm glad we were able to spend some time together. I will go up to your room to get my beautiful negligee."

"I needed to see you, April, even though I didn't get to make love to you. Soon, my Love, soon, we'll be together... forever! I promise. Please wait for me ... just three more years. Then, we'll get married; I always keep my promises..."

"I want you to have this, Jared. It's my little Bible and my favorite spiritual tape. Someday, when you're alone on your boat, read the sections I've marked in Romans, and listen to the tape. Listen with your heart, Honey. Let God talk to you. He's calling you, Jared."

He took the things from her hand and pulled her into his arms. As they stood by the door, embracing, they shared a final kiss. April pulled away from him and stepped into the hallway.

"I'll catch ya' later, Kind Sir!"

"You bet, Princess," he said, bending to kiss her once more. "Wow, what a woman!"

After she'd left, Jared took another bottle of Jack Daniels from his luggage. The room suddenly seemed devastatingly lonely...only April's fragrance remained.

As Jared drank himself into a stupor, he said, "I'm a lucky man to have her love. I hope she'll wait for me."

Jared's business dealings went well the next day; and he left Tampa, remembering how special the weekend had been.

CHAPTER SIXTEEN

THREE MONTHS LATER - MIDDLE OF THE NIGHT

April is awake, restless, wondering why she hasn't heard from Jared. She prays, "Lord, things were so special and he made promises, convinced me he still loves me. I don't understand, Lord, why do we have such a strange relationship? All these years I've waited for him to fulfill the promises he made—that we would get married. If we can't be together, why can't I put him in the past and find someone else? You've put so much love in my heart for Jared. I pray continuously for his salvation. Help me understand why he hasn't called, Lord. Our relationship is in your hands. I pray, Lord Jesus, you'll give Jared Walker another opportunity to accept you in his heart before it's too late. Put him under conviction; don't give up on him yet, Lord. Your will be done regarding our relationship. In Jesus' name, I pray. Amen."

April had a strong feeling in the pit of her stomach the next day. She was facing a lonely weekend because the boys were going camping with the youth director from church.

She picked up the phone and called information to obtain the number for Jared's sporting goods store in Boca Raton. She wrote the number on a piece of paper, stared at it for a few minutes, and shoved it into her purse. "I'll never have enough nerve to call him..." she said.

April stretched out on the couch, emotionally exhausted. Soon she was asleep...dreaming of Jared's arms around her. When she awoke and discovered it was only a dream, she cried. She needed Jared to hold her, to reassure her. "Oh, Lord, help me," she prayed, "Please give me the strength to hold on...."

After a few minutes of quiet tears and meditation, April grabbed her purse and fished through its contents until she found the scrap of paper with Jared's phone number written on it. She quickly dialed the telephone number before she lost her nerve.

"Walker Sporting Goods....how may I help you?" The friendly voice said.

"Is Jared Walker there?" April asked.

"No, I'm sorry. Mr. Walker is not in the store today. Can someone else help you," the operator asked.

"I've known Mr. Walker since we were twenty years old. I wanted to say hello...to talk to him for a few minutes." she replied, as the words clumsily stumbled out of her mouth.

"Well, normally, I wouldn't tell you, but his phone number is listed in the telephone directory under his daughter's name. If you know his daughter's name, you can get the number from directory assistance."

"Oh, thank you. I do know her name! I appreciate your help."

April called information and asked for the phone number for Kristie Walker. Then, taking a deep breath and drawing from all her available nerve, she dialed the number. A woman answered...

"Is Jared Walker there, please?" April asked quickly.

"No, he isn't home right now. This is his wife, Penny Walker. Can I help you?"

April was shocked by the response; but, she quickly regained her composure. "No, thank you. I wanted to speak to him for a minute. I'm just an old friend. I'll call again. Sorry to have bothered you."

"Is this April?"

The tone in Penny Walker's voice sent chills down April's spine. "Yes, how did you know?"

"My husband talks about you in his sleep, you Bitch! Why don't you leave him alone? He's a married man!"

"It is my understanding that he's no longer your husband, Penny, you ARE divorced! I'll leave him alone when HE tells me to. I don't have to take orders from you." April retaliated.

"Jared and I are together and happy. Now, leave him alone, you Slut! You're shit under my feet, chasing after a married man. You should be ashamed of yourself. Jared's happy now. Leave him alone, WHORE!" she shouted into the phone. The line went dead.

"What a real b-i-t-c-h!" April muttered, spelling out the word she normally didn't say. "Lord, you gave me an answer, didn't you?"

Tears streamed down her cheeks as she remembered how wonderful she'd felt in Jared's arms.

"Well, Lord, I prayed for YOUR will to be done. I guess Your Will was shown to me. With Your help, Lord, I'll get over him, once and for all. Please comfort Your child. I need Your heavenly compassion to help me get through this. Thank you for showing me the truth...the pieces of the puzzle finally fit together.

The reason we're not together is simple; he's still with his ex-wife. After all these years, the marriage, which ended in divorce, would probably be considered common law. He'd have to get another divorce to be free of her. I'm not a home wrecker. Somehow, Lord, I'll get over him and make a new life for myself...find a good Christian man to love."

April walked to the stereo and turned it on. Sandy Patti's "You Shall Behold Him" was playing. April knew she'd survive her encounter with Penny Walker. Jared could have her! If SHE was what he wanted, she didn't want him.

April listened as Sandy Patti sang the beautiful song. "Thank you, God, for this heavenly song. Someday I WILL behold YOU. Thank you for loving me...for saving me...for being with me, no matter what. I pray for Jared to know the peaceful security of Your love, Jesus."

April re-affirmed her faith, once again picked up the pieces of her meager life, and put one foot in front of the other. She would survive! There was nothing she could do about the past. She had no assurance she would be alive the next day. She had carried the torch for Jared Walker for the last time. So, in essence, all she has is TODAY, and her incredible faith in God. Her boys were the treasure of her life. She'd put Jared Walker completely out of her mind... once and for all!

THREE MONTHS LATER - SATURDAY AFTERNOON

April and the boys were watching a movie on television when the doorbell rang. It was a florist delivering a box of beautiful red roses. April took the box from him, thanked him, and handed him a dollar bill.

"Wonder who sent me flowers, Boys," she said.

As she opened the box, the boys started to tease her by singing, "Mama's got a boyfriend...Mama's got a boyfriend!"

April read the card: "To the Love of my life. I'll be in town Monday. Want to see you. All my love forever, Jared."

April's mind was racing as she put the beautiful roses in water. The boys were still chanting their little song, and April laughed at them.

"No, Mama doesn't have a boyfriend. He's just an old friend." she explained.

Monday evening, April paced the floor as she waited for the phone to ring. In her mind, she was rehearsing what she would say when Jared called. She prayed for the right words.

Finally, the phone rang. April answered it on the first ring, anxious to say the words. She knew she'd always love Jared; but, she needed to end their relationship, once and for all, so she could get on with her life.

"Hey, Beautiful! It's good to hear your voice." Jared said.

"Hi, Jared. Thanks for the flowers and the compliment. We need to talk. I've got a few things to say to you."

"Well, come on over to the hotel. I'll buy your dinner."

"Thanks, but no thanks. I've already eaten. I'll come by for dessert. Go ahead and order your dinner, though. I'll be there in about an hour, after I pull myself together."

"You're the most together person I've ever met!" he said, playing on her words. "I'm sure you're as radiant as ever. I can't wait to see you."

"I'll be there in about an hour or so; then, like I said, we need to talk."

"Great! Catch ya' later, Princess!"

April, of course, was ready to leave. She was wearing jeans and a red knit shirt. Every hair was in place, and her make-up was perfect, as usual.

During the drive to Jared's hotel, she rehearsed exactly what she was going to say...how she was going to say it... and imagined how he would react to her words.

As soon as she knocked at the door, Jared opened it and pulled her into his arms. "You feel so good, Woman! Boy, I'm glad to see you again."

April hugged him, savoring the feel of his body next to hers. It would be hard to say what she'd come to say. Remembering Penny Walker's harsh words, she pulled away and walked to the window of his room, staring silently out the window, trying to find the strength to say the words she HAD to say.

Jared came up behind her and put his arms around her waist. She suddenly had a flashback, remembering when he'd first done that when they were dating as she stood washing dishes at the sink in her first apartment.

"Is everything okay, Princess? You feel angry. I've never known you to feel angry," he whispered, holding her as if he knew it would be the last time. "I love you."

"Like I said, we've got to talk, Jared." April insisted. "I don't plan to stay but a few minutes; so, I'd better say what I've come to say before I lose my nerve. This is the hardest thing I've ever had to do...." her voice broke.

"What's wrong?! Has something happened? Is there someone else in your life? Don't you love me anymore?" he battered her with questions.

"No, there's no one else in my life; but, I think you've lied to me all these years about Penny. Not long ago, I was worried about you. You know, Jared, we've always been able to communicate without words. I had a strong feeling you were in some kind of danger. I wanted to talk to you... to be sure you were okay. I needed reassurance that we'd be together. I got your home phone number from directory assistance. When I called, Penny answered. She said you two were together and very happy. She called me some horrible names, told me to leave you alone, and slammed the phone in my ear..." she said, her voice breaking.

Since April had blurted out all the words without taking a breath, she had to quit talking for lack of oxygen. She trembled and tears filled her eyes.

Jared said nothing. He couldn't believe what he'd heard. He stared at April's tear-filled eyes, her quivering shoulders, for what seemed like an hour, but was, in reality, only a few seconds. The muscles on his face began to twitch. He diverted his eyes and stared through the window, which overlooked the Gulf of Mexico.

"April, I don't love Penny. You're the only woman I've ever loved!" he whispered. "What did she say to you?"

"She called me by name...said you sometimes talk about me in your sleep. She said you two are together... and very happy. I don't know if I care to repeat the names she called me before she slammed the phone in my ear. She shouted at me to leave you alone."

"What did she call you, Honey?"

"She called me a slut....a bitch...and a whore! I don't think I resemble any of those character judgments."

It sounded strange to hear April say the words. Jared winced and turned to look at her facial expression. Her pained expression reminded of the night so long ago at Frisch's when Ramona got into his car. He put his hands on her shoulders and tried to pull April into his arms.

"I'm sorry, Princess. She's the one who deserves those names. You're certainly not like that!"

"I want the truth, Jared. If you and Penny have been together all these years; and, you've been using me ... taking advantage of my love for you, I'll understand, provided you're honest with me. You can say anything from *'I love you'* to *'I hate you'* and I'll understand, provided you're telling me the truth."

"I DO love you, April—and only you. I've never loved anyone but you. You've got to believe me? I can't stand the thought of never being able to see you again. You and Kristie are my reason for living. From your tone, it sounds as if you don't want to see me again. Is that right?"

"Before I answer that question, answer me this, Jared. Do you buy Penny gifts on Mother's Day? Her birthday? At Christmas? Do you celebrate an anniversary? Do you take her to your Christmas party at the store and introduce her as your wife? Do you file a joint tax return?"

Jared didn't answer. He stared at April's angry face for several minutes, searching his mind for an acceptable answer. Then, he looked away and stared at the floor. "You don't love me anymore...."

"You fool, I've always loved you. I've been obsessed with loving you. I would have done anything for you. I've never asked for anything in return. You've always had money. I've had a rough time bringing up my boys alone; but, I never asked you for a thing, have I? You said it yourself, 'YOU should have been the father of those boys'."

"I've never known you to be angry, April."

"You said once that it scares you that I've never gotten angry with you all these years. That was a mistake. There were many nights I had to cry myself to sleep from wanting you. You put me off by saying.....'JUST ONE MORE YEAR'! I don't understand why we're not together."

"That'll change in a couple years...."

"I need you NOW....the boys need you now. They've never had a good father figure in their lives."

"I'm sorry. Isn't there a way I can make amends?"

"No, I'm afraid it's too late. I've got to end this lifelong affair once and for all before I can find someone to build a life with. I'm tired of waiting for you, Jared Walker. I pray for you every night, ask the Lord for patience; but, I need you beside me..."

"I appreciate your prayers, Honey. Somehow I know, God hears your prayers. I need you, too. Please believe me when I say there's nothing between Penny and me. I can't stand the thought of never seeing you again. The thought that someday we'd be together was the only thing holding me together...."

Tears welled in Jared's eyes as he pulled April into his arms. She was stiff and unresponsive.

A slow love song started to play on the stereo. Jared began to sway to the music, trying to coax April into dancing with him, to somehow recapture what he was losing. He felt the tension leave her body and felt her tears on his neck when she put her head on his shoulder.

They didn't say anything, just clung to each other as they swayed, in perfect rhythm, to the music.

When the song ended, Jared whispered, "Oh, God, April, please don't walk away from me. I need you as much as you need me...even more. You can't imagine what my life is like. I pray you'll be patient just a little longer. I dream about you while I'm sleeping in my bed....ALONE! I swear, Princess, I never touch Penny. I need you desperately right now. I need to recapture what I'm afraid you're throwing away. It's been so long since I've made love to anyone. I don't want anyone but you...."

"Then, help me understand why you can't walk away your ex-wife. Are you still living together as man and wife? DO you file a joint tax return?"

"Yes, you've got me. We file a joint tax return; and, I guess I'd need some kind of legal agreement in order to walk away from her. You believe me when I say I love you with all my heart, don't you?" he pleaded.

"I believe you mean it now...but, I'm not so sure what you say when you get home. I was warned about you when we were only twenty years old. I threw caution to the wind and fell in love with you anyway. This is an impossible situation. Only you can change it, Jared. I'm not going to wait any longer. I'm going to find a good Christian man and build a life for myself ... for my boys ... find someone to hold me in his arms... to care for me ...to cherish me.... all the things I've missed for so long. I'm not sure I've ever been more than a 'piece of strange' to you. Do I even cross your mind once you leave Tampa..."

"Why do you put yourself down...calling yourself a 'piece of strange'? Besides, I don't recall our making love in years; so, I don't see you just to 'cheat' on my wife. Physically, I don't have a wife. I've always thought of you as you wife."

"Then we have a rotten marriage...." she quirked.

"Boy, I'm not sure I like what you have to say; but, I have to give you credit for sticking up for yourself. It shows me you're determined, and have self-esteem."

Jared sat down on the bed and buried his face in his hands, wiping away his tears. Shaking his head, he said, "You've got to believe me, April, you're the only woman in the world that I trust. I've never told Penny about my experiences in 'Nam. You're the only woman I've trusted enough to allow my fears to show. You're special ... please tell me you believe me. I'm not sure I can survive if you walk out of my life. I need to know you'll be waiting for me when I finally get Penny out of my life."

"Jared, think about it! Is that fair to me? You want to put me on a shelf while you work out your personal problems. I want to help you, to hold you, to love you through them. Is it fair for me to be alone? I have needs, too. Sometimes I get so lonely; I think I'm going to go crazy. I need someone to take me in his arms and tell me everything's going to be okay. The only way I can get through the day, or the night, is my faith in God, and my love for you. My faith in God has helped me overcome the horrible emotional scars of my childhood; and, of course, they have helped me get past the brutal rape. I've been through a personal hell. I've suffered my own 'tragic war' experiences; but, I'm a survivor."

"Yes, you are. I'm proud of you for that. Have you made love to anyone since the rape?"

"No, of course not."

"I wish you'd let me make love to you. You need a pleasant memory to wipe out the horror."

"Where were you when I needed you?"

"Loving you....missing you....wanting you. Can't you see, our lives have been hell so far? Once we're together, our lives will be heaven."

"Just out of curiosity, did you ever listen to that tape I gave you, and read the scriptures in the little Bible?"

"No, I'm sorry to say I haven't. I put them in my boat, though, I've got good intentions. I haven't forgotten them. I'm waiting for the right time."

"I pray you will listen—soon; but, in the meantime, I have to tell you. I'm going to do my best to get over you. I want to get married again."

"Marry me....just a couple more years to wait." he pleaded.

"It's too bad we can't be together because I know you really love me; but, I not going to wait any longer. I've waited too long as it is. I'm going to put the pieces of my life together and do my best to move forward. I'm sorry, Jared. You'll never find anyone who'll love you as deeply as I do; but, I deserve happiness, too. I'm a lovable woman. I've taken care of myself, and think I'm still desirable. I'm very lonely, too!"

"You sound like you've already found someone..."

"No, I haven't; but, when Penny was so snippy with me on the phone, something died in me. I've known too much pain. I know you love me; but, I have to walk away from this destructive relationship. I'll be praying for you 'cause I want us to be together in eternity, especially since it looks like we'll never be together on earth. The gypsy was wrong....."

"The gypsy?" he asked.

"Yes, I went to see a gypsy a few years back, after you went to California, and then Penny showed up, remember? She seemed to know all about us and said God wants us to be together; but, we can only find happiness in the 'sunshine by the seaside'. Well, we're in the 'sunshine by the seaside' now and I don't feel very happy, do you?"

"April, that's amazing. Let's make her prediction come true."

"I'm sorry, Jared. I'll always love you. My phone number will always be listed with directory assistance. If your marital situation changes, or after you have Kristie raised and on her own, see if you can find me."

"You will wait, then?"

"No, until that time, and not meaning to put pressure on you to leave Penny, I'll be looking for someone else to love...a man with whom I can build a life. My boys are practically grown. I have nothing of value on this earth but the shirt on my back; but, I believe it's possible to have heaven on earth. We could have been together all these years. We may have even been able to reverse my tubal ligation and have a baby. I would have been willing to take a chance."

"It's not too late, Princess...."

"It's too bad we didn't realize the potential of our love when we were twenty years old. We could have been very happy. We could have had it all!"

"Yes, we could have....we still can. April, I'm worth millions. If you'll wait a little longer, you'll never want for anything. We can be together as soon as Kristie's on her own. Then Penny can't use her against me. I'll give Penny anything she wants to be free of her. Penny and I are together in name only. I haven't touched her in years! I swear. What words can I say to convince you to wait just a little longer?"

"There are no words. I've thought it through. I have a super relationship with my children. They know they can always count on me. I've always tucked them into bed, listened to their prayers. I've been there for them. They think I'm pretty special; but, they're almost grown. We need a life of our own. I'm being selfish, I guess; but, I have to tell you, Penny's words cut me to the core. She wounded me. I didn't deserve those words. I'll never tolerate anyone talking to me like that again...."

"Your boys think you're special because you are. I've always known how special you are. I really messed up when we were young. Because of something my Dad said, I thought I had to make love to you before we committed to a lifetime of being together," he explained. "I apologize for Penny's words; but, remember, I didn't say those things. You should hear the way she talks to me; but, my relationship with Kristie is worth putting up with her verbal onslaughts. She's going to die a miserable, vindictive, lonely old woman some day."

"You'll get no argument from me on that one...."

"As soon as I get Kristie on her own, Princess, I'm history as far as Penny's concerned. But, for now, tolerating her is the only way I can be with my daughter. Can't you wait just a couple more years? Isn't our love worth the wait?"

"I've waited too long now. I'm glad you care so much for your daughter that you pay the supreme sacrifice by tolerating her mother. I understand, and I appreciate your fatherly duty. It's probably one of the reasons I love you so much. Find a way to be happy, Jared. As for me, I've got to get enough courage to walk out that door and build a life for myself, without hanging onto empty promises from you...." she said, as she started for the door.

"They're not empty promises, My Love. I mean every word. Once Kristie is on her own, I fully intend for us to be together. Please don't go. I'll order some cheesecake and Sangria. Stay long enough for some dessert....talk a little, and dance a few dances, maybe. Please!"

"I've lost my appetite. As far as talking, we've said enough. As far as dancing, how could we possibly dance to that song?" she asked, referring to the fast tune which was playing on the stereo.

Jared laughed, relieved to break the intense tension between them. "Wait long enough to see what the next song is....I need to hold you, just for a minute before you walk away from me..." he pleaded.

April shook her head and sat down on the bed. Jared sat down beside her and took her hand in his. They stared at the floor, emotionally drained, saying nothing.

After four commercials, the song, *"After the Lovin'"* started to play—their song!

"Did you have this planned, Jared? It's the song you dedicated to me when you left for California."

"I wish I could take the credit; but, it all goes to God. He must have planned it!"

Jared stood to his feet and pulled April into his arms. They clung to each other as they swayed to the beautiful tones of "their" song. Neither could speak because of the tears that were streaming down their cheeks.

Jared frantically searched for the words which would dissuade April from walking away from him...."

April broke the silence, "I've got to get out of here, Jared. I'll always love you. Please listen to the tape I gave you and read the scriptures. It's my favorite tape. It says exactly how I feel about God. I'll be praying for you. Maybe someday, our paths will cross again!"

"You'll see me again....soon, I hope. I love you, April. Take care of yourself. I'll catch ya' later, Princess, I promise...."

Jared didn't know if April heard his words or not because she had disappeared down the hallway. He was tempted to run after her. He closed the door, leaned against it and slid to the floor.

Reaching into the nearby bathroom, Jared pulled an unopened bottle of Jack Daniels from his overnight bag. He opened it and took a big drink straight from the bottle.

April pushed the elevator button after turning around to make sure Jared wasn't following her. Finally, the elevator door opened and she stepped inside. She was alone in the elevator with the exception of a nicely dressed gentleman. He watched as April fumbled in her purse for some tissues so she could wipe her eyes.

"Are you okay, Miss?" the kind stranger asked as he handed her his clean handkerchief.

"Yes, thanks for asking. I'll be fine. I've just had the strength to walk away from a destructive relationship. It's only taken me twenty years to get up enough nerve to break it off..."

"God bless you, Miss. He'll help you if you ask Him..."

April smiled and stared at the man. "Yes, I know. Thanks for your concern. God bless you, too. He's already blessed me."

The man's words were kind and gentle. April gained strength from his blessing as they ascended to the first floor in the closed elevator.

"God has already blessed me as well, Miss. I hope he'll grant you a miracle. It looks like you could use one right now. Will you be okay to get home? Can I get you a cab or something?"

"No, thanks. I have my car. I'll be fine....really; and, the miracle's already happened. I was able to walk away from him for good this time. I feel great; at least, I will as soon as I get my tear ducts under control! Thank you for your kindness."

"Tell you what....why don't you let me buy you a cup of coffee. We'll talk until you're calm enough to drive your car. It'd be a tragedy if you had an accident. You're pretty upset. They have a nice coffee shop in the lobby."

"That's a good idea. Thank you. God's worked another miracle in allowing you to be in this elevator. I was able to draw strength from your faith...."

April allowed the kind stranger to buy her a cup of coffee and they talked for about a half hour.

Before they parted, he asked for her phone number. The kind stranger was a minister who'd recently begun pastoring a church on the west side of town. He was single, 43 years old, tall, dark and handsome, with salt and pepper-colored hair.

April couldn't help but think as she sat watching share his joy at being a pastor ..... God works in strange and miraculous ways!

As April stepped into the cool night air to go to her car, she felt like a fifty-ton weight had been lifted from her frail shoulders. Her tears had stopped. She was at peace.

"Thank you, Lord, for the strength and direction to walk out of that room tonight. May Your will be done regarding Jared Walker, his relationship to You, to me, to his daughter, to his ex-wife, and to my boys. I pray utmost for Jared's salvation, Lord. Help him as only You can. I can't help him."

As April drove home, "The Gypsy Cried" was playing on the car stereo. She remembered the old gypsy's words and wiped away a final tear.

I guess we'll never find our happiness in the sunshine by the sea, she thought. I'll be fine, though. God will bless me with a good Christian husband someday. If not, I'll be fine 'cause I'm a survivor. I AM loved! God loves me dearly!"

In Jared's room, the bottle of Jack Daniels was now empty He had drank himself into a stupor. He spent the night on the carpeting of the hotel room. He couldn't face the thought of losing April. Surely, somehow, he'd be able to regain her love.

THE END

CHAPTER SEVENTEEN

WRITER'S LIFE - PRESENT DAY

When Suzie finished the novel, she felt a great sense of accomplishment. In her story, she could do or be anything she wanted.

"Oh, David," she said, even though she was alone. "I should do the same thing in our relationship. I need to put our relationship in the past and get on with my life. But, my character, April, is bigger than life. She's a figment of my imagination. I'm not like her. I don't have her strength. I wonder if I could walk away from you. Even though, in my heart, I know I should, I don't know how to end our story because you've never allowed it to end. You keep me hanging on with your endless promises."

"My friends encouraged me to fulfill my dreams in this book; to end our story the way that I want to see it end. Although I don't understand why we're not together, I know we love each other. I can't help but hope someday we'll be together." Suzie said, to herself.

As she read and re-read the passionate love episodes in the book, tears ebbed in her eyes. Of course, she'd taken bits and pieces of several men she'd known to create Jared; however, the love between Jared and April was real.

She wondered if the love story was believable. Is it possible for two people to love each other so much that their love spans the years even though they're apart? It's a known fact; a writer's first novel is often the author's story. Well, Suzie thought, this isn't exactly my story; but, it's a small part of the whole picture.

I've personally experienced most of the pain in the book, she reasoned. I inserted religion into the book to subtly depict that Jesus became more important to me than David. I've given my life to Jesus; and, I would love to be with David right now. Although I haven't seen him in years, I pray for him every day. I pray for his salvation, and ask God to guide and protect him. In my heart, I can't be with him unless he makes a commitment to God.

She re-read portions of her book, pondering, wondering if the religion in the book was too much. Is it believable? I'd hate to turn anyone away from God because of my feeble words. Were the sensual scenes too sexy? Would they be a turn-off for readers? God had created her as a sexual being, and had so much love for David. She said a quick prayer for God to use her words to bring people closer to him rather than turn them away.

April proofread her novel, made her corrections and decided to send the book to a publisher before her birthday in two weeks. It would be a birthday gift to herself.

Two weeks later, Suzie's birthday. She didn't notice the date as she diligently worked on the book, putting in the final touches, making sure the punctuation and capitalization was perfect, and the story flowed smoothly.

She was startled by the doorbell and somewhat irritated at being interrupted. She was on a roll and the doorbell had broken her concentration.

When she opened the door, a florist was delivering a dozen long-stemmed red roses, intermingled with white daisies.

She pulled the card off the flowers. It read: "To the Best in the West! Happy Birthday! See I remembered! Please call me, at 305-555-3321. Love always, David."

Suzie walked to the telephone and immediately dialed the number on the card. There was no answer.

She paced the floor for over an hour, trying the phone number every few minutes, anxious to talk to David. She wondered how he'd found her. The last time they had talked, he was out west in Phoenix. She was still in Ohio. She wondered how he knew she had recently moved to Florida. She also realized the 305 area code was in Florida as well.....in the Miami area.

Suzie dialed the number again and listened as the phone rang several times. Just as she was about to hang up, she heard David's voice...."Hello!"

"David? Hello, thanks for the beautiful roses! How in the world did you find me?"

"Suzie?!?! Oh, God, Suzie. I'm so glad you called. You're a hard person to find. I had to hire a private detective. He tracked you to Florida; but I could only get your address. They wouldn't give me your private number. How'd you end up in Florida?"

"My Mother retired and moved here. I was the only one of her four children who wasn't married; so, I moved with her so she wouldn't be alone. She bought a beautiful house just a few blocks from the beach. We live in an apartment...."

"WE?"

"The boys....they're almost grown, David!"

"Oh, Suzie, I've hungered for the sound of your voice, to feel your arms around me once more. I miss you! Let's never lose touch with each other again. I still love you, you know. Not a day goes by that I don't think about you. Soon, Suzie, I promise, if you'll wait, we'll be together. When you said 'we' I was afraid you had found someone ... else. "

"You keep saying that you want us to be together."

"You're not involved...or married....or anything, are you?" he asked.

"No, David. I date once in a while; but, there's no one special in my life."

"Good! I can't wait to see you, Suzie!"

"That'd be nice. Do you get over to the west coast of Florida very often?"

"Yes, in fact, hum....let me check my appointment book. I'll be in Tampa in a couple weeks. If you'll give me your phone number, I'll call you as soon as I get in. I'll take you out to dinner...."

"Okay, David. My number's 813-555-7072. I work five days a week, Monday through Friday. I normally get home about 5:30."

"I can't wait, Honey. How's life been treating you? Are you doing okay?"

"Well, I've become quite religious. That's changed me somewhat. I'm different than the last time you saw me. How about you?"

"I'm fine. I'm glad you found God. He and I have an understanding. I could never have survived in 'Nam if it wasn't for him, and thinking about you. I'm different, too, Suzie. My hair's turning gray and I've gained weight. You might not like me anymore...."

"I'm sure you're still very handsome, David. What are you doing in Florida?"

"We've opened another store in Ft. Lauderdale. I've been in Florida several months, opening stores in different malls. If everything goes well, we'll open one in Tampa soon at the University Mall. Do you know where that is?"

"Yes, it's a nice mall. Is there anyone special in YOUR life?"

"No, just my little girl. She's the light of my life. AND, I have a 100-foot sailboat. We go sailing almost every weekend. I want you to meet her, Suz...."

"I'd like that. What about your ex?"

"Well, unfortunately, she lives in Florida, too. We're still sharing custody. She lives across the street in a condo; but, there's nothing between us but Karen. Peggy works.... has her own friends."

Suzie's heart sank when she heard that Peggy lived across the street from Jared. After all, she'd tried to kill her. Suzie was shocked to discover that the story she had written was becoming real. Was she dreaming, she wondered. Are we headed for a goodbye in real life as well?

"Well, call me when you get into town, David, maybe we'll get together."

"There's no maybe about it, Love. By the way, Happy Birthday! I wish I could give you a birthday kiss. I'll make it up to you when I see you in a couple weeks, okay? I'll call as soon as I get to Tampa."

"Your flowers made it a special birthday, David. Thanks, again. It'll be great to see you...."

"Catch ya' later, Princess! I still love you...more than you'll ever know." he said. The phone line went dead.

A week later, David called to let Suzie know he'd be in Tampa in three days. They finalized their plans for dinner the first night he would be in town.

Suzie felt both excited and apprehensive as she dressed to go to the hotel. When she was finally ready to leave, she wasn't happy with the image she projected in her full-length mirror. She'd gained weight, and the royal blue silk dress did little to hide the extra pounds.

"I wonder if David will be repulsed by me..." she whispered, "It's been so long since we've seen each other; but, somehow, just like in my book, we need to end our love story. Because we've never had closure in our love affair, I've never been able to move on. I've hung onto a dream for too long. There's always been something special between us, though. Maybe that's why we've never ended our relationship...and never been able to find someone else to love."

Suzie was shaking with excitement and fear when she knocked on David's hotel door. She wondered what she was doing there and chastised herself because she didn't make him come to her apartment. Why does she always have to come to him....she wondered.

The door opened. There stood David, in all his glory, smiling at Suzie as only he knew how to smile.

"Suzie, you're still the beautiful woman I've known and loved for so long...." he said, taking her in his arms as if she was a delicate piece of porcelain. "After all these years, I'd have known you if we passed on the street. You're still the girl of my dreams."

David kissed Suzie lightly on the lips, then ushered her into his room. The suite was exquisitely decorated. There was an elegant table for two set up in the corner.

"How do I look to you, Suzie, after all these years?"

"Terrific, just like I imagined." she said, observing the deep set wrinkles around his eyes. "I love the gray touches in your hair, David. Gray hair is so sexy in a man's temples... just like Omar Shariff!"

"I don't see any gray in your hair. Is that your natural color?" he teased.

"Of course, I've never dyed my hair."

Staring at her without speaking, David was filled with emotion. "God, you're beautiful, Suz. I can't take my eyes off you!"

"It's a good thing you said that, David, or the evening might have ended rather quickly. I was feeling apprehensive about being here."

"Why? It's wonderful to see you." he whispered as he pulled her into his arms for a loving embrace.

They said nothing further for several minutes...just held each other gently, staring deeply into each other's eyes, drinking in the long-awaited view of each other after so many years of separation.

"Boy, Suzie, you look so young. I don't see any wrinkles around your eyes. If someone saw us together, they'd think you were at least ten years younger than me. My wrinkles come from spending too much time on my boat in the hot sun. Life's taken its toll by wrinkling my face, graying my hair. It's been tough, Honey, facing life everyday without you by my side..."

Tears welled in Suzie's eyes. How she'd longed to know if David still cared after all the years of being apart. It felt wonderful to be in his arms. She felt as if they were married. She had a momentary fantasy they were together again after a separation of some kind...reuniting after him being in an enemy prison. She definitely had a writer's imagination! The words she'd written in her novel, however, were becoming real! It was awesome!

There was a knock at the door. "I hope you don't mind, I ordered dinner. I didn't want any distractions or interruptions so we could talk....catch up on things."

David had ordered shrimp cocktails, steaks, baked potatoes, salad and strawberry shortcake for dessert. He'd also ordered a bottle of Dom Perignon.

Suzie watched as David dimmed the lights and lit the candles on the table. Then, he walked to her side; and, in a very gentlemanly way, offered her his arm, saying, "Your dinner, Madam!"

The dinner and conversation was superb, the ultimate of evenings for them both. They hungered to share every aspect of what had happened in their lives since they'd last seen each other. The emptiness and loneliness soon spilled into the conversation. "And, you've never found anyone to love?" David asked.

"What can I say? I'm a one-man woman! I fell in love with a very special young man when I was only twenty years old. I've never gotten over you, David."

"Princess, you deserve to be loved...pampered. I'm sorry I haven't been there for you all these years. My Darling, it's amazing, being together like this. It's like we've never been apart...our feelings for each other are the same!"

"Why do you think we've never found anyone else? We're both lovable, caring people. We deserve to be loved."

"Suz....I don't know. Hardly a day goes by that I don't think about you. In all the years we've known each other, we've never had an argument...not one cross word has passed between us. If we had gotten married, we could have made our marriage work, and been very happy, don't you think? Why haven't you found anyone else?"

"Because no one I've met can come close to standing in your shadow. When I care, I care deeply. Somehow, our love affair never ended. Maybe we need to do each other a favor and end it now, David."

"Don't say that! I can't stand to think about never seeing you again. I love you, Suzie. By the time we found each other again, Karen had been born. You couldn't have any more children. In order for us to be together, I would have had to give Karin up. She means as much to me as you do. She was my whole life. I was wrong to ask you to wait all these years, though; and, I hope you will wait a little longer so we can be together. You should have been Karen's mother. I kick myself every time I think about what I've missed...how I messed up our lives."

"Well, David, it takes two people to make a relationship work; and, it takes two to mess it up. You didn't mess it up alone. I didn't have enough confidence in myself to fight for you when we were twenty. I gave up without a fight because of some insecurity problems stemming from my childhood....some hang-ups. I've never told anyone;

but, when I was only five years old, my Dad's best friend molested me. My Dad laughed about it."

"Oh, God, Suzie, did he hurt you?"

"No, he just sort rocked me up and down on his penis. I had clothes on and so did he; but, I knew it wasn't right. My Dad laughed at his friend. Did I ever tell you my Dad was an alcoholic; and, they'd been drinking. My Mom wasn't home at the time."

"I'm sorry. Why didn't you tell me before?"

"I was afraid. Then, when I was a teenager, I got my own apartment, remember? Well, My Dad said some terrible things about me. He said a different guy spent the night with me every night. He said I was an evil, hot-to-trot, slut, David. You, of all people, know I was a virgin. If I'd let anyone get to me, it would have been you. I was adamant about remaining a virgin until my wedding night."

"I never doubted your virginity, Honey. I tried like hell to change that fact, though. I'm sorry you had a rotten father."

"David, when we were twenty, remember the last time I saw you.....you know, you were with HER! I'd made up my mind I was going to give in to you; but, the next thing I knew you were married. I was devastated; so, I accepted the next marriage proposal I received after that."

"How did things work out with him?"

"He was so stupid, he accused me of NOT being a virgin the first time he touched me. I almost bit off my thumb to keep from screaming. One night, he raped me in a drunken rage. After we were divorced, I tried to find you."

"I wish we'd found each other. It was probably about the time I was getting back from Vietnam, right?"

"Yes, about the same time. I called your mother. She said she remembered me....said she'd thought I'd be her daughter-in-law someday. Oh, well, I can't continue to ramble about the past..."

"Wonder why my Mom didn't tell me you called."

"I asked her not to..... She said you were trying to work out your problems with your wife. She told me about your little girl....."

"Oh, Suzie, let's make a pact....a pledge, to be together as soon as we can. It won't be more than three years before I'll be free to marry you. Will you wait?"

"Why can't we be together now? You said you were opening several stores in Tampa. We could live here, work things out with your ex-wife for joint custody. I have full custody of my boys....they're practically grown. Douglas is going to get married this spring; and, my youngest, Jason, is graduating this year. He's enlisted in the Navy."

"Several of my friends have gotten married when step-children were involved. It didn't work out. I want us to be happy. If we get married and have problems because of the children, I couldn't stand it. Say you'll wait...just three more years. We can spend weekends and vacations together until then. What do you say, Suzie?" he pleaded.

"There's no doubt that I want you, David; but, I want to be your WIFE....not your weekend lover. Because of deep religious convictions, I can't make love with you again until we're married. I can't tolerate a cheap affair. I want to be your wife, not your weekend lover."

"I'm proud of you for sticking up for your beliefs; even though, I don't like what you said. It's almost like, so many years ago, when you told me 'no' for a different reason. Tell me more about your religious experience...."

"After I moved to Florida, my life was sad because I didn't have any friends. I was a nervous wreck and sought the help of a doctor because I was so depressed and frustrated. He had the gall to suggest I have an affair with a married man, and even volunteered to 'do the job!' I refused, of course, but, I started to date one of my co-workers....married, of course. I couldn't handle the situation. I didn't like having to sneak around. It made me feel dirty. I chose to get on with my life.... alone."

"I'm glad to hear that!"

'Well, after I received a raise and bonus at work, I was able to move into a larger apartment. A group of men from work, who had pick-up trucks, offered to help me move. I bought the beer and pizza; and, they supplied the trucks and manpower. We invited some girls, too, and made it a party. It was a lot of fun. I laughed. I needed to laugh. One of the movers singled me out. He'd recently separated from his wife."

"Ut, oh. What happened?"

"He stayed after the others left. He was a very dynamic, out-going guy who was formerly a professional football player. One thing leads to another; and, before I knew it, we ended up in my bed. I was lonely and his arms were nice. It'd been a long time since I'd felt a man's arms around me. I hadn't heard from you in a long time; and, to top it off, it was my birthday! I was especially vulnerable."

"Stop, Suzie. I don't want to hear anymore. I can't think about you being with someone else."

"There's a reason for telling you this...bear with me for a few more minutes."

"Okay...."

"When I went to work the next Monday morning, everyone was laughing at me. They'd been told every detail of what had happened between us. He bragged about everything...even the most intimate detail! I was extremely embarrassed; but, somehow, I was able to make it through the day. I stuck it out.....and the bragging backfired on him. I dare not repeat the horrible things some of the men said to me. I was so humiliated and heartbroken; I swore I'd never date again."

"Oh, Suzie, I'm sorry. If we'd been together, this would never have happened...."

"My heartbreak lingered, and my depression increased. My health suffered. I sought professional help. A Christian counselor helped me work through the sordid details of my life. He found NO fault with our relationship, however."

"Great! I'm glad to hear that. Our love is the real thing...."

"During our counseling sessions, he introduced me to Jesus Christ; and, I made a complete commitment to Him. He's everything to me. Because of my commitment, my life reflects this love. I have to set a good example for the world to see. Jesus touched me in a special way, David. He saved me. He forgave me for the sins I'd committed, and promised to forgive me for every sin I commit in the future. All I have to do is ask. He's my Savior, my Confidant, and my daily Inspiration."

"Suzie, you make it seem so real. Do you realize you're almost glowing? You started to radiate when you began to talk about your religious experience. It makes me jealous, makes me want what you have...."

"Oh, David, it's so easy....a simple act of faith. A total surrender of your life; and, then, you strive to walk in His footsteps to represent Him to the world. When I die, I'll go to heaven. I want you to be there, too....in heaven!"

"Oh, I don't know about that. My sister's constantly after me, trying to convert me to her religion. Her nagging has caused me to be turned off about God. You make it sound like something I'd like to have...and I'm envious of you. Like I said, you're glowing!"

"Oh, Honey, I'm glad I found Jesus. I'm happy to see you again. I love you so much."

"Will you dance with me, Suzie? Like we used to?"

"Sure."

Suzie watched as David walked over to tune the stereo to a local station. He returned to the table, took her hand and said, "May I have this dance, My Lady?"

She melted in his arms. It was terrific to be together again. Suzie could have easily made love with David. She knew her passionate longings and knew God would forgive her for making love with David outside of the bounds of marriage; but, if David wasn't a child of God, would the coals of sin be piled upon his head, she wondered. In her heart, she couldn't make love to him until they were married.

"Suzie, will you stay with me tonight? Let me hold you in my arms. I swear, I won't make love to you unless you want me to. I'll hold you close. It's been so long since we've been together."

"I'd love to stay; but, I can't. I've like you to come to dinner and see the boys. They were kidding me about you when I was getting ready for our date."

"I'll only be in town tonight and tomorrow; but, I'll be back in a few weeks to finalize our deal. I'd better wait until

I come back to see them. If we're all together now, I may never want to leave. You know, I always wanted a son."

"They should have been your sons...."

Tears welled in David's eyes. He quickly looked down at the floor. "Just a few more years, Suzie, I promise. If you'll wait for me, we'll be together....get married."

"Let's take it one step at a time and not make any promises we can't keep. It's hard for me to understand your relationship with your ex-wife. Wherever you go.... whatever you do, she seems to be part of your life. Are you sure you two aren't together?"

"No, we're simply bringing up our daughter. I think about you all the time. Every night, when my head hits the pillow, I want you there. I drink to drown my memories of holding you....loving you. I need you, Suzie, more than ever. What for me until I get Karen raised..." he pleaded.

"Like I said, David, let's take it one step at a time. Call me when you get back to town. We'll see how it feels after a few months. But, don't expect me to sleep with you until we're married, okay? I can't do that right now. Besides, I've been writing a love story, and this conversation is scaring me because it's almost identical to my written words in the novel."

"Really? Hum....that's interesting. Does your story have a happy ending?"

"That depends on the reader's viewpoint of life. Some will think it's a happy ending, others will feel sad, I suppose."

"Well, you'll see, our story WILL have a happy ending. I'll call you. You'll hear from me soon...."

"David, the hardest thing I have to do is walk out of this room. I want you...."

David grabbed Suzie and crushed her body to his, smothering her face and neck with kisses. Their passion was overwhelming. Suzie finally pulled away.

"I'm sorry, David. I want you; but, I can't.....uh, I just can't. For once, someone means more to me than you. Regardless of whether we end up together or not, we can be together throughout infinity. I'm certain one of my last thoughts on this earth will be about you. I'll be praying for you with my dying breath!"

"Will you meet me for lunch tomorrow...so we can talk some more...make some more plans?"

"I can't. My company is hosting a sales meeting tomorrow and I have to coordinate a luncheon for about thirty people. All I have to do is instruct the caterers; but, I have to be there. I can leave work early, though. Do you have a car? We could have an early supper before you leave town."

"Well, no, I don't have a car. I flew over in the company jet. I use a cab or limousine for my transportation; but, I'll be happy to provide transportation. What do you have in mind?"

"You'll see. I'll pick you up at the hotel at four o'clock. Okay?"

Sure, my plane's scheduled to leave at seven. I'll delay departure until later."

"Fine. Until then, David, goodbye....."

Kissing her sweetly, David said, "Never say goodbye. Remember, always say I'll catch ya' later. Until tomorrow, then. I can't get over how wonderful you look after all these years!"

David and Suzie stood in the doorway for several minutes, holding each other, not saying a word. Finally, she pulled away. "Thanks for dinner, David. It was delicious. Catch ya' later!"

"You bet, Princess!" he said, blowing her another kiss.

It was late when Suzie got back to her apartment. The boys had cleaned up the kitchen and left her a note: "Hope you had a nice time on your date, Mom. How come you're so late!!!!"

After Suzie showered and crawled into bed, she pulled a small Bible from her nightstand and started to read. She quickly wrote the "Romans Road Map" scriptures to give to David the next day. She decided she'd give him her favorite Christian tape... just like in her book.

It was past three o'clock when she finished her project and said her prayers.

"Lord," she prayed, "I commit David to you. Give him another chance to accept you as his Personal Savior. Work Your Will in his life. Your Word says You'll give me the desires of my heart. It's my desire that David and I spend eternity with you in heaven. Use me, Lord, if I'm worthy, to help David understand how wonderful YOU are..."

After finishing the Lord's Prayer, Suzie's mind was calm and her heart was peaceful. She drifted into a beautiful, dreamless sleep.

The next day, the luncheon went smoothly for Suzie so she was able to leave at three-thirty to pick up David. Traffic was unusually heavy; and, it was starting to rain when she arrived at the hotel. David was carrying his briefcase and overnight bag, waiting patiently for her in the front of the hotel. When he saw her, he waved and smiled.

Suzie pulled her Cougar to the curb and raised the seat so David could put his bags into the back seat. He leaned across the seat and kissed her as soon as he sat down.

The Gaither Trio was playing softly on the car stereo; but, Suzie turned down the volume so they could talk as she drove to a local restaurant.

When she pulled into the parking lot of the restaurant, David smiled and looked at Suzie with surprise.

"Frisch's! very clever, Princess. It's been years since I've had a Big Boy!"

"I read your mind. I thought it would be a pleasant surprise."

"You're so thoughtful… We are truly soul-mates."

It was fun eating together in what used to be their favorite restaurant. The decor was old-fashioned, sixty's-type. Their big boys and onion rings were scrumptious. The cherry Cokes provided pleasant remembrances of days gone by. The conversation was light and fun-filled, almost as if the years had been erased.

"Since you have your bags with you, David, I'm assuming you'll allow me to drive you to the airport."

"If you don't mind. We'd better leave soon, though. The jet's gassed up and the pilot's waiting. I can't tell you how wonderful it's been to see you. This time, we're going to stay in touch, Suz…"

"You'd better or I'll be knocking on your front door!" she teased.

"You're welcome anytime. I'd love to show you off, take you out in my little boat…."

"Didn't you say your boat was a hundred feet long? That's not a little boat!"

"Well, I guess not; but, I'd love to take you out for a weekend of fun and sun....just the two of us."

"Maybe someday..."

"Well, you know, I've got plenty of money. I've had everything I want from life except you, Princess. I want to make you my wife soon. Promise you'll wait for me...just three more years..."

"We'll see, David. It could happen. I'm not interested in anyone else."

"Good, let's keep it that way! Be sure to go to church on Sunday so you'll stay as sweet as you are right now..." he feigned, thinking it was what she wanted to hear.

"Since you brought up the subject of religion, David, I have something for you. I stayed up late last night and wrote down some verses from Romans that spell out the Romans Road—the Road to Christ. I know you're turned off to religion because of your sister's nagging; but, it's really so simple. Someday, when you're on your boat alone, read my note and the scriptures I've written down in the front of the little Bible that I'm giving you. I also want you to have my favorite Christian tape. After you listen to it, if you don't want it, don't throw it away. Send it back to me. Listen with your heart; and, remember, I'm giving you these things in love. I love you very deeply...a love that grows stronger every time I see you. I'll pray for you, and for God to work things out so we can be together."

"I hope so, Suzie. Thanks for caring enough to lose sleep over me last night to write these things down. I'm touched."

"Babe, I've lost plenty of sleep over you through the years; but, this was a labor of love...pure love!"

They hugged each other, and Suzie kissed David as he helped her get into the car. The drive to the airport was swift; and, before they knew it, they were sharing a final embrace....a final, lingering kiss. It was hard to pull away from each other."

"I'll call you soon, Suzie..."

She nodded, unable to speak as he disappeared into the large-size jet. She stood motionless as the jet revved its' engines and taxied onto the main runway. She waved, unable to determine if David could see her or not. Tears were streaming down her face as she prayed for the "*Wings of Protection*" to surround the plane today and always.

Inside, David watched Suzie wave. He wiped a tear from his cheek. There was no doubt in his mind that he loved her. She was somewhat different than he'd expected; but, he didn't really mind the religious jargon. In his mind, he could see them making love the next time they were together. He'd break down her resistance. After all, it was clear she wanted him. She'd give in to him, he reasoned, the next time.

David smiled confidently to himself. He opened his briefcase and dropped the notes, the small Bible, and the cassette tape into one of the compartments, smirking to himself, "I don't know about this religious crap, though....."

As Suzie drove back to her apartment, she thought about her novel. Should she leave the ending as she'd written, or allow April and Jared to be together? In her heart, she wanted the "real story" to end with the lovers being together.

Thinking to herself, I'd love to be his wife. We could move to a rustic cabin in the woods so I could concentrate on my love stories. I've got so much love bottled up inside me...so many stories that need to be told. I've never had enough romance in my life."

About halfway home, Suzie turned on the car stereo to W-H-B-O, which plays old love songs. As she turned into her parking space at the apartment, "*The Gypsy Cried*" started to play on the radio. Suzie listened to the station simply because they played the Lou Christie golden oldie on a regular basis.

As she listened, tears flowed from her eyes. "This would be the best title for my story. I'm going to finish the rewriting tomorrow and send it to a publisher!!!!"

CHAPTER EIGHTEEN

Two Months Later

Suzie couldn't sleep. She had an overwhelming inner peace because she'd finished a major project in her life. She surmised no one, except David, would be able to determine exactly what was truth and what was fantasy in her book. Some parts of her novel were pure fiction...others were elaborated truths....others were factual.

Suzie got out of bed, picked up her pen and started to proofread the novel again, checking for misspelled words and punctuation errors.

At eight o'clock the next morning, Suzie was waiting for the post office to open so she could mail her treasured manuscript.

Suzie had the clerk weigh the package, making sure there was ample postage on both the manuscript and her return envelope. Then, she walked to the mail drop, said a prayer, and dropped her novel into the mail slot.

Everyday during the next month, Suzie ran to the mailbox every day, hoping to hear from the publisher. Nothing!

Finally, after six weeks, the phone rang, "Person-to-Person call for Mrs. Suzanne Phillips...." the operator said.

"Operator, this is Suzanne Phillips."

"Go ahead, Sir." the Operator said to the calling party.

"Mrs. Phillips, this is Joe Waterson, editor of Doubleday. Could you come to New York to discuss your manuscript?"

"How's next week! I'm a secretary; but, I'll arrange to take some time off....a short vacation."

"Perfect, Mrs. Phillips. There'll be a first-class ticket for Delta's Sunday afternoon's flight 3244 to New York. I'll make a room reservation for you at the Plaza. Take a taxi from the airport. Get a receipt and I'll reimburse you when I see you Monday morning. I'll leave a message at the hotel with my private phone number. Call me Monday morning, okay?"

"Sure, no problem. Did you like my book?" she asked quietly, knowing she couldn't wait until Monday for his response.

"First, tell me, have you written any other books?"

"I've got about a dozen written in my mind. I've not put them on paper yet. This was my first attempt at writing."

"Well, be prepared to discuss your ideas at greater length when we meet, Mrs. Phillips. I'm very excited about your manuscript. We'll discuss it when we meet. Until then, I look forward to meeting you..."

The phone line went dead. Suzie cradled the phone in her hand, deep in thought.

The week passed quickly as she made arrangements to take a week's vacation. She bought a week's supply of food for the boys to eat while she was away. She chuckled at their excitement at being left to fend for themselves. She wondered how creative they would be with their new found freedom; so, they were as excited as she was about her trip.

The flight to New York was uneventful. Suzie felt luxurious being pampered in the First Class section of the plane. She'd never flown First Class. She'd always been cramped into the Coach Section. When she arrived at the Plaza, it was a dream coming true for her.

After Suzie checked into the Plaza, the Day Manager informed her that Mr. Waterson had left an envelope and instructions that she could order anything she liked from Room Service. He had also arranged for fresh flowers, fruit and iced champagne to be delivered to her room. There was a small refrigerator that contained a variety of foods.

Suzie's first night in New York was memorable. She enjoyed the delicious food and the elegance of the hotel. Her room had a breath-taking, panoramic view. She was so excited that it was difficult to sleep.

When she was finally able to drift off, David filled her dreams. She dreamt he was beside her, that he was enjoying her victory. She had no idea what to expect the next day. She was thrilled, scared, excited....feeling all these emotions at the same time.

The next morning, Suzie was taken by limousine to Mr. Waterson's office. As soon as she entered the outer office, Helen, his personal assistant, met her.

Helen immediately ushered Suzie into the publisher's impressive office. The man sitting at the large desk was tall, slightly-balding, a handsome-figure of a man with a powerful aura. He shook Suzie's hand firmly, and they small-talked while Helen got them some coffee. Joe asked about Suzie's trip and exhibited all the courteous niceties she had expected. Suzie nervously smoothed her skirt, anticipating the conversation they had ahead of them regarding her writing ability.

"Tell me about yourself, Mrs. Phillips...."

"Please, call me Suzie, Mr. Waterson."

"Agreed, but only if you will call me Joe."

Shaking her head affirmatively, Suzie told Joe she was divorced, a Christian country lady, a secretary, and the mother of two boys.

"I've been alone for many years, virtually raised my children alone. They're practically grown, though. My youngest son, Jason, is graduating this year; he's joined the Navy. My oldest son, Douglas, is getting married in June to a really sweet girl. So, my nest is almost empty!"

"Good, you'll need time. Tell me about the other ideas you have for novels. Let's see, what you said on the phone ....'Stories you've written in your mind'?"

"They're mostly love stories. One is about Jane Ables, a legal secretary, who's having an affair with the governor of the state. He's very married, if you know what I mean. Their relationship gets complicated when her pocket is picked by a sleazy character named Snake Monroe. Snake discovers a secret compartment in her wallet that contains a photo of her and the governor, and motel receipts. He starts to follow her, without her knowledge, and confirms his suspicions. He then starts to blackmail her. The governor ends their relationship after Snake gets murdered. Jane's boss, Ron Gould, an attorney, who has secretly loved Jane for years, defends her when murder charges are filed against her. Ron, of course, will get her off by the skin of her teeth, and they get married at the end of the book. I like a happy ending."

"But you didn't give this book a happy ending."

"In a way I did. April pulled herself together and walked away from a relationship that was emotionally damaging... one she'd nurtured for years. Now, she's free to love again."

"That's what I thought, too. You left it open for a sequel. You can allow her to find a husband. Have you given that any thought?"

"Oh, yes, I have several stories I'm planning in my mind right now. A sequel to *'The Gypsy Cried'* is only one of them."

"Do you have another example to share?"

"Victoria Baxter, a socialite housewife, is disgraced by the town when George, her political husband, is murdered. She's cleared of all charges; but, the town no longer accepts her and her two children, a boy and girl. They are forced to move to the outskirts of town to a rental home to try to pull her life together. The owner of the house is a well-known Hollywood director/writer. Let's name him Robert Fielding. He comes to town in the middle of the night, unaware the house, which has sat empty for years, has been rented by the leasing company. By now, Victoria has the house in perfect shape. At first, they hate each other; but, agree to live together, yet separately, in the large house, ignoring each other. They end up falling in love, of course. I'm creating a disagreeable actress, a real floozy ...maybe name her Mattie, or something, as a love interest for him. Robert discovers he likes the sereneness of the housewife ....a thought which, at first, disgusted him."

"Any others come to mind?"

"Yes, I've got an idea I've been tossing around about a very lonely widow....hum, let's name her Callie, who wants to visit Disney World in Florida. She can't get anyone to go with her so she takes the trip alone. While going through the turnstiles, she accidentally trips over a massive, red-headed Irish gentleman, Eric Talman, who's also visiting Disney World alone. He suggests they spend the day together. At first, she's reluctant; but, finally succumbs to his charms. They, of course, end up falling in love and get married. She doesn't find out he's a billionaire until they go back to his castle in Ireland. I'll have to do some research about Ireland, castles, such as that."

"Suzie, I'm impressed with your divisibility and creativity. Are you prepared to quit your job and write exclusively for me?"

"That's a big decision, Joe. I've got to give it some thought. Would I have to move to New York?"

"No, not necessarily. I could send you to my cabin in North Carolina. It's pretty remote; but, you'd be supplied with everything you need. I've got a maid and caretaker who oversee the house. I'd want you to do some minor rewriting on this first book; and, then, I'd like to contract you to write four more books. Since it'll take almost a year to get your first book on the market once my re-writing requirements have been fulfilled, how many books do you think you can write in a one-year period?"

"In a year's time, without any distractions? I suppose I could write several books. But, what about my expenses... like insurance? You realize, I'm not a wealthy woman. I only have my income. I've got to look out for myself...cover the bases, so to speak."

"Don't worry, your expenses will be paid. We'll provide insurance for you by enrolling you into our group health insurance plan. Mabel and Jake, the maid and her husband, live down the road from the cabin where you'll be living. They've taken care of my place for years. She cooks and cleans; he does the maintenance and yard work. If you need anything from town in the winter, I have a four-wheel Land Rover that'll take you anywhere you need to go. Like I said, it's remote; but, of all the real estate I own, it's my personal favorite. While you're there, you'll have complete control of the place....no interruptions. I'll be a phone call away. How does this sound?"

"Scary...I need a little time. My son's graduation and his subsequent military enlistment; my oldest son's wedding. What do I do with my apartment? My furniture? Should I take a leave of absence from my job, or submit a resignation?"

"You won't need an apartment...or furniture. You can cancel the lease on your apartment if you like. We'll pay any expenses involved. I'd like to see you quit your job because a year is too long to ask an employer to hold a job; besides, I don't think you'll have to work as a secretary again. I have a hunch you'll be a very successful writer. Can you be at the cabin in....what do you say....three months?"

"Wow! What an opportunity. My head is spinning. Three months will work well, I guess. You're not going to change your mind, right? You don't have any reservations about my writing ability!!?? You're definitely going to publish my first novel?"

"Suzie, I'm so certain I have a winning novelist in my office right now, I'll have my attorney draw up an overview of our first contract; and, I'll authorize a $10,000 advance to help pay your expenses until you arrive at the cabin. Any expenses you incur will be reimbursed once you get to the cabin. You can then put your money in the bank and write for me on a full-time basis, all expenses paid, while you're at the cabin. You'll receive written confirmation, re-writing instructions and an airplane ticket in about three months."

"I can't believe this is happening!"

"It is....but, for now, I want you to enjoy New York. Why don't you join me for dinner and the theater tonight? I've taken the liberty of ordering tickets for the Broadway play, 'CATS'. In the meantime, my chauffeur, Morgan, will take you anywhere you'd like to go. Some sightseeing perhaps? Some shopping? I'll pick you up at the Plaza at six-thirty. We'll dine there so we'll be able to get to the theater by the eight o'clock curtain. I'm sure you'll enjoy it, Suzie."

"This sounds like a dream. Am I dreaming?"

"I assure you, you're not dreaming. I wonder where you've been hiding all these years; and, I'm glad you sent ME your manuscript. I'm impressed with your creativity. I can't spend the day with you because of other commitments. I'll have my attorney draw up a contract. But, as for today, enjoy yourself and I'll see you tonight."

"Let's see, I'd like to see the Statue of Liberty first. I'm proud to be an American; and, I've only seen it in pictures. When we landed last night, I was on the wrong side of the plane to see it."

"Morgan will take you there first. Why don't you take the ferry over and tour the inside?"

"That's a great idea! I just might do that ..."

Suzie lavished in her first day in New York and was a typical tourist. She toured the Statue of Liberty; then, she went shopping. She purchased a red silk evening dress to wear to the theater, some shoes and a purse to match. Then she asked Morgan to drive her to Sassoon's for a complete makeover ... hair, nails, facial, and haircut ...the works! She was so excited by Joe's offer, she felt she could splurge; luckily, she had room on her charge cards to do everything she wanted.

When Suzie returned to the Plaza, heads turned when she walked into the lobby. Suzie felt gorgeous, confident, and it showed!

When Joe saw her that night, he was surprised by Suzie's transformation. They enjoyed a delicious light supper. The pleasant conversation allowed Suzie to find out everything that she needed to know about the publishing industry.

"You know, Suzie, it's easy to talk to you. You'll do well on your publicity tours. Once your book hits the market, I'll more than likely arrange an appearance for you on most of the major talk shows. I have a hunch the public will love you! Your natural beauty and charm are refreshing."

"Me...on television?!?! Oh, I don't know."

"If your other novels are as good as your first, you could easily be a millionaire by the time they're all published. Hollywood could pick them up. Who knows, maybe a movie ...a play ...television, et cetera? It's hard to tell, at this point, just how far you'll go. I feel, however, we'll all be wealthier in a couple years because of your novels."

"Oh, I hope so, Joe. It would mean the fulfillment of a dream I've had since I was a little girl. I've had a tough life; but, I think I was meant to experience life so I could write about the things I've seen. I've got so many ideas floating around in my head, waiting to be put on paper."

"That why I'm setting you up in the cabin in North Carolina. You'll have so much peace and quiet; you'll probably have the four books written in no time."

"I can't imagine not having any interruptions. My life has been so hectic."

"I'll contract you for five novels, including this first one; however, our relationship doesn't have to end there. We'll renegotiate once your first five books are completed."

"Fine, Joe, whatever you say."

"You'll like the cabin, Suzie. It's not very big; and, it's rustic. There's an ocean inlet almost at your front door; and, at your back door, you have a magnificent view of the mountains and a rushing stream. The change of seasons is absolutely breath taking! There's a deck in the back that you can use for writing on nice days. Hopefully, you'll be so inspired by the view that the words will flow. I go to the cabin often when I need to escape the smog of New York."

"I'm sure I'll love it, Joe. I'm a country girl who's been forced to live in rental apartments most of my life. Your cabin sounds heavenly. I'll be able to clear my mind and concentrate on my writing."

"Of course, you will; but, for now, we'd better leave for the theater. You'll enjoy this play. I've seen it several times."

"I have two cats myself! I've heard the soundtrack. My youngest son loves the music from the play. He has posters plastering his bedroom walls. Maybe someday, he'll get to see the play, too!"

"Sure, let me know if he's going to be in New York and I'll get him some tickets. Didn't you say he was entering the military when he graduates?"

"Yes, he wanted to go to college; but, it's pretty hard for someone with my income to pay college tuition. I sent my oldest son to technical school, with the help of a scholarship. My youngest son's grades didn't qualify him for any kind of financial assistance; so, he chose to let the Navy educate him. I'm trusting God for his safety. He's excited about going off to see the world...."

"He'll be fine. I served six years in the Air Force myself. It was the best thing I ever did."

The play was fabulous; however, Suzie was exhausted when they returned to the Plaza. Joe handed her a folder of contract papers.

"Suzie, I want you to review these contracts. If you'd like, call an attorney for legal advice. I'll send Morgan to get you in the morning at ten o'clock to take you wherever you'd like to go. Meet me for dinner and cocktails tomorrow evening at let's say, seven, to discuss the contracts." Joe instructed.

"Great! I'll see you tomorrow, Joe."

Joe waited until Suzie was safely inside the building before he instructed Morgan to take him home.

When Suzie got to her room, she reviewed the contracts. They were fairly standard; but, contained a clause wherein she had to sign away the future rights to the books. If a movie was made from her novels, she wouldn't get a cent. She remembered the old gypsy's words and knew she couldn't sign away the rights. She wondered if Joe would agree to her retaining the future rights. Would the deal be off?

Suzie spent the next day buying small gifts for her family, and doing some sightseeing with Morgan's assistance.

Her dinner meeting with Joe went well until he brought up the subject of the contracts.

"I'm sorry, Joe, I can't relinquish my future rights to the stories. If any of my books are made into movies or plays,

I'd like to do the screen writing. I can't cut myself out of the profits! Even though you're making a great monetary offer, I can't sign these contracts. I've never been impressed by money. What will your offer be if I retain the future rights?"

"Well, you're not just a country girl, after all, are you? You're a pretty shrewd lady. I'd better be on my toes from now on. Let's leave the dollar amount the same, give you a smaller percentage of the profits, including future rights. How does that sound?"

"Absolutely not! I will not sign away any of my future rights. I'll gladly cut you in; but, I have to retain the rights!"

"Suzie, I have to tell you. I usually don't have such a hard time with a first-time writer. They're usually so happy to get published, they don't even read the contract, let alone think about future rights." Joe said angrily.

"Well, I'm not just ANY writer. I am adamant about retaining the future rights. I'll be happy to write exclusively for you, Joe. You'll always get a hefty cut of the profits; but, I MUST, I repeat, I MUST, retain future rights."

Exasperated, Joe motioned for the waiter, "Give me a magnum of your best champagne. We've just made a deal that will make us both millionaires!"

Suzie smiled at the waiter, then at Joe. The waiter hurriedly left to get the champagne after offering his congratulations.

"Suzie, I have another suggestion for you..." Joe continued. "I suggest you use a pseudonym....uh, a pen name, for security's sake."

"That not a problem either. I'd like to use the name 'Michelle Wynne.' The name came to me one day while I was sitting in church. I want my private life to remain private."

"Michelle Wynne...hum, that sounds nice. Sounds like the name of a winner!"

After the waiter filled the champagne glasses and handed Suzie a glass, Joe toasted, "To a very shrewd lady. A writer with a refreshing creativity; and, I accept her, without question or doubt, totally. You have a bright and prosperous future. Welcome to the world of writing, Michelle Wynne. Soon your name will be a household word ... known in every home in America!"

"Wh-o-o-o-o! That's pretty scary..."

"Enjoy it, Suzie; but, don't let success change you. Stay as you are now. I've seen people destroyed by this business. They let fame go to their heads. Since you're not impressed by money, perhaps you'll be smart enough to ignore the money-hungry people who say and do anything to get some of your money. You're a single woman; you won't believe the good-looking roaches that'll crawl out of the woodwork, hoping for a piece of the action. They'll say and do anything to get close to you."

"Thanks for the warning. I won't forget your advice, Joe."

"It's refreshing to meet someone like you. You truly are a sophisticated country girl!"

"Thanks, Joe."

"Are you going to stay in New York all week?"

"No, I don't think so. If I'm going to move to your cabin in a couple months, I need to get home. There's a lot of preparation ahead of me."

"I'll have the contracts drawn up and delivered to the Plaza in the morning. Morgan will take you anywhere you'd like to go until you leave New York. We can meet to finalize our deal, or you can send the contracts back to me via the messenger who delivers them. You can trust me, Suzie. The contracts will be in order...just as we discussed."

"I'm a very perceptive person, Joe. I know they'll be in order."

"How about tonight? I can get more theater tickets, or perhaps tickets to the opera or ballet; or, if you'd like, we could take a carriage ride through Central Park."

"The carriage ride through Central Park sounds wonderful. Let's keep the evening simple...remember, I'm a country girl. Big cities scare me!"

"Good idea. I don't want to take you to the hot spots yet. When your first book is ready to hit the market, we'll make the rounds then so I can show you off."

After the carriage ride, Joe suggested, "I know where we can get great chili burgers. I don't know about you; but, I'm a little hungry."

"Okay, Joe. I loved the carriage ride; so, I'm sure I'll enjoy the chili burger, too!"

The burgers were hot and spicy. Joe took Suzie to Rockefeller Plaza; and, then, he showed her the view from atop the Empire State Building.

Since she'd enjoyed the first carriage ride so much, Suzie asked Joe if they could end their evening with another ride through Central Park.

While they rode around the park, Joe said, "Suzie, I'm not ready for the night to end. I probably won't be seeing you for quite some time...."

"Are we far from the hotel? It's such a beautiful night, maybe we could walk back. Is it safe to walk the streets at this time of night?"

"As long as Morgan follows us, I don't think we'll have a problem. It's a great suggestion, Suzie."

Morgan drove alongside them as they walked to the hotel. Joe told Suzie about his rocky marriage. "I still love her; but, I don't think our relationship is going to make it. She's nothing like you, Suzie. She's become obsessed with money and power. I wish she were more like you. Somehow, we've lost the romance we once had in our marriage. She'd never enjoy a simple evening like this...."

"If you really want to, it's possible to put the romance back into your marriage, Joe. Do you send her flowers? Do you take her out for special evenings?"

"No, sad to say, not any more. I spend most of my time with clients."

"Isn't she your best client?"

"She should be. Maybe if I set aside one evening each week for her... Maybe I could get her to join me for a quiet evening like this. Our marriage is worth it."

"Do you have any children, Joe?"

"Three. A boy and two girls."

"How wonderful. Well, Joe, it takes two people to make a marriage work; and, it takes two people to break it up. You should try to make it work for the sake of the children. Be kind to each other. Always hold onto the romance; then, when the children are grown and gone, you'll still be lovers. Make her feel special. She'd have to respond and eventually let you know how special you are to her. You have to work AT a relationship to make it work. The work begins before the honeymoon ends."

"You should be married, Suzie. Is there anyone special in your life?"

Suzie got a far away look in her eyes. "Yes, Joe, there's a very special man. I love him more than life itself; but, we're not together. I don't understand why; but, he got pretty messed up in Vietnam. Well, who knows, maybe someday...."

"Do you ever see him?"

"Once in a blue moon. The relationship in the book is obviously based on our real love affair."

"Well, be prepared. When you become famous, men will flock to you. They'll be good-looking men, who'll know exactly what to say to get your attention. They'll try to make you fall in love with them so they can control your millions...."

"Wow! My millions!!! That seems so far from my grasp."

"Believe me, my Dear, it isn't unrealistic. Maybe you'll find someone to marry. A pretty girl like you shouldn't be alone."

"Well, I'm too old to be referred to as a girl. My chances are getting slimmer each year...my biological clock is ticking away....tick, tick, tick!"

"Tell me, this special man. Was his name Jared? Is your book based on a true story?"

"I tried to be a little bird in a tree, tell a love story from both viewpoints. I took a few aspects of several men's personalities, blew them out of proportion and make him larger than life. The 'love of my life' wasn't nearly as romantic as this fictional one. His name is actually David Knight. He did, however, request the song, 'After the Lovin'' for me when he went away once; but, that was a long time ago."

"Suzie, what about the bartender? Did that rape actually happen?"

"What do you think?"

"You made it seem real. I would guess it actually happened."

"It was a figment of my imagination. I needed an avenue for April to seek God. Most of the story is fabricated. The emotions and love, they're real. Ah, the gypsy, that actually happened."

"The gypsy is real!"

"Yes, if you remember, she told me to write a book and not give away my future rights."

"Suzie, you're fantastic. I'm glad you sent me the book!"

"Me, too, Joe, me too."

When they got back to the Plaza, Joe said, "I feel as if I want to kiss you, Suzie, but, I don't want to offend you. Maybe you'll let me kiss you on the cheek. It's been a pleasure spending time with you....getting to know you. Hopefully, we have a long, successful relationship ahead of us. I'll send my signed contracts to the hotel in the morning. The messenger will wait while you read them. If everything's okay, sign one and give it back to him. They'll be in order, I promise. I don't want to blow this deal now. I'll send you my re-writing suggestions for your first book to the cabin prior to your arrival. Jake, the caretaker, will meet you at the airport when you arrive in North Carolina."

"Thanks for everything, Joe; and, I know the contracts will be in order. It was a pleasure meeting you, too." Suzie said as she quickly kissed him on the cheek and dashed through the door at the Plaza.

Joe smiled and brushed his cheek where Suzie kissed him. He looked up just as Suzie turned around and waved to him through the glass window. He smiled, waved, and then signaled for Morgan to pick him up.

Early the next morning, a messenger arrived with the contracts. Suzie asked him to wait while she reviewed them.

Finding everything in order, she signed one copy and completed the insurance enrollment form. Keeping her copy of the contract, she gave the envelope back to the messenger.

"Please tell Mr. Waterson that my flight leaves at three twenty-five today. He said he's send his driver to take me to the airport. I'll be ready to leave at one o'clock. Be sure to tell him!"

"Yes, Miss. Right away."

"Thanks." she said, handing him a ten-dollar tip.

Morgan arrived at one o'clock. Suzie had her bags packed and checked to make certain everything was in order for her bill. Just as expected, Doubleday had taken care of everything.

The take-off allowed Suzie to enjoy another breath-taking view of the Statue of Liberty. The return flight to Florida was uneventful. Suzie's mind raced with anticipation. There was so much to think about; her son's wedding, the upcoming graduation and leaving for the Navy for her youngest; and moving to North Carolina. Her life had certainly taken on a new and very exciting twist!

CHAPTER NINETEEN

Suzie could hardly wait to tell her children about her trip to New York. They were as excited as she was regarding the prospect that she might become a famous writer. Since they were pretty wrapped up in their own lives, they were fairly receptive to the news she'd be moving to North Carolina to work on her books. She was confident she'd be a successful writer and gave all the credit to God.

Suzie took the necessary steps to prepare to move out of state. She attended the graduation ceremony and the wedding. She gave both her boys a party to celebrate the happy milestones in their lives. She saw Jason graduate and took him to the airport to catch an airplane to the Great Lakes Naval Training Station. She said goodbye to her friends and co-workers at a party held in her honor. All in all, the transition went smoothly.

Suzie wanted to let David know she was moving to North Carolina for a year, and to let him know her great news about getting her book published. She called the phone number he'd given her. After the phone rang five times, the operator announced the number had been disconnected.

When she checked with directory assistance, Suzie was informed David's phone number was unlisted. She angrily slammed the receiver down..."Huh! And he said we'd stay in touch this time! He's history. I've opened a new door in my life!"

Joe sent Suzie the re-writing suggestions, and pertinent information regarding the cabin. He explained in his note it would be fully stocked with food; and, for her leisure time, it would contain a television and V-C-R, and various movies so she shouldn't have to take anything but her clothes and personal needs. He gave her permission to take her cats to the cabin, too.

As agreed, exactly three months to the day after Suzie left New York, she was on her way to the remote cabin location in North Carolina.

Jake, the caretaker, met Suzie's airplane. When they arrived at the cabin, the sun was setting and the view was breath taking.

Suzie found Jake and his wife, Mabel, to be a delightful couple who instantly took a liking to her....

As they showed her around, Suzie could hardly believe her eyes. "What a beautiful place; but, this is hardly what I'd call a cabin! I can't believe I get to call this place 'home' for the next year!"

One wall in the living room consisted of a huge fieldstone fireplace. Another wall offered a panoramic view of the mountains that were situated directly behind the house. The cabin itself consisted of a large living room, decorated with over-stuffed colonial furniture.

In one corner of the rustically-furnished room was a big-screen television and V-C-R system. The cabinet next to the television contained approximately two hundred movies.

The book shelves where loaded with classic Doubleday novels. Just off the living area, there was an office with a word processor and a complete reference library. It was a dream come true for Suzie. She laughed at her two cats, as they explored the crevices of their new home.

Off to the right of the living area was a large master bedroom that included an enormous walk-in closet and master bath. On the other side of the room was an atrium, with an enclosed hot tub. The king-sized, four-poster bed was a masterpiece of perfection with its' thick comforter. There was even a small step stool beside the bed because the mattress was three feet from the floor. She smiled as her cats jumped up on the bed using the step stool.

On the other side of the living room were two guest bedrooms, each containing its own bathroom. The kitchen was small, but well organized. The refrigerator was built-in and looked like part of the wall. Next to the refrigerator was a fully stocked, walk-in pantry, loaded with canned goods and paper goods of all kinds. Behind the pantry was a walk-in food locker, fully stocked with meats, juices, vegetables, fruits...anything she could want. Even the linen closet was the walk-in-type, containing every personal product she could possibly need during her stay in North Carolina, including various brands of canned cat food. She smiled, Joe had thought of everything.

Mabel had prepared a large pot of beef vegetable soup, freshly baked cornbread, and an apple pie. She showed Suzie how the security system worked, and pointed out the intercom system. If Suzie needed them, all she had to do was pick up the telephone. Suzie shook her head in amazement.

"Mr. Joe, that's what we call him..." Mabel explained, "Took great pains to be sure you'd have everyt'ing you need.

If you get scared or anythin', just pick up the intercom and Jake'll be here in a minute. It's very quiet here...sometimes too quiet. I'll be comin' over ever mornin' to cook and clean, and tend to your personal needs...."

"Thank you both. I'm going to like the peace and quiet. I've wanted to be in a place like this for so long...I'm overwhelmed by the beauty and serenity of this place."

"Would you like me to help you unpack?" Mabel asked.

"No, let's do that tomorrow. I'm tired from the trip. I think I'll just eat, take a shower and relax tonight."

"Well, then, we'll see you tomorrow. Call us if you need anything." Jake said, as he ushered Mabel to the door.

"You just put your dishes in the sink. It'll be my pleasure to wash them for ye tomorra'."

"Okay, fine, Mabel."

After they'd left, Suzie quickly changed into some shorts and a knit shirt so she could take a walk. When she walked down to the pier, she was overwhelmed by the beautiful view in every direction. She felt like a small child as she explored the cracks and crannies around the cabin.

A large meadow, filled with deer, squirrels and birds, stretched out from the back porch to the mountains. In the front, Suzie could see the ocean inlet, which was surrounded by large pine, oak and maple trees. There was a large dock in front of the cabin. The mountain air was clean and fresh.

Suzie loved the sounds around her, sea gulls, chirping crickets and croaking frogs, as well as the peaceful sound of the water lapping the sandy shore.

When it was finally dark, Suzie explored the bookshelves inside the cabin. She read part of a classic novel as she ate, soaked in the hot tub, and curled up on the couch. There were several large overhead-ceiling fans situated throughout the cabin. They were pulling in the cool evening air. Suzie shivered.

On a whim, Suzie built a fire in the fireplace. She was relaxed, calm. She wanted to get herself a place exactly like that one as soon as she could afford it.

That night, for the first time in years, Suzie slept all night, without waking up once, which was her usual habit. The next morning, she was totally relaxed, refreshed, and ready to begin working on her stories, ready for her new life.

The phone rang. It was Joe. "Is everything to your liking?" he asked.

"Oh, yes, Joe, I love it here! I'm totally inspired. I'll send you the changes for my first book before the month ends. I want to make lots of money so I can get myself a cabin, just like this one...."

"Good Girl! That's what I wanted to hear. Call me if you need anything. Is the word processor system okay?"

"Sure, it's perfect. I've used the system before. It's one of the easiest systems I've ever used...perfect for writing. Thanks for everything, Joe."

"I won't keep you. As soon as you get several chapters ready, send them to me. There's some labels and postage in the desk drawer. As soon as I receive them, I'll start the publishing process."

"Great! You should receive the first batch sometime next week. If you're unhappy with any of the work, please let me know."

For the next few months, Suzie worked diligently every day. She re-wrote the original novel in two months, spending about ten hours a day writing or proofreading.

Normally, she would start to write as soon as she finished breakfast and work until lunch.

After lunch, Suzie would take a relaxing walk; or, sometimes, she would take some tear-sheets that needed to be proofread into the meadow, where she'd read it, out loud, to the squirrels and birds.

Occasionally, a deer would stumble into the meadow and stare at her precariously before pouncing away.

After her evening meal, she'd take another walk until dusk; then, often, she'd spend a couple more hours working. Sometimes she'd read or watch a movie, just as a distraction, especially if she was temporarily stumped by what she should do with a particular novel.

Usually, when a plot stumped her, she would lay awake all night until she knew what direction the story should take.

She finished her second and third novels with relative ease. By taking a break a couple times a day and taking a walk, she could work diligently, earnestly pursuing her desire to please Joe with her stories.

Even when she was sitting on the dock, relaxing, she was thinking about one of her stories.

Joe was thrilled with the quantity and quality of the work she was cranking out.

Everything was right with Suzie's world...everything, that is, except David. When she lay down in her bed at night, she couldn't help but think about him. Sometimes, the loneliness was overwhelming. Suzie wondered what was happening in David's life. Soon it would be Christmas... Christmas was a time for lovers!

Each new season had inspired Suzie more than the last. She loved summer's greenery, fall's brilliant colors; and, now, the freshness of feathery snow falling, capturing the trees in delicate beauty, overwhelmed her. She longed to feel David's arms around her, sharing her joy.

Suzie discovered Jason would receive a leave of absence at Christmastime; so, she invited her family to the mountains for a real country Christmas. They were amazed how terrific she looked when they saw her. She was trim, tanned and relaxed.

They bought gifts at the local stores. Douglas and Jason cut down the Christmas tree from the meadow, and they all decorated it with natural, homemade decorations.

It was a very special Christmas....only David was missing.

COCOA BEACH, FLORIDA—CHRISTMAS DAY!

David slowly edged his yacht away from the moorings at the dock, revved the motor, and pulled away from the shoreline to spend a few quiet moments alone. He was troubled by the upsetting day.

Why do I bother? He wondered, it's impossible to have a family get-together. The family is split up by our problems. No one is happy. I've done everything I can do to please Peggy. The expensive diamond tennis bracelet I gave her didn't impress her. What'd she do? She looked at it, smirked, and tossed it aside. Oh, how I wish I could take Karen and get her away from that bitch. What a mess! A family is supposed to be close on Christmas. My relationship with Peggy is worse than my nightmares of Vietnam...

After David pulled into his favorite cove, he put bait on a hook and dropped a line into the water, awaiting his first catch of the day. Fishing is my only recreation, he thought, I love being on the water.

He stretched out in a deck chair so he could watch his fishing line, and reached into a storage compartment for a fifth of Jack Daniels. He removed the cap, raised the bottle to his lips and poured the liquor down his throat. Then, raising the bottle to the sky, he said, "Merry Christmas, David... Merry Christmas, Jack Daniels. You're my only true friend..."

Full of self-pity, David pulled his hat over his face and closed his eyes.

No, he thought, I DO have a friend...a good friend. Suzie. Why didn't I marry her? She was so cute when I met her.... If we'd gotten married, I might not have had to go to Vietnam. Man, I really messed up our lives. She's never been happy either. I thought I could put her on a shelf... sow some wild oats.

She wouldn't let me touch her. I needed to touch her... to make sure we were compatible. Then, what'd I do? I messed around and knocked up another woman—a woman I didn't even like, let alone love. She wasn't even pregnant. Because of her, I missed having the best wife a man could want.

Then, at the lowest point of my life, we ran into each other again. When no one else gave a shit about me, Suzie loved me... cooked for me...accepted me, unconditionally, no matter what, without change. She accepted me with all my inadequacies.

Then, stupid me, when I had my shit together so we could be together in California, I messed up again by letting Peggy move there. Maybe it's not too late.

Oh, hell, I don't know, he continued to think, Suz was different the last time I saw her. I don't know about all that religious crap; but, on the other hand, she had that peaceful glow. Although it's hard to imagine, she was more beautiful than ever. Wonder if she knows how beautiful she looked?

I wanted her so badly I ached. God, it'd been so long since I'd made love to a woman. She held her ground, though, and wouldn't let me close to her. She wanted it, too; but, she kept talking about Jesus Christ....what rubbish!

David remembered Suzie's words. Curiosity soon got the best of him and he pulled the tape Suzie had given him out of one of the compartments of the yacht, and pushed it into the tape player. The singers were harmonizing..."*You are loved, you are loved.*"

David smirked and started to jerk the tape out of the player. Then, he hesitated, leaned back in the chair, and listened to what each song had to say. The final song talked about a "*king coming...that all work would be ended...all pain would cease...*"

Oh, if only that could be, he thought. My pain from Vietnam is so real I still wake up screaming. This destructive relationship with Peggy, just so I can be part of my daughter's life, is devastating. And, this pain of needing Suzie in my life is real....

David picked up the bottle of Jack Daniels and poured another swallow down his throat. The alcohol seemed to taste sour. He slammed the bottle down on the floor of the yacht..."All right, let's find out what this Romans' Road crap is all about!"

Hours passed as David read and re-read the plan of salvation, to simply believe in Jesus. The little Bible told him God loved him. No matter what sins he'd committed, God would forgive him...wash them away.

How could this possibly be...he wondered. I killed so many times when I was in 'Nam. Can that be forgiven? Some were only children?

David started the tape again and turned up the volume, listening with his heart to each song. He needed something substantial in his life. He was searching for an element of feeling loved. Did God really love him? Would he really forgive all his sins? "But, God," David said aloud, "I'm such a mess!"

The tape was still playing..."*Hold on, My Child, joy comes in the morning...*"

"Oh, I want to feel good in the morning....and MY CHILD??!! Does God really want me? Is God trying to reach me?"

Deep in thought, David picked up the Jack Daniels and took another drink. Again the alcohol soured in his throat. He quickly spit the foul-tasting liquid over the side of the boat. "What's wrong with me? I'd planned to be wasted by now?"

The tape continued to play..."*I am loved, you are loved. I can risk loving you.*" It was almost as if God himself was speaking directly to David. David put his face in his hands and wept like a small child.

"Will you forgive me, God, for my multitude of sins? Those lives I took in Vietnam? It seems like an eternity ago;

but, many were young boys, women, and babies. God, I do believe in You."

David sat motionless, deep in thought, for hours in the boat, remembering the sins he'd committed, as he called each to God. He asked forgiveness for the man that he'd killed in the auto accident when he was only a teenager. He asked God's forgiveness for the people that he'd hurt, especially Suzie.

"Thank you, God. I feel Your love and forgiveness. I DO believe, beyond a shadow of a doubt. It's crystal clear now, just like Suzie said it would be...."

Jumping to his feet, he took every bottle of alcohol he had on board and poured them over the side of the boat. "I don't need this crutch anymore. I've never felt so good in my life! All I need is God, Suzie and Karen, in that order."

The next time the final song played, *"The King is Coming"*, David was on his knees. Layers of goose bumps prickled his skin. He was worshipping and praising God. His chest was about to explode with joy as the Holy Spirit filled him with love.

David spent the night on the yacht, listening to the tape over and over until he had every word memorized.

"Oh, Lord, I hope it's not too late to find Suzie...to make things right with her. I believe You created her for ME! She should be my wife. We were meant to be together. She's never been happy or fulfilled in any way on this earth, except through you, God. If it's Your will, allow us be together for the time we have left on this earth; then, we'll spend eternity with you in heaven. I felt my burdens being lifted when I gave my life to You, Lord. My Vietnam nightmares are over, I know it! I don't need alcohol to get through the day—or the night. Thank you, Lord!"

When David got back to his house, Karen was home alone. He explained to her that he could no longer live with her mother. "I'll always love you, Karen. You'll be welcome at my house anytime...wherever I end up; but, I can't continue this farce any longer. I hope you understand."

"It's okay, Daddy. The constant fighting is a real drag. It gets me down. I'd rather see you two live apart...the fighting grosses me out!"

David packed his clothes and told Karen he'd call her as soon as he had a place of his own. They enjoy a precious moment of goodbye.

When David walked out of the house he'd shared with Peggy, he felt free. After all, what example of "marital bliss" had Karen seen from their relationship? She'd seen a bad example of marriage. What kind of emotional damage would she suffer as a result of this fiasco, he wondered.

David freed himself of his obligation to Peggy; but, it cost him dearly. His relationship with Karen, however, grew stronger and she visited him every weekend at his condo. They still took their weekend excursions on you yacht.

David picked up the pieces of his shattered life. He studied the Bible every day, and asked God to help him find Suzie. This time, however, even a private detective couldn't locate her. "Oh, God, help me find her....if it be your will!"

Several months passed, with no word of Suzie.

David kept a television set on in his office, watching for his advertisements. That morning, Phil Donohue was interviewing a new author, Michelle Wynne.

David ignored the screen, engrossed in his sales reports, not aware Suzie was appearing on the television screen in front of him. Then, suddenly, he heard her voice...the

The Gypsy Cried

sweet, familiar voice he knew so well. The voice he longed to hear.

David stared at the screen. He couldn't believe his eyes. Suzie was talking about her book, a love story, about a couple who'd loved each other their entire lives. It was their story! She looked young and beautiful, like an angel. She was more than gorgeous, she was radiant! He wanted to crawl into the television set and hold her.

The show was almost over when Phil asked Michelle what her future plans were.

"Michelle....?" David said, somewhat confused. "I know that's Suzie!"

"Well, my publisher gave me a beautiful cabin in the woods, by the sea, after I completed my fourth book. My schedule has been cleared so I can spend fall and winter in the cabin, writing. In the spring and summer, I do publicity tours for my books; but, I love being in the woods. I've done most of my writing in the beautiful mountain cabin. Phil, writing is a lonely occupation. You have to get deep inside yourself and shut everything else out. I strive to create characters that are so realistic; I actually miss them once the novel is finished. In the woods, I'm able to do just that...."

"What's your next novel going to be about?" Phil asked.

"I'm going to write a sequel to 'The Gypsy Cried'..." she replied.

The audience applauded loudly.

"Phil, I'd love to get some input from the audience as far as what they'd like me to do with the sequel...." Suzie completed once the applause had quieted.

"Good idea! Folks," Phil said, turning to the audience, "If you read 'The Gypsy Cried' and want to make a suggestion about the sequel, let's hear from you."

A lady in the front row held up her hand. Phil put the microphone in front of her...."I think you should get Jared and April back together...." There was a loud applause.

A man in the back row held up his hand...."Why don't you have April hire a hit man and do the ex-wife in....." Everyone laughed.

A woman in the third row suggested...."Why don't you have her marry the minister who was so nice to her at the end of the book....that would be interesting."

"I'd like to see her with Tom Wilson....." a young girl in the center section suggested. "He could come back into her life. I liked him. I never understood what she saw in Jared!"

Phil came back to Suzie. "Well, Michelle, you've got some input. What do you think you'll do with the book?"

"I'm not sure right now, Phil. We'll see...." she said, mysteriously.

"We look forward to the book..... Good luck in your future endeavors."

As the program ended, the publisher's name and address appeared on the screen. David quickly wrote down the information and called to get the phone number. He talked with several secretaries before he was able to speak to Joe Waterson.

"Mr. Waterson, I just saw the tail-end of the Phil Donohue show. I need to get in touch with Suzie Phillips. Would you give me the number, please?"

"Suzie Phillips? I'm sorry, I don't know a Suzie Phillips..." Joe said, protecting his client.

"Michelle Wynne must be her pen name. I know her as Suzanne Phillips."

"No, I'm sorry. She's traveling and has a very tight schedule. I probably won't be able to get a message to her until she returns to the mountains. She'll be there in about a month..." he explained.

"How are her books doing?"

"They're selling like hotcakes." Joe exclaimed. "She's really something..."

"She sure is...Mr. Waterson. I'm the man from her past. We've loved each other since we were twenty years old. I'd love to surprise her. Can I get directions to the cabin?"

"I'm sorry, I'm afraid I can't do that over the telephone. I must be certain you ARE the man from her past. We must be very careful now that she's so successful. I've become very protective of her. I'm sure you understand...." Joe replied.

"I'll be glad to be her protector if I can find her...and if she still wants me! I pray she still wants me. Listen, Joe, I'm a marksman, served my country in Vietnam. It'll be my pleasure to watch over her...."

"If you are the 'Jared' in her life, I owe her this one. She helped me turn my life around and literally gave me the advice that saved my marriage. She needs a man in her life. I've never met such an incredibly lonely woman. She's so beautiful, and that inner glow makes her one of the most attractive women I've ever met. I definitely owe her one. Why don't you come to New York and meet with me? If you can convince me you are, indeed, the man she's loved for so long, I'll give you directions to her cabin."

"Let's keep it between us, Joe. I want to surprise her..." David instructed. Joe agreed.

David immediately left his office and went to a bookstore to purchase the book. He ended up having to go to three different stores before he found one. He was told the book sold so fast, they couldn't keep it on the shelves.

After making his purchase, David went to his condo. He prepared himself a sandwich and filled a glass with Coca-Cola. Then, settling into his favorite chair, he read Suzie's book from cover to cover. The beauty of their relationship overwhelmed him as it was detailed in the pages of the book. At the end, when April told Jared she was ending their lifelong affair, David cried.

"I wonder if this is how our relationship will end. I've got to find her. Help me Lord." David prayed. "I'm thankful she never actually said those words to me; although, I certainly had them coming. I'm not sure I like myself when depicted through her eyes. I pray it's not too late for us... Help me, Lord."

Meeting Joe Waterson was an enjoyable experience. It took David two hours and an expensive lunch to convince Joe that he was, in fact, the "*Jared*" from Suzie's book.

"To tell you the truth, David, I'm secretly in love with Suzie myself. She's a real beauty! She's the most unusual woman I've ever met. You can imagine how many people I meet in my profession. Success hasn't changed her so far; and, I hope it doesn't. She's had a chance to date some very influential and famous men. She prefers not to date.... doesn't drink or use any recreational drugs which are so common in this business."

"She looked great when I saw her on Phil Donahue's show. I can't wait to see her, Joe. If you'll help me find her, I'll take my yacht and arrive by sea...."

Reluctantly, Joe gave David instructions to Rachel's Inlet, which was directly in front of the cabin. "She'll arrive home on the first of October, and will stay at the cabin until spring. It'll be up to you to make this work between you; and, I'm trusting you'll leave if she doesn't want you there. If you plan to arrive on October first, I'll call on October the second to make sure everything's okay. I have a caretaker who looks after her.... if things aren't right, he'll let me know right away."

"There won't be any problem. If she sends me away, I'll have no choice but to leave. I pray things will work out; that she'll give me another chance."

"Promise me you won't keep her from writing. She plans to crank out another story this winter."

"No problem. If it works for us, we'll honeymoon right in the cabin. Boy, Joe, I can hardly wait to surprise her!"

"Well, like I said, David, she's the loneliest person I've ever met; but, she's lonely by choice. I know at least a dozen men who'd give their eyeteeth for the chance I'm giving you. I hope it works out for you...."

"Thanks, Joe. I hope so, too. I'll call you from the cabin and let you know how everything works out."

David obtained the nautical maps he needed to pinpoint the exact location of Rachel's Inlet, on which the cabin was located. He took an extended leave of absence from his job; after all, he'd hired several first-class management employees. The business practically ran itself.

David shopped for some warm winter clothing and had his yacht stocked with his favorite food. He could hardly contain his excitement as he began his journey—to claim his precious treasure.

CHAPTER TWENTY

OCTOBER 1ST - CABIN, RACHEL'S INLET

Suzie was weary when she arrived at the cabin; grateful Jake and Mabel had stocked the pantry for the winter months which lay ahead. She was too tired to think about supplies.

She took a refreshing soak in the hot tub, remembering the very lonely promotional tour she'd just completed. She had been especially lonely for David and searched for his face in every crowd. Why hadn't she heard from him, she wondered,.... maybe he is dead!

That winter, Suzie had to write a sequel to THEIR love story. What will she write about? Love seemed far from her grasp. She was burnt-out, desperate for David's touch....to feel his arms around her. She needs some romance in her own life.

"Maybe David IS dead! It's been so long since I've heard from him. Oh, Lord, I can't stand that thought. Lord, please, put the Wings of Protection around him...keep him safe."

After dressing in her most comfortable pair of jeans and a warm sweater, Suzie walked outside and sat down on the dock to relish in the calmness of the sea and woodlands around her.

The mountains are already snow-capped, and there is a chill in the air. The Farmer's Almanac was predicting an especially cold winter.

Suzie was thankful that Jake had left some firewood because she'd want a fire later that evening. Right then, she didn't want to do anything but relax, and enjoy the chili and homemade cherry pie Mabel had prepared for her. What a precious couple they are, she thought, thanking God for them.

The publicity tour she'd just completed had been horrendous. She loved her fans; but, she's signed entirely too many autographs, and given too many speeches. She's appeared on every talk show on television and radio. Her name had become a household word, just as Joe predicted.

Suzie had accumulated enough money in the bank that she could live in financial security for the remainder of her life. She probably had so much money there'll still be some left for her great-grandchildren to spend if she never banks another dollar. The money kept rolling in ... movie offers, personal appearances.

Suzie was a generous person, and gave freely to any needy soul who came her way; but she helped in such a manner, they never knew who had helped them. She didn't want them to feel as if they had to repay her. She had plenty to share, and she willingly shared.

Suzie had everything she needed in life except David's love. "I guess the old gypsy was wrong about David. I DID become a successful writer, though, just as she predicted; and, by not giving up my rights, I've maintained control of my stories. Unfortunately, she was wrong about David and me. I'm alone....very alone. I guess I'm just tired; feeling sorry for myself. Even after all these years, I can still feel David's arms around me. I can still taste his kiss," she said as she brushed her finger across her lips, remembering it so well as if was actually happening.

Suzie closed her eyes, allowing the in her eyes to roll down her cheeks. As if it was only yesterday, she could remember being in David's arms.

"I wonder if this is how I'll spend the rest of my life.... feeling lonely, wanting David, and never having him?"

Suzie visualized the first time she'd seen David when he was spraying the security guard with his windshield washer. She affectionately remembered his first kiss. She remembered how precious their first lovemaking had been. She remembered watching him leave on the airplane.

She remembered the night they had a date to meet for a drink at a local bar. Suzie had arrived early and David didn't see her sitting behind the waitress stand.

David was so handsome, that night, just thinking about it still took Suzie's breath away. She told the waitress to send him a drink, and let him know the lady who bought it thinks he's mighty handsome. Suzie would remember the look on David's face until her dying day. He was so cute as he smiled through his mustache.

Boy, she thought, David would love this place. We'd curl up in front of the fireplace and watch the snow fall this winter. He needs this peaceful experience. Oh, well, maybe someday!

Suzie notices a large yacht was entering her inlet. She decided to ignore it, surmising they were probably looking for a place to anchor for the night, so, she ignored the approaching boat.

When it edged even closer and invaded her "space," she angrily turned around to watch. Suddenly, she noticed a familiar silhouette.... "Oh, God, can it be?"

Her heart started to pound rapidly. She jumped to her feet. There is a large sign on the front of the yacht...."Suzie, I love you. Will you marry me?"

Suzie's knees grew weak. She was light headed and felt faint.

"Oh, Lord, thank you!" she said, tears streaming down her cheeks. "You've blessed me so much, and now this! I'll forever be your servant!"

The water at the dock was deep enough that David could drop anchor next to the pier. David was so anxious to get his arms around Suzie, he literally jumped onto the dock and threw his arms around her as soon as he'd dropped anchor.

Suzie and David were embracing with such vigor; they lost their footing and fell into the ice-cold water.

Laughing and crying for joy at the same time, they swam ashore so they could get out of the icy cold water.

They run to the cabin, shivering from the cold, and from seeing each other again.

Once they were inside and Suzie had found a warm velour robe for David to wear, she pointed him in the direction of one of the guest bedrooms so he could take a warm shower and get out of the wet clothing.

Suzie ran to her bedroom, shivering and crying; and, she stepped into a steaming shower to warm her cold body. She dried off quickly with a Turkish towel and pulled on a fluffy robe.

Suzie dried her hair and tried to put on some make-up. She was cold and excited. Her hands kept trembling, and the eye make-up washed off as soon as she put it on because of the constant stream of happy tears that continued to run down her cheeks.

It seemed like a dream. Suzie expected to wake up any minute to discover she was simply dreaming. She pinched herself to make sure it wasn't a dream, leaving a red mark on his skin. No, she wasn't asleep!

When Suzie returned to the living room, David had built a roaring fire in the fireplace. The room was glowing, and toasty warm.

"I'm glad to see you, David. Are you hungry? Let's have some hot chili and apple pie by the fire so we can catch up on things...."

"Sounds good, I've got a lot to tell you...." David said mysteriously.

While Suzie prepared the tray, David walked over and put his arms around her waist. They recalled the other times in their lives when that had repeated that activity, his walking up behind her and slipping his arms around her waist.

"I'm glad to see you, Suz. Pinch me; make sure this isn't a dream. I love you, Lady. I'm proud of you and your success."

"How in the world did you find me?"

"Well, you'd vanished again. I was afraid I had lost you forever. Then, as luck would have it, I saw you on the Phil Donahue show. I called your publisher. He made me fly to New York and prove who I was. He's a tough one!"

"Tell me about it!" she laughed. "I'm glad you found me, David. Before I left Florida, I tried to call you; but, your number had been disconnected."

"I'm sorry. A disgruntled customer started to call me night and day. I had to change the number to an unlisted one."

David and Suzie enjoyed their chili by the fire and continued to talk. Then, finally, the conversation became serious.

"Suzie, you didn't answer my question...."

"What question is that?"

"The sign on the boat, remember? Will you marry me?"

At first, Suzie couldn't say anything. "David, before I answer, did you ever listen to my tape?"

"Yes, my Darling, and I thank God you cared enough about me to give it to me. Thanks to you, I found God on Christmas Day on my boat. You shared your innermost feelings with me. I haven't had a drink since Christmas. If you'll have me, I'd like to spend THIS Christmas right here, with you, in your beautiful cabin, as your husband."

"Surely, after all these years, you know what my answer is; and, of course, I'll have you. This could get complicated, though. I have to write another novel this winter, and make another round of publicity tours next spring and next summer for Joe. What about your business...?"

"It can run itself. We've been apart long enough. Suzie, I'll gladly go with you, wherever you go, as your husband. I've got a lot of making up to you. I want to spoil you the way you deserve to be treated. I think your next novel should be a sequel to your first book.... our story, get us back together again."

"That's funny, that IS my assignment for this winter."

"If you'll have me, I'll travel to the ends of this earth with you. I pray you'll give me the chance to prove my love. Let me spend the rest of my life making up to you for a lot of mistakes, here, in this beautiful cabin."

"It's mine now....Joe gave it to me as a bonus."

"You deserve it, Honey. How about allowing *Jared*," David said, pointing to himself, "Claim April in your sequel ...both in the novel, and in real life!"

Suzie sat quietly for several minutes. David stared at her longingly, savoring the moment. Tears well in his eyes and roll down his cheeks. She knew the passion they felt for each other had multiplied a hundred-fold throughout the years.

David touched Suzie's shoulder and thrills washed through her body. She knew what her answer would be....

"Excuse me for a minute, David. I'll be right back. I have a surprise for you...."

Suzie went into her bedroom closet and pulled down a dusty box she had sealed years earlier, just like a wedding gown. It was preserved for eternity. She quickly dressed in the beautiful silk negligee, sprayed on some cologne, and returned to the living room.

David's mouth fell open when he saw the vision of Suzie in the negligee. "You've still got it! That's the one I sent you from California, isn't it??!! I was touched that you included it in your book..."

"Yes, tonight feels like a honeymoon, don't you think?"

"A much-needed, long-awaited honeymoon."

David took Suzie's hands in his, kissed each palm, and placed them on his cheek. "There's so much I want to say to you, Suzanne Phillips. I hope I can say them without crying.....I NEED to say it...to set things right between us. I didn't like myself very much in your book.....but, you were right to say what you did about me."

"I'm listening, David."

"Oh, God," he prayed, "I accept this beautiful woman as my wife, my love, to keep her safe, to cherish her dearly, in sickness and in health, so long as we both shall live. I thank you, God, for allowing so much love to flow from such a beautiful creation as this dear woman allows. She's my soul-mate and I pray she'll agree to love me forever, to live with me, to be my wife..."

"Oh, Lord, I DO accept David as my husband, my love, to keep him safe, to cherish him dearly, in sickness and in health, so long as I live. I also thank you, God, for allowing so much love to flow from this beautiful man, my soul-mate. We knew it so long ago but we were too scared to take that next natural step in our relationship. I pray we'll always love each other as much as we do right now..."

"In God's eyes, Suzie, we're married. Let's make it legal, in man's eyes, tomorrow. I don't want to wait any longer because we've waited too long now. Tonight will be the beginning of a honeymoon without end. You couldn't have a more beautiful wedding gown than this...your negligee. I want to make love to you tonight, my Love...my wife. We'll never have to cry ourselves to sleep again. We'll always be together. Remember, I keep my promises; and, I hereby promise you my undying love forever. I plan to spoil you rotten, beginning with this..."

David handed Suzie a little velvet box. Opening it carefully, Suzie found a five-caret diamond ring, with a matching eternity diamond ring for a wedding band. She stared at the rings.

David took the rings from the box and said, "With this ring, I thee wed, Suzie. I promise to love you, to cherish you with a never-ending love, even into eternity."

David slipped the rings onto the third finger of Suzie's left hand. Suzie couldn't speak.

"By the way, Suzie, did you notice the name of my yacht?"

"No, you have to realize you were quite a distraction. I saw nothing but you! What did you name it?"

"What else... *'The Gypsy Cried!'*"

Their lovemaking that night was sweeter than ever; and, they were legally married in a small country church the next morning, with Jake and Mabel as their witnesses.

Christmas was spent in each other's arms, in the cabin, where they made love on the bearskin rug beneath the Christmas tree, in front of the roaring fireplace. They fell asleep while snuggled under a blanket, watching the snow fall through the panoramic window.

The novel Suzie wrote that winter, *"The Gypsy Loved Me!"* was an even bigger success than all her previous books put together. Hollywood immediately picked it up to make it into a motion picture, with Suzie doing the screen writing.

Suzanne "Michele Wynne" Knight won an academy award for her writing ability the next year, both for the original novel and the screen play.

David proudly accompanied her to the acceptance ceremony, and was protectively by her side as she appeared at the numerous scheduled bookings. Their prayers had been answered, and the promises they made to each other were fulfilled, triple-fold.

THE END—
A writer's fantasy!